THE MARRIAGE AT THE RUE MORGUE

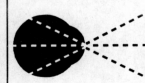

A RUE AND LAKELAND MYSTERY

THE MARRIAGE AT THE RUE MORGUE

JESSIE BISHOP POWELL

WHEELER PUBLISHING
A part of Gale, Cengage Learning

GALE
CENGAGE Learning·

Farmington Hills, Mich • San Francisco • New York • Waterville, Maine
Meriden, Conn • Mason, Ohio • Chicago

LIBRARY OF CONGRESS CATALOGING-IN-PUBLICATION DATA

Powell, Jessie Bishop.
 The marriage at the Rue Morgue : a Rue and Lakeland mystery / by Jessie Bishop Powell. — Large print edition.
  pages ; cm. — (Wheeler Publishing large print cozy mystery)
 ISBN 978-1-4104-7358-5 (softcover) — ISBN 1-4104-7358-9 (softcover)
 1. Women detectives—Fiction. 2. Marriage—Fiction. 3. Large type books. I. Title.
PS3613.O87965M37 2014b
813'.6—dc23
2014031539

Published in 2014 by arrangement with Jessie Bishop Powell

For Scott, who made me believe in true love. For Caroline and Sam, who encourage me with their own creativity. I couldn't ask for a better husband or more amazing children.

ACKNOWLEDGMENTS

I owe a debt of tremendous gratitude to the family, friends, and professionals who helped bring this book to life. First among these is my husband. Scott is a brilliant man whose actual field is history. But when he's conversing with me, he can demonstrate expertise in just about anything I happen to ask. It's an invaluable asset in a spouse. He's also my first reader, and he gives honest critique where others dance around flaws. My love and admiration for him are boundless.

My children are vibrant reminders to me of *why* I write. I want Caroline and Sam to know the importance of doggedly pursuing dreams and of knowing their own hearts. I hope that they understand that by writing, I am also asking them to be passionate, to throw themselves into the things they love with ferocity. I am so proud of them already.

My sister's daughter Kaylee reminds me

so much of myself. She's independent, smart, and ready to tackle the universe. But she's very much her own person. She's got a wicked laugh, a keen eye for drama, and a knack for being *good* at everything she tries her hand at.

In fact, I admire all of Scott's and my nieces and our one nephew. (Ryan was the only boy for several years before Sam came along.) Elizabeth is a smart athletic young woman; Courtney has the courage of Joan of Arc; Ryan's energy and creativity fuel our family gatherings; and Meghan's quiet enthusiasm is contagious.

But they are not the only people who helped me bring this book to life. I had help from the outset from Melanie Bond of the Center for Great Apes in Florida. She took time out from her busy schedule to correct misunderstandings and misapprehensions, and to direct me to numerous resources that primate caretakers would use regularly, such as the *Orangutan Species Survival Plan: Husbandry Manual* edited and compiled by Carol Sodaro. Any apeish (or monkey-fied) errors that remain are entirely mine. For more information about great apes, and to find out how to help ensure the species' survival, take a look at the end of the book.

Detective John K. Schadle, Chief Deputy

of the Brown County Sheriff's Office in Ohio, gave me insight into Ohio policing. I grew up in Brown County, and it was particularly fun to connect with a member of the law enforcement community from my home area. The fictitious towns of Ironweed and Granton are rural, just as Brown County is, making him the perfect expert for this book. I'm sure errors remain. They are entirely my fault, so I pray you heap contumely upon my head, not upon that of one who tried to steer me to the correct path.

My first readers, like D. L. Bass Kemp, Jennifer Richmond, Jennifer Southcombe-Harmon, and Linda Myers, have been so kind to my drafts. Other friends, like Kristi Jones and Karen Mannion, have done everything from watching my kids so I could write to taking my picture for the cover. Readers of my blog *Jester Queen* have given me encouragement along my road, even though they've never seen the book. Stephanie Ayers, Cameron Garriepy, Deana Burson, Lance Burson, Lisa Harvey, Kirsten Piccini, Carrie Rogozinski, and Andra Watkins are just a few of the people who I consider colleagues and friends. In fact, my blogging community represents the first writing community I've had outside of school, and I would be remiss if I didn't thank them.

I need to thank my parents and in-laws as well. I will never live through half the things my mother has endured. She will surely fuss at me for being melodramatic, but when I look at what she has withstood, and how she has somehow come through with a joyful attitude toward life, I am awed and humbled. I admire you Mom, more than I can say. Dad, too, is always supportive. He's a creative force of his own. He gives me honest critique, even when I don't want to hear it, and I return the same to him, because we both know we're doing each other no favors to lie.

I'm delivering no spoilers to tell you the mother-in-law in this book is an awful person, but I want to state up front that she is *in no way* based upon my own mother-in-law. My mother-in-law is patient where I am fiery and kind where I am judgmental. She has always been a solid rock that Scott and I can rely upon. Indeed, I have often said that if I had to choose my husband based on my in-laws, I'd still be married to the same man. My husband's family, from his mother, through his sisters, and to his father and stepmother, has been universally loving to me. I can't believe I lucked into such a close-knit group.

Finally, thank *you*. If you're reading the acknowledgments page, you are a truly dedicated bibliophile. If you'd like to get in touch with me, I'd love to hear from you. You can find me online at http://jesterqueen.com. That's a stable Web address where my most recent e-mail address should always be posted if you want to drop me a line.

CHAPTER 1

Lance Lakeland dodged as a well-aimed fecal mass sailed past him.

"Thanks for the warning, Noel," he called as he headed toward me. "Integration not going so well?"

"Slow." I had been toting breakfast to the enclosures before I stopped to check in on our newest monkey. The pungent smell of overripe fruit mingled with the earthy scent of Ohio forest as I leaned across the chow bucket and Lance bent down so I could peck his cheek. "Anyway," I asked, "what's up?"

Lance's hairy right hand crept up to the top of his head. Though I couldn't see it from my own height of barely over five feet, I knew he was scratching his bald spot. His left thumb started drumming on the dial of his two-way radio, and he hunched in what I called his gorilla pose. "Bub got in," he finally said.

"What?" My sympathy for his stress faded fast. "I thought your brother wasn't coming!" I thumped down the chow again, primates temporarily forgotten in light of this new personal crisis. "What are we going to do with him?"

"I don't know," Lance said. But he did know. We both knew. His right hand moved down to the back of his neck, and he looked at the bucket of food like maybe the answer was fermenting in the mangos and bananas.

Around us, the din of primate chatter edged up a notch. The animals were restless, perhaps keying off of their caretakers' moods, or maybe reacting to the distant racket of mall construction. In one enclosure, chimpanzees emitted their characteristic high-pitched screeches with lower huffing-hooting accompaniment. In another, the red-ruffed lemurs' chatter periodically erupted into chirps and croaks. In front of me, the rhesus macaque screamed bloody murder. It didn't seem at all repentant about throwing its excrement at my fiancé.

Above the animal ruckus, a car honked. The animals increased their volume. "Wonder who that is," Lance said. "We're not expecting anybody at the visitors' gate, are we?"

14

"No."

We looked at each other. I said, "That better not be your brother."

Simultaneously, Lance said, "If that's Bub, I swear I'll kill him."

"Tell me you didn't invite him to stay with us."

"No, no!" Lance held out his arms, palms open. "I told him you and I would have to discuss it."

"Making *me,* of course, the bad guy if we say no." I trained my glower over his shoulder and tried not to be angry. The anger boiled down to stress and the fact that we should have listened and taken the entire day before our wedding off work.

The horn blared again. I looked toward the barn. "Art will get it," Lance said. "He was sitting up there fiddling with paperwork when I left him. Give him something to do."

Thinking about Lance's brother again, I said, "I love you." But I was thinking *Perspective, perspective, perspective* to keep myself from shouting.

"Good thing," Lance replied. He lowered his eyes to the bucket between us.

Since Lance was taken up with scrutinizing the meal, I turned my attention to the monkey. Although he looked starved, his real problem was an inappropriate diet. He

15

smelled better now that we had regulated his insulin levels and gotten his kidneys under control, but his body still showed signs of his former circumstances. Most of all, the neglect could be seen in his face, where his prominent nose seemed too close to his sunken eyes.

This knowledge didn't fix the problem of my future brother-in-law. At forty-two, I was far from the typical first-time bride. It was difficult enough getting around the fact that Lance's brother Alex was very much a volatile ex-boyfriend of mine, without dealing with the landmine of my future mother-in-law's fury should she feel *I* had denied Alex hospitality. She already considered me monstrous for leaving one brother for the other, never mind that it happened ten years ago and I had good reason.

Sophia's willingness to make herself comfortable in Lance's and my guest room in the days leading up to the wedding had initially given me hopes for a less tense relationship. But my hopes of her acceptance faded considerably when the first words out of her mouth off the plane last week were, "He's finally gotten you to change your name, has he?" Nor had she been happy to learn that my name would still be Noel Rue, even after my title became

"Mrs." I had not reached middle age without becoming firmly attached to my own identity, and I didn't plan to change the paperwork on everything from my driver's license to a bevy of graduate degrees.

Lance clearly hadn't thought of who would be portrayed how and in whose eyes, should Alex be consigned to a hotel. In fact, it was doubtful he had thought of seriously turning his brother down at all. More than likely, he had said anything to get his younger, more athletic, more financially successful sibling off the phone so he could come break the news of the arrival to me.

"Where is he now?" I asked. "How long do we have to come up with something?" It was always possible he had flown in at the more distant Dayton, or even Cincinnati, airport, not up the road in Columbus.

This time, Lance didn't say anything. He looked around me. Then his hands went down to his sides and our eyes finally met.

"He called you from our house, didn't he?" I asked.

Lance nodded once, an infinitesimal slump of the head, and then he resumed his examination of the food bucket.

"Which means," I went on, "it's a good bet that whatever *we* say, your mother has already counteracted it." We'd invited Alex to the wedding as a courtesy to Lance's parents, and now that he had accepted our grudging offer at the last possible moment, I wanted to move back in time and rescind the invitation.

Now, Lance put his hands in his pockets and nodded.

I blew out a loud breath, trying to decide if anything could be done. Nothing came quickly to mind, and instead I looked over at the monkey I was trying to socialize. Maybe *he* had some ideas.

Darting glances at the humans, the rhesus crept over to the food I had so recently delivered to his bowl. Out of the corner of my eye, I watched as he slid a hand into the mix. He checked again to make sure neither of us planned to snatch his selection back. Lance assumed the same nonchalant pose that I had suddenly adopted, pretending to look at everything *but* the monkey. It scurried over to the cage's far corner to eat, and I tried to think rationally about my future in-laws.

"If Alex contributed to this guy's normalization, I might be willing to forgive him quite a lot," I finally said. "Maybe I could stay the night with my folks."

Lance sagged in total defeat. "Maybe that would be best," he said quietly. Then his shoulders came up again. He said, "If you do, I think I'll come with you." It was the first time since I'd seen him coming down from the barn that he'd looked even remotely happy.

"Seriously?" I asked.

I had hoped my question contained a hint of *are you crazy?* But Lance missed my tone or chose not to hear it. "It's perfect!" he said. "Mom hasn't spent a night in the same house as Bub since he left for college. We'll leave the two of them alone and see who comes out alive."

I hissed, then picked up my bucket and headed toward the other cages, where hungry primates hooted and warbled in anticipation of their meals.

Behind me, Lance continued, "Maybe she'll . . ." He trailed off, seeming to realize I'd walked away.

I called back, "Great. That's going to fix everything."

The squirrel monkeys twittered and scolded while I filled their bowl and shook some crickets on top. If we didn't mix their diet up on a regular basis, they would get bored and stop eating.

Lance caught up to me and said, "It's not like he'd seriously hurt his own mother. Bub isn't the same guy we used to know."

"I don't want to hear it. Don't you *dare* tell me how fabulous he suddenly is." Now I felt as frustrated as Lance had looked when he first arrived beside the rhesus's cage.

We stared at each other across the squirrel monkey feed for a few more moments. I picked the bucket up, but Lance took it out of my hand. He set it down behind him, out of my reach. "It's all going to be finished tomorrow," he said. And then he kissed me.

I had seen the kiss coming, but I still nearly lost my balance when he pulled me toward him. He's quite a bit taller than I am, and his arms encircled my shoulders as he drew me in close. I wrapped my own arms around his waist and felt my initial flush of surprise turn into one of desire. A lot of our friends seemed startled when we opted for a ceremony to formalize the union we had known was permanent for a very long time. But when I imagined kissing Lance like this, in front of our assembled relatives, colleagues, and comrades, I knew it was exactly the right thing for us.

When we finally broke apart, Lance said, "Allow me, madam," as he bowed down to collect my bucket for me.

"Oh!" we both said.

Lance had put the bucket entirely too

close to the spider monkey enclosure. Although none of them could reach it with their arms or legs, a very determined tail had crept down to wind around the bucket's handle. The little animal was now straining mightily to lift the prize it felt it had won. Lance deftly unwound the tail and pulled the food out of reach. I rewarded the intrepid explorer by feeding that group next. Then, Lance still carrying my bucket, we headed over to the colobus area.

Before we could deliver to that group of primates, Art came on the radio. "Sally, Lance, Noel, Trudy, Gary, Janie, Allen, Pat, Linda, all of you, whoever's here today, get up to the entrance fast."

"Art," Lance said, "what's wrong? You're paging last spring's interns. And Sally and Gary both graduated!"

"Never mind that!" Art shouted. His voice breathy, and urgent, he went on, "There's an orangutan up here!"

CHAPTER 2

Lance dropped the bucket and started up the hill, trying to raise Art again. I raced along in his wake, but his long legs easily outpaced my short ones.

"Art! Arthur!" Lance said. "Can you hear me? Is anybody closer to the gate than I am? Noel and I are under the barn down by the chimps." Under the barn was our quaint way of describing much of the sanctuary's property. The barn was at the highest point, and everything else sloped down from it. The phrase most commonly referred to the area down around the enclosures, where the barn was always directly visible. We were past the chimps now, rapidly moving up to the barn doors.

Trudy, the only intern on Art's list who was still with us over the summer, came on. "I'm inside. I was getting lunch together, but I'm going to the gate as soon as I can find keys." It didn't matter that it was only ten a.m. and I was currently delivering the last round of breakfast. Food prep was probably the biggest job we did at the center. Trudy was working up lunch so our next round of volunteers would be able to step up to a table and start chopping as soon as they arrived around noon.

One of our daylong volunteers, Darnell, entered the conversation. "I'm on my way up there now. I can't see anything but the trees yet." For a moment, he went silent, though we could hear his engine rumbling in the background as he failed to let go of the "send" button. Then he said, "Oh . . . man. You gotta . . . Art! Turn your sound back on!" Another pause, then, "He sees me talking on this thing and he's waving me to put it down. He's out of the cart." The cart would be one of the center's two golf carts, which we frequently used to move around the property. Darnell continued, "He's exactly right. There's an orangutan outside the gate, and it's loose."

"Get Art back in his vehicle!" Lance shouted. "Carry him if you have to."

"I'll do what I can," Darnell said. "But he's got the gate open."

"Who opened the gate?" Lance demanded.

"*He* did," Darnell said. "Art did. Just now.

And he's walking toward it."

Lance said, "Get Art in *your* vehicle if you can."

Darnell didn't answer, perhaps having finally obeyed Art's instructions. Lance reached the barn and fought with the door, too impatient to treat the frame as gently as was required to open it rapidly. I took his hands off the handle, jiggled it gently, then twisted and pulled.

The outside smells gave way to contrasting odors of hay bales and veterinary disinfectants as we passed the clinic inside the barn. Although we shared our veterinarian with the animal husbandry department at Ironweed University, most of our larger primates were conditioned to present their body parts for shots, blood drawing, and light wound care without leaving their enclosures.

The clinic's antiseptic smell faded and Lance strode in ahead of me. "What does Art think he's doing?" He jammed his radio back in its holster. "If there's seriously an ape . . . and if it isn't in a cage . . ." he spluttered to a halt in front of Trudy, who was holding her keys up, waiting for us. She jingled the set, and the two of them walked out of food prep together.

Lance continued, "He cannot confront an

orangutan on his own. How can he think of opening the gate and letting it in?" There was no time for me to answer *because he's Art, and when has logic or common sense ever stopped him from doing whatever crossed his mind?*

"Come on!" Lance took the keychain out of Trudy's hand, but then seemed to realize what he'd done and handed it right back. "Sorry," he said. "I didn't . . . we can't . . ."

"I know," Trudy said. "We're in a rush. Come on."

Neither of them even mentioned Lance's and my truck, the keys to which were in my pocket. I took a different route, detouring to the offices beyond the food prep tables. I grabbed a smaller key and motioned them both to the other golf cart, the one Art hadn't taken with him to the gate. "If Art has the radio off, it's for noise. Our cars are going to be too loud. If Darnell didn't already spook it in that SUV, we'd be sure to if we came roaring up in Trudy's . . . car." I'd nearly called Trudy's worn sedan a wreck.

"We need to ensure our own safety!" Lance pointed out.

"Then we'll climb in with Darnell," I said. "Do not stand there arguing."

Trudy jumped in beside me, and Lance

ran ahead to open the larger sliding doors that we use to get vehicles into and out of the barn. As Trudy and I drove by him, Lance jumped onto the rack we normally use for carrying food or sedated primates to and from the farthest enclosures. We didn't waste time closing the doors as we hurried down the service road.

Our preserve is located in an old-growth forest with a lot of burr oak and maple trees. So our ride was a shady one, spent in the company of trunks and loamy earth. A golf cart goes at about fifteen miles an hour even when it is absolutely racing. So, in spite of my jamming the accelerator pedal to the floor, it felt like eons before we pulled up behind Darnell's tan SUV.

Darnell's SUV completely blocked the view in one direction, and the trees crowded in on either side, preventing us from assessing the situation from our distance. Once I stopped the cart, we all sat for a moment. "What now?" Trudy whispered.

Lance swung down from the rack and moved ahead on soft feet, motioning Trudy and I to stay put. "Now, we wait," he whispered as he passed us.

"Damned machismo," I muttered, and climbed out to follow him, Trudy close behind.

He stopped to the left of the SUV's hood, arms raised like he wanted to grab Art and pull him back. I had to peer under one of those lifted arms while Trudy stood on her tiptoes behind me and tried to look over his shoulder. To our right, Darnell still sat at the wheel, doors shut, windows up. He was so focused on the scene unfolding in front of him that he didn't seem to notice our arrival from behind.

And really, it was impossible not to stare. Darnell was right on both counts. Art's orangutan was real, and there was nothing separating us from it, because Art had opened the gate. Art walked slowly forward, beckoning in gentle welcome. A textbook case of why we don't invite tourists on the premises, but the behavior was coming from the facility director. Good that the animal was too busy pulling apart the wooden crate it had apparently been transported in to pay attention to much else. It seemed the arrival of our vehicles hadn't signified anything worthwhile. Which meant we might have time to get Art back to safety. He knew we couldn't walk up to an unknown ape and strike up a friendship.

We interact with our primates, but we do it in a controlled way. And we *don't* do it without the safety of a solid enclosure or cage between ourselves and our charges. We also don't handle orangutans at all, and I only seemed able to remember tidbits about them. So much of my recent knowledge came from experience with other species. What I needed right now was a good book. Or, that failing, an orangutan handler. But aside from zoos, the only accredited facility in the US that handled these great apes was in Florida.

Art murmured to the orangutan as he moved. I could hear his voice, but not the words, though I knew from his tone the things he would be saying. "Poor guy, looks like you've had a rough day. Bet somebody took you out for a ride and then left you here. But it's fine now, because I'm here. I can help you out." It was the kind of thing he said to every primate that came into our care. The kind of thing we all said to our new charges. The rest of us said the words to focus ourselves and establish some kind of vocal interaction. Art said them for the animals.

Art meant the orangutan to hear and understand him, even though his intellect must have been telling him that he needed to shut up and get in, if not Darnell's SUV, then at least the golf cart he had driven down to the gate. But he didn't even look behind him, and the SUV sat sandwiched between the two golf carts on our little service road, quite as if it had been parked there for the long term.

Earlier, I had thought that this kind of behavior was Art at his most batty. Now, I thought it was Art returning to his childhood. When he was a boy, Art's mother gave him a monkey for his birthday. By the time the creature was a few years old, it had to wear a muzzle except when it was caged. Realizing that his parents were planning something dire, the young Art ran away to the zoo with it. He happened onto a sympathetic keeper who made room for Art's little animal. And from the day he met that kindly zoo director, Art had been on his way to a career in primatology.

With that much experience, Art knew that the animal at our gates couldn't possibly understand him. His conversations with the staff always came back to the fact that we needed to follow established patterns of positive reinforcement using rewards and target and clicker training to achieve desired behaviors in our own captive population. It wasn't that the primates lacked intelligence. Rather, they didn't think like humans, and we, as their caretakers, had a responsibility to communicate with them in ways they could understand. But Art, in spite of what he knew, still believed the right tone and body language could convey a complete message. He was still healing the little kid who had to donate his own pet to save it from euthanasia. He was still personally rescuing all the other primates facing down similar fates.

He took seriously his role as a caregiver to unwanted creatures who had outgrown social roles they never should have been assigned. He wanted them to know they had found a true home at last when they entered our enclosures. Which was fine, except when he did something stupid.

Lance muttered, "You're going to get yourself killed, Art." But he spoke so softly that even I barely heard him. Art was too far ahead. Reaching out to pull him back was impossible. And none of us wanted to spook the animal the man was trying to cozy up to. Not to mention nobody brought a dart gun to the party.

We owned them. Sometimes, especially if we were called into a bad situation by the police, wary animals could only be sedated with darts. But estimating the weight of a full-grown orangutan would have required seeing it first. Not to mention that this whole adventure had started with honking.

That creature arrived in a car, and it was in the middle of an adrenaline rush, which could completely neutralize the tranquilizer. A dart would probably only startle it and make it mad. I was relieved we'd forgotten the guns.

But then, it was pretty clear we needed *something*. The orangutan didn't look or smell like it was having the most winning day so far. Even from a distance, I could see that its orange hair looked dull and dirty. More than that, the hair was obviously tousled and matted, the back hair trailing down to the ground in dreadlocks that must have been collecting excretions. A rank odor of feces and decay emanated from the animal so strongly that I couldn't imagine coming into close contact with it without first putting on several layers of facial mask. It was like standing next to garbage.

Possibly, it would be so exhausted that Art could coax it through the gate, and we could get Art into Darnell's SUV to talk about the situation. If it was conditioned to humans, it would consider the fence a barrier, even though it could easily vault over it. Maybe we could get it in and work from there. It wasn't a healthy animal, and I wished I could recall the list of diseases it might be carrying. I found myself simultaneously hoping that its bad health would prevent it from hurting Art and fearing that those conditions would make it more likely to lash out. But Arthur Jamison Hooper was not considering these things. He was walking forward with the very clear intent of getting the newcomer in.

"Jesus, Art," I muttered.

The center was Art's creation. It was his baby. He was a true conservationist who understood that monkeys and apes are not at all like the differently-sized humans television shows and films would have us believe. Even as youths, they can have behaviors that seem erratic to untrained eyes. But youngsters are smaller, less likely to break skin and bones when they act outside human expectations. And this was no youth. Yet Art was an impulsive man, somewhat unpredictable himself, and quite convinced of his own charms. Like all of us, he talked to the animals in our care while he tended to them. But he was demonstrating his most prominent trait right now, a complete lack of common sense. Or rather, a complete inability to prioritize common sense over love. Art considered himself personally responsible for everything that happened at the center. He thought he could fix anything. Rather than wait for the rest of us to arrive after his hurried call on the radio, he had taken action.

"Where can we even put it?" Trudy whispered.

That was another problem. We weren't equipped for orangutans. We had no enclosure, except for the one already home to fifteen chimpanzees, that could house a primate this big for any long term. And we couldn't dump a new housemate on the chimps. The newcomer needed to be quarantined until we could get him, if not directly to Florida, then at least to a zoo.

In fact, a zoo sounded like an excellent idea. All of the regional zoos had orangutans. Perhaps one of them could house this animal until the folks from down south could collect it. Our first call would be to the Ohio Zoo, where our friend Christian Baker worked as a keeper. He and his staff had been part of the crew that had intervened to save the lives of several animals when a couple of angry former employees in Michigan managed to turn loose an entire private zoo. Many animals were shot when they gamboled into town, but the keepers had saved a few. Perhaps *they* could lure in and trap this orangutan.

We had acted as intermediaries in the

past, when an orangutan in an Indiana roadside zoo had suddenly become an inappropriate attraction. But again, in that case, we'd quickly gotten help from our friends at the Ohio Zoo.

The orangutan turned. The plate-like cheek pads that gave the top half of the animal's face its squashed appearance rotated away from the crate and toward our director. Art shifted his own body seamlessly into reverse. The big ape took one step, then another, and a third to follow before it stopped again, looking around at its environment in complete befuddlement.

And then it bellowed, a furious belch vocalization that startled me backwards several steps.

The animal's meaning was clear. It considered Art an intruder into its territory and wanted him out. When Art suddenly stopped moving backwards, the orangutan charged, screeching threats as it ran. It used both its hands and feet to surge forward. Before any of us could act, one great hairy arm shot out and batted Art out of the way before the animal passed him and bolted into the trees, still vocalizing loudly.

Art staggered a few feet and landed beside the road with a soft whuff. Darnell shoved open his door and jumped out to race forward with Lance. Art jumped up almost as soon as he hit the ground and hobbled toward the SUV, his common sense seemingly restored by the rough landing. So Darnell scrambled back in and leaned across to open his passenger door instead, while the rest of us piled gracelessly into the back.

Art reached the vehicle as I dragged myself out from under the pile of me, Lance, and Trudy. Art was scolding us: "You came too soon! You came too soon!"

The orangutan had stopped short at the tree line, and it now stood huffing at our vehicle, deciding whether or not it was, in fact, a threat.

Art and Lance slammed their respective doors simultaneously, suddenly dampening the ape's noise and cutting back the smell.

"We came too soon?" Lance said. "You wanted us to let that thing mangle you in the cart?"

"What?" Art seemed to shake something off to hear Lance. "I wanted you to . . . no . . . no . . . of course I needed help." Then, Art's face cracked open in a grin. "Did you *see* that? It was so *gentle* putting me in my place. It could have *killed* me instead of pushing me out of the way. Ha ha!" He ended on a gleeful laugh that suggested he hadn't learned much of a lesson from getting too close.

"We need to lure it down to the barn," Art went on, strategizing now. "It's not ideal. But until we can . . . until something more appropriate . . . with food . . ."

While Art was talking, the orangutan offered one last shout at the SUV, then took off into the trees.

"There he goes," Lance said as we watched it vanish. "Now what?"

"It's fine," Art said. "It's all right. It looks half starved. My God, it needs our help. Did you see its backside? I think it should be pretty easy to draw in. I thought, but I never expected . . . something like *this* to happen. Darnell, can you take us back up?"

Darnell put his SUV in reverse, but he stopped immediately when we all felt a thump.

CHAPTER 3

"Oh damn," Lance said. "We forgot about the carts."

I hadn't set the brake, so the golf cart rolled back a few feet and one wheel bumped off the road. We waited until we were at least reasonably sure the orangutan wasn't coming right back, and then Lance and I got out and pushed the one cart back onto the road while Art returned to the other. Lance performed a cursory inspection. "It's fine." We led the parade back up to the barn.

By the time we arrived, Art's good humor had been fully restored. He zipped around to park first, then jumped down and clapped his hands. "Now," he said, leading us all into the barn. "Here's what we need to do. Noel and Lance, you've only got a couple more hours today. This could take all afternoon." He paused, laughing. "Did you see that beauty?" he asked us. "My God, when we get him back in shape he'll be three hundred pounds. He was so close. He touched me."

"I'll say he touched you," Darnell said. "He almost ripped your head clean off."

"No, no, no." Art chortled his way over to food prep, where he continued the work Trudy had been engaged in before the orangutan's arrival. "That's the thing. It *didn't hurt me*. It could have done exactly that, Darnell. One smack. Boom. I'm gone. It pulled its punch, on purpose. It spooked," he said. "If it hadn't . . . Well, we'll find him."

I didn't cut in. Now wasn't the time for lectures, but Art had one coming. I met Lance's eyes, and I knew we were thinking the same thing. If anyone else on the staff had precipitated such rank stupidity, personal affection wouldn't have stopped Lance and I from firing that person on the spot. Art was very lucky he outranked us both.

Now that he was happy again, Art began zestfully hacking a number of fruits while giving us instructions. It didn't seem to matter to him that the food had not yet been organized or that others would be arriving in the near future to address this project. His hands clearly wanted for action. Lance backed quietly away from the tables and into our office. I followed him as Art began to think out loud.

"I'll get a call in to Florida," Art said. He meant he would call Richard Norris, our contact at the sanctuary we would be sending the orangutan to once we caught him. Art had more ideas. But I didn't hear him because I shut the door.

"Talk fast," I told Lance, "because he's going to want us back out there in a minute."

But Lance seemed disinclined toward conversation, instead pausing to breathe deeply, arms crossed over his chest. Art might have recovered fully from his encounter, but Lance was still frightened. Me, too. I walked around behind my fiancé and reached up to rub his shoulders. Slowly, his muscles relaxed, and he rolled his neck from one side to the other.

We could see into the barn through an internal window. Art was using the butcher knife as a pointer to indicate people as he spoke. Since he only had two people to indicate, he waved it back and forth between Trudy and Darnell until he buried it in a watermelon. Lance shook his head. "This is extreme. Even for him."

Our office had a good view of the rest of

the barn. We could also see pretty clearly out into the woods, thanks to the vehicle doors that we still hadn't bothered to close. Through these, we watched the fruit truck lumber up the employee drive to the parking pad with our weekend delivery. "We need to warn Olivia to watch out," I said.

Lance nodded agreement, and I left him alone in the office.

"Trudy and Darnell, get ready to come with me," Art was proclaiming, as I went through the barn. He wanted to talk to me, too. "And you two, Noel, Lance," he said. He had dislodged the knife from the melon and was using it as a pointer once more.

"Not now," I snapped. "Fruit truck's here, and I want to be sure the driver doesn't get any surprises." Even as I spoke, Olivia swung the truck around to back it up to the open doors. The orangutan was riding on her tail, standing on the back lift holding onto the door's handles like he was taking a ride on a trash truck.

"Noel, you have to —" Art began again.

"Art!" I snapped. "Dart gun."

"What?"

I glanced his way, then pointed. When his eyes followed my gaze, they widened.

"Look at that," he breathed. "So smart."

"So dangerous." I cut quickly away from

him and ran toward our medical clinic, hoping I could sedate the animal before Olivia even knew her danger. "Lance! Come out! I need help!"

"He knows," Art said, not referring to Lance, but delivering Trudy and Darnell a classroom lecture about an animal that was going to come charging through the doors in a few seconds. "He associates us with food, and he knows the food comes on a truck."

Lance didn't emerge, and I couldn't worry about why he wasn't listening to me right then. "Trudy, Darnell, shut the door before it gets in." Their feet thumped rapidly across the floor. If the orangutan associated the sight of the truck with food, I could only imagine what it would think of our prep tables.

I ducked into the clinic and reached for one of the two dart guns stored on the wall. Although it was similar to a rifle in appearance, its long barrel meant it was unlikely to be mistaken for a firearm. We kept the immobilizing agents in a locked cabinet, and I fumbled with my keys in my hurry. Cabinet open, I took out two darts and a dart-loading syringe, hoping that I was guessing the animal's weight accurately. I prepared a dose large enough for a full-grown male chimp, but I couldn't be sure it would work for the behemoth out front. I needed two shots if I was going to be sure.

Then Lance joined me.

"I was afraid you weren't coming for a minute there," I told him.

"I had a couple of calls to make," he said. "I got Olivia on the phone and now she knows to sit tight."

That coupled with the sound of the doors sliding shut brought me a measure of relief. We had contact numbers for our vendors and volunteers, but mostly we needed them for more mundane reasons. This was about as far from mundane as things got. Personal safety was the number-one concern when dealing with apes, and I knew that even if my hastily assembled darts reached their intended target, there was a possibility that I would not have prepared a strong-enough solution, and that I would only make the orangutan angry or woozy.

"And," he went on, "I couldn't get anybody in Florida on the horn, but I got to Christian at the Ohio Zoo. He says we're aiming for the shoulder or the outer thigh. Otherwise we'll injure it without doing any good." Typical, but good to be sure. These primates didn't have many concentrated muscle masses to make for good darting targets, and those that existed were small. Making it all the better that Lance had reached Olivia first on the phone.

"And try not to let the animal see the darts. It probably knows what they are."

I thought that last thing would be impossible. "Thank you," I said and hugged him tight. Any minute now, I expected to wake up again and have to redo the whole morning because this had all been a dream.

Lance returned the embrace. "We're good together," he told me. I wondered, *In general or with run amok apes in particular?*

I shouldered one of the rifle straps and Lance took the second from the wall, along with my second dart. "Let's go."

Out in the barn, I realized we had another problem. With the big doors closed, I had lost my visual on the animal. I placed a quick call of my own to Olivia. "Is it still there?" I asked her. "Can you tell?"

"Yes," she squeaked. "I see it in the rearview. Its butt is sticking out. My whole truck is rocking. Noel, can that thing get to me in the cab?"

"You should be safe where you are." I didn't add, *As long as it doesn't notice you.* Because if the orangutan decided it wanted in the front of the truck, window glass wouldn't be much of a bar to its gaining entry. Olivia didn't need to know that.

I hung up and outlined a plan to Lance. "We're going for the outer thigh," I said. "Let's go out the back door and try to come up from behind."

"Great!" Art said. I hadn't even heard him join us.

"Great what? You sit tight and don't put your body in danger."

My annoyance with his attitude must have shown, because he adopted a more serious tone to say, "I'm going around the other way. I'll distract it so you and Lance can get a clear shot before it sees you have darts."

"Art, no!" I snapped.

"Noel," he said. "I haven't completely lost my mind. I was far too excited, and I put all of us in danger. If I had settled down and waited for the rest of you, it would have sat there tearing up its crate for another twenty minutes at least. We would be able to do this without further stress to the animal or danger to ourselves. This is my fault. Let me make it right."

I might have argued him down, but Lance said, "Fine, it's not a bad plan. You carry out half that watermelon you were so busy hacking up and throw it away from the barn, then run back to the door. We will signal you on the *radio* when you need to

44

do it." Lance reached over and turned Art's radio on before patting him on the shoulder. Then he repeated, "Let's go."

Trudy stood inside, holding the sticky back door almost shut so we wouldn't have to either leave it wide open or fight the frame and knob if we had to beat a fast retreat.

Lance and I circled around one side of the barn while Art went the other way. We moved quickly. The primate noise down below us had reached cacophonous levels. The chimps in particular were screaming warnings to everyone in their vocal radius. We didn't think silence on our part was either necessary or particularly prudent. Olivia sounded terrified. She needed rescue, and she needed it quickly. As soon as we split off from Art, Lance and I started running. He was polite enough to slow his feet to a trot so I could keep up, but we still moved fast.

We could smell the orangutan long before we came around to see it. That rotting fecal odor was unmistakable. By the time we arrived, it had foiled the truck's simple padlock (via the expeditious method of ripping the padlock off) and let itself into the back to have at the fruit. It was still distracted, all right, but now it was a much harder target to reach, and a mobile one to boot. Its hindquarters, which should have been conveniently facing us, were disappearing into the truck's open bay as we arrived.

My cell phone rang right then, the noise falling into a momentary silence in the ruckus. I answered without looking away from the truck. Olivia whispered, "It's in the back now. I heard the door go up."

"Yes," I said. "It is. You should be able to see us, too." And I hung up on her. Lance waved.

At the sound of my ringtone, the orangutan stuck its head back out the door. Apparently, cell phones meant something to it. It was easy to imagine that the animal's head was a giant pancake as it glowered at me, thanks to those cheek pads. But my pancakes had never looked at me like *I* might be on the menu. It squinted as it stared, and I held my gun behind me. I thought now I might be able to hit a shoulder.

"Art," Lance had his radio. "Watermelon."

The ape jerked, now looking at Lance.

"Oh! Right! Hang on there," Art crackled back.

Two things happened simultaneously. Art popped around the other side of the building, the melon held aloft in both hands. I could see him in the distance, but I tried not to lose my focus. At the same time, the orangutan brought out one of its massive hands from the back of the truck. It held a melon of its own, this one a cantaloupe.

"Hey, big guy!" Art shouted. "Dinner's on me!"

Art and the ape threw at the same time. Art hurled the melon as far as he could make it go, then took off rapidly in the other direction, exactly as Lance had instructed. But I had already been unnerved by the way the animal was looking at me. Long before it threw the cantaloupe, I had to let it see my dart gun, pulling it up to make a rapid shot. The gun jerked as I squeezed the trigger, and I missed my shot entirely. The cantaloupe sailed over and smacked the ground right at my feet, knocked only slightly off course by my dart, which met it halfway to its destination. I groaned.

Art's champion hurling days, if he had ever had any, were clearly several years in his past. The watermelon only went a few feet before it splatted on the pavement. But it was a sufficient distraction that the ape jumped down and shambled off to investigate the fruit, the fetid aroma increasing as it presented us with its dreadlocked back.

Beside me, Lance's rifle popped softly,

and the second dart took wing. "Damn, I should have waited," he said. The dart made contact somewhere around the animal's buttocks and bounced off its fecally-armored dreadlocks. If the orangutan even noticed, it didn't show. It pursued the watermelon exclusively, having reached accessible food at last. Although orangutans are geared up to explore their meals, the wide open watermelon appealed to the ape even more than the closed cantaloupe it had thrown from the truck.

While it ate noisily, Lance signaled me to keep an eye on the animal and sped over to Olivia's passenger door. He mounted the running board and knocked on her window. A few seconds later, she emerged and they ran to me. The orangutan never lost interest in Art's melon. Lance even had time to run over and shut the truck's back door. It wouldn't stop the orangutan from climbing back in, but it might slow it down a little, maybe long enough to target its shoulders, which weren't clotted with feces.

Although the orangutan looked up briefly when Lance pulled the truck closed, it didn't get up to act, and we all three ran back the way Lance and I had come. "Art, we need two more darts," Lance said into the radio as the three of us sped around the building again. "We both missed."

"You didn't," I puffed, stretching my legs to their fullest to keep up with his easy jog. Olivia had outpaced both of us, fear spurring her on to safety as soon as we came around the side of the building and she saw Trudy standing at the back door waving us in.

"Might as well have," Lance replied.

"That poor creature."

"I know. I could smell it when we were down by the gate. I could *see* it. But we were all more concerned with Art then. The full impact didn't hit me. I hate to admit it, but I can almost understand why Art tried to let it in like that."

I said, "Almost."

Back indoors, Art said, "Let's do this differently." Trudy had taken Olivia under her wing and led her into Lance's and my office to sit out the shakes. And Lance had explained how his dart had simply failed to penetrate the thick layer padding the animal's whole lower back. Art continued, "I think we need to step back. We aren't going to catch it this way. We're going to stress it out, and possibly expose it to the heat of the day when we don't have enough muscle between us to get it inside. We need to lead it off a ways so we can get our lunch crew in here safely, and pretty soon we need to get lunch out to the enclosures."

He outlined a perfectly reasonable plan delegating lunch details, explaining how staff should go about safely delivering food to the enclosures, and fleshing out a process to lure in the orangutan in the evening. We would set out a series of tempting treats and blankets, then dart it when we had a better chance of making our shot. "So," he wound up, "Lance, you and Noel go get your marriage license so we can have a ceremony tomorrow."

"What? We can't *leave* right now!" Lance protested. "We have to work as a team to get it to go far enough away so we can unload the truck and Olivia can get out and everybody else can get in."

"We'll be fine," Art said. "Please. I'll be so sad if something stupid *I* did stops the two of you from getting married tomorrow." As he spoke, he tilted his head and opened his eyes wide, so he looked already bereft. When Art had that expression on his face, I knew who was going to win.

CHAPTER 4

In any case, I agreed with Art. If we didn't get out of here, the wedding we were so concerned about wasn't going to take place. "You should still call Florida," I said. "The Ohio Zoo gave Lance good tips for darting an orangutan." Perhaps the Ohio Zoo could house this big guy for us until transportation to Florida could be arranged.

"Very right," Art agreed, his countenance lightening as soon as he saw that we would comply with him.

"But Noel and I need to be setting the bait out with you," Lance protested, not at all distracted by this talk of who needed to be informed and who might help.

"Not nearly as important as getting married!" Art said. His smile returned. "The ape arrived in a crate. It is conditioned to humans. We will be able to lure it with food."

"But . . . ," Lance began.

51

"Art's right," I said. "If we don't get that license today, the whole thing is off. And honey, we have a hundred things we need to be doing right now, starting with that planning lunch at my parents' and ending with our houseguest invasion."

"Oh, right." Lance's face fell a little.

We had been lazy planners in general, but the list of things we needed to finalize seemed infinite. We had ordered chairs, and tables and tents to set up around my parents' yard for the reception. But we needed to go out and buy or rent at least twenty centerpieces to go on those tables, get started assembling those, and at some point rehearse the whole ceremony. The afternoon was going to be full. We needed to face the wedding.

"Ugh. *Alex,*" I said. Lance groaned, too, and I knew we would not be looking for Art's orangutan this afternoon or any other time. If we delayed our wedding, it was unlikely to happen at all, and really, we were too far committed to the event to back out now. We were simply formalizing something for our families that was already real for the two of us. So why was my stomach in knots about it?

"Everything OK?" Art said.

"Yes, fine," I told him.

Lance added, "Bub decided to come to the wedding after all."

"Oh dear," Art said. He knew who Alex was. "Do you need my guest room?"

He knew. Without being told or asked or anything else, Art knew how unlikely Lance or I would be to either throw Alex to the hotel wolves or stay overnight in our own house with the younger Lakeland brother. "No, we're probably staying with my parents," I said.

"If you change your mind, you've got the key," Art said. "Now, Lance, help me draw our hairy friend off with food so you two can get going."

While the two of them went out back, I commandeered Trudy and Darnell on the phones. We got in touch with everyone scheduled to come in for lunch, and I spent a couple of minutes in conversation with the slowly calming Olivia.

"It scared the devil out of me," she said. "I almost didn't even answer my cell, except I was parking and your people closed the doors instead of opening them. I tell you what, I didn't even feel it climb up there, but it must have jumped on."

"Maybe you were going over a speed bump," I suggested. "When you wouldn't have noticed it."

"I guess so," she said. "But I'm sure I've never been so glad in my life as when your knight in shining armor ran up to my cab."

I filed Olivia's description away to amuse Lance later. Then Lance himself returned with Art, both of them shaking their heads. "That was pointless," Lance grumbled.

"Looks like it grabbed a few more melons off your truck and took off for the woods on its own," Art explained, nodding to Olivia. "We couldn't see it anywhere."

"Couldn't smell it very strongly either," Lance added.

"OK, let's go then," I said.

Trudy said, "Yes, do!" with such force that we all turned to look at her.

"What?"

"I'm sorry if I'm speaking out of turn here," she said. "But you are the weirdest people I've ever met!" Trudy was our only intern who stayed for the summer. She had spent nearly as much time up at the center as we had for the last two weeks, so I didn't see how she had any room to talk about people with too much work dedication. She went on, "When my sister got married last month, she took the whole *week* before the wedding off. I've got other friends who didn't do anything for a *month* except get married. I don't *get* you."

Art laughed at her little tirade. "Oh my goodness, Trudy," he said. "You won't meet anyone stranger than those two."

I restrained myself from saying, *Except maybe you, Arthur.*

Trudy continued, "Now I'm going to do what I was doing before and keep working on lunch."

Lance rallied for a final round of protests. "But Noel and I hadn't finished taking around breakfast."

Trudy countered, "Tell me who to finish."

And Darnell said, "Go on. None of us wants to see you again before six tomorrow evening. And I hope you've both had showers by then. You're starting to smell pretty ripe yourselves." Darnell had been our sense of humor for the past year. I didn't know much about him, except that he had been in the building industry before getting laid off and that he was volunteering with the center while he job searched. But when he planted himself in front of the fruit table, arms crossed over his chest, I knew his muscular frame wasn't one that either my fiancé or I would be challenging.

We went.

We should have at least picked up the license sooner. But the last two weeks had been pure chaos at work. Art had hardly been into the center as he got everything ready for commencement up at the university. Two of his doctoral students had graduated, and at Ironweed U, the dissertation advisor handed the graduate the diploma, moved said graduate's tassel, and made a speech about that graduate's work. The last time Art had two graduates in a single year, it had been Lance and me. Art had been completely consumed with making things perfect for this new set.

Thinking about their graduation made me think of my own. Lance and I had only been together for a little while. We had still been more lab partners and good friends at that point. Art, of course, insisted we were a couple in graduate school and didn't know it. Now that we were getting married, Art claimed complete responsibility. He certainly deserved some credit. Indeed, he was going to be our best man tomorrow.

My mind drifted back to his distracted state of late. Sally and Gary were planning to go on to careers elsewhere, and Art had helped secure them grants and licenses. We kidded that Gary and Sally were going for a bit more funding with their PhDs than Lance and I had opted for, when what we really meant was that they had only interned here throughout their degree program, where Lance and I had both already been full-time employees. Our jokes also meant that Sally and Gary wanted a different working atmosphere. They were frustrated by Art's constant flights of imagination, and they both wanted a larger income.

Ours was not an undertaking for financial gain. It was a career chosen for love. Sally clearly loved the work too, even though she was looking for a bit more money. Gary, though, seemed afflicted by burnout at every turn. The only person who seemed genuinely dismayed by his departure was our board chair, Stan Oeschle, and that was probably because he and Gary were related. Rumor had it that Stan paid Gary's tuition outright.

We rode into town in Lance's little blue truck, which we had dubbed "the primate mobile." It *looked* like the sort of vehicle one would drive back and forth from an animal sanctuary. It hated first gear, only ground reluctantly to life in the winter, and groaned alarmingly in left turns. Its paint hadn't been shiny in years, and patches of rust on the tailgate and body suggested we might need to replace it long before we actually wanted to get rid of it.

At the wheel, Lance said, "This whole

thing is a little like planning your own funeral."

"What do you mean?" I shifted in the passenger seat and hooked the seat belt down around my shoulders so it wasn't actively choking me. My height had disadvantages.

"Think about it. We had to plan who would speak and think about what they might say. We had to invite the preacher, and we all wear formal clothes."

"True." Rather than contemplate the formalities of our wedding, Lance and I had thrown ourselves into the daily running of the center with extra gusto.

Of course, it didn't hurt that Art had been a busy leader and we had a small staff. Mostly, Art didn't handle the center's day-to-day operation anymore. He had filled that role in the beginning, but more and more, he was the one who interacted with the board and maintained a strong campus presence to show the university what a rescue center affiliation could do for it. Like offering plum work-study opportunities and internships, among other things. Lance and I were used to being in charge here.

But normally, by the time university graduation rolled around, Art would have been ready to spend a few months more involved out at the center. Lance and I had planned our wedding nearly a year in advance thinking this would be the case. We were quietly grateful that circumstances had changed when Sally and Gary suddenly accelerated their dissertation research. Art had been grumbling and working around the clock getting ready for them to graduate.

This year, it seemed like the closer we got to our wedding, the crazier things got at the center. For one thing, we could hear construction for the new mall for most of the day. It was one of those "out" malls that was really a whole bunch of strip malls all connected. I hated it already, and it was only half finished. In fact, they started the thing before the economy went south a few years ago. Construction halted not long after the project was begun, and it had only started up again in the last few months.

I didn't remember hearing the first wave of building at all, or even the first few weeks of this new push. But in probably the last month, it seemed like every jackhammer was in the center's backyard. The fact that we were on two hundred square acres of woodland and the mall was a good two miles away didn't seem to dampen the noise at all.

We humans found it a minor annoyance, but it drove the primates wild. Quite frankly,

I had thought the noise would stay further away. It had made Lance's and my work for the last couple of weeks far from routine, particularly as we had acquired the fecally dexterous rhesus right at the beginning of this period.

Art's graduates had walked last Saturday, at which time they had stopped working for the center, leaving us even shorter of staff. And Art himself had only really gotten settled back into his summer schedule here yesterday. Which meant that whether we were using it as an avoidance tactic or not, Lance and I had been needed at the center. And that our current schedule couldn't be helped. We had four hours this afternoon to pick up our marriage license, get center-pieces for twenty tables, shower, and get dressed for the rehearsal on my parents' lawn.

Friday afternoon did not appear to be a popular day at the probate office, and parking was easy. "Marriage license, please," I said to the man behind the desk. Then I added, "Oh, hi Matt!" as I belatedly recognized an old high school classmate.

"Application," Matt corrected me. "You get the license after you do the deed."

I said, "Um," and he burst out laughing.

"Having a little fun on a slow day." Matt

pushed the appropriate form across the desk to Lance and me. But his joke was technically correct. The form we completed today wouldn't be valid for anything unless we submitted it back to the court within sixty days with the signatures of our officiant and witnesses.

"When's the wedding?" he asked us. Like many in the town of Ironweed, Matt had a country accent, and "wedding" became "weddin'."

"Tomorrow," I answered. Lance filled in a dozen lines about himself and his parents in silence, then pushed the form over to me.

The clerk was reading upside down as I wrote. "Cutting it mighty close, aren't you? Most people do this part a little sooner."

We shrugged and didn't make eye contact, either with him or with each other. The silence grew heavy as I completed my own information. I glanced up from the sheet once and saw Lance rubbing his bald spot again. Quite a bit of his hair was still thick and black, and he wore it in a short taper cut. But the spot of scalp in the center of his skull was not something he could call "thinning" anymore. We kidded that he would ultimately bald out in the shape of his right hand, since he spent so much time worrying it over. But then, if my hands hadn't been busy with the paperwork, I would probably have been working up some female-pattern baldness of my own. We *were* putting this until late in the game like everything else. After a decade, a change like this didn't come gently to us.

Finally, I finished, and we pushed the form back to Matt. "All right," he said. "Fifty dollars, and you're on the brink of no return." He chuckled at his own joke and didn't seem to realize Lance and I didn't laugh along.

"Do you take debit cards?" I asked. "Or does it have to be credit?"

"Cash only."

"What?" Lance and I asked in unison.

For an answer, Matt pointed to the top of the form we had hastily completed. Very clearly across the top we read a demand for fifty dollars. Cash.

I said, "I don't carry that much cash."

"Didn't you look into this at all before you came down?" Matt asked.

Lance and I exchanged a glance that said *no* more plainly than if we had spoken. I rummaged around in my purse, and Lance fished in his billfold, and between the two of us we came up with forty-six dollars and change.

"I guess we'll be right back," Lance said,

patting his pockets one last time, like there might be four dollars hidden somewhere.

Matt rolled his eyes. "Look," he said, pulling out his own wallet, "I'll kick it in for you. Wedding present. I think if I send you out of here, you won't be any kind of right back."

Lance seemed dumbstruck.

I said, "Thank you," and made a perfunctory offer to repay him. He declined, and Lance and I left the office hand in hand.

Out of the office, Lance asked, "Why wouldn't we be back? There's a bank machine around the corner. Doesn't he think we want our license?"

I didn't answer. I don't know what my old classmate saw in my face, but Matt was right. If I had left to get money, I would not have come back. Living together was comfortable. It didn't involve influxes of relatives, and it didn't force us to abandon the center when we were very clearly needed there. Art had seemed so rational telling us why we had to go, how he had it covered. And he had lied. If that clerk hadn't ponied up three dollars and sixty-five cents, we wouldn't have had time to mess with this marriage nonsense today.

"Lance, we have to get back to the center

now. Art's about to do something stupid," I said.

CHAPTER 5

"No." Now Lance was the firm one. "We're going to have to trust him on this one. We have a wedding to get ready for, and right now we're late for your mom's." It was almost humorous to see how seamlessly the two of us changed roles. Back at the center, I had been so sure that the wedding was more important, so sold on Art's argument that we didn't want to exhaust and then dart the animal in the heat of the day that I hadn't seen that Art planned to do exactly that.

He might not have been an Olympic watermelon pitcher, but Art *was* a talented marksman. He had been using a dart gun when Lance and I were in elementary school, and he wouldn't be waiting idle when he could be neutralizing the orangutan. Or else trying again to lure it. I hoped his recent close encounter with the ground had put an end to that attitude, but it was impossible to be sure.

"We need to be where we can keep an eye on Art!" I argued.

Lance shook his head. "Nope. Art can take care of himself. He knows he did something stupid, and he wants to make up for it. And the more I think about it, the more it doesn't make sense for us to be there today. Orangutan or no, I'm getting married to you, Noel, and I don't want to spoil that. Remember, it's all going to be over tomorrow." And then he pulled me into another one of those kisses like the one that had nearly made me fall over in front of the squirrel and spider monkeys.

All right then. Wedding it was.

It wasn't that his kiss erased my doubts and worries about Art. Brave words aside, I knew he had to still be concerned. But he refocused me, reminded me that the wedding was more than a time-consuming hassle. It was a chance to smooch like high schoolers in front of our collected friends and relatives. And Art was sure to cheer us with his patented catcall.

As we left the building, my purse snagged in the security gate. The strap jerked me backwards and an alarm whooped. I pulled, but the purse remained looped.

"Hang on there." The security guard loped

over. I snaked my arm out of the offending strap, and my purse fell to one side, but not to the ground. The guard picked it up and lifted it off of a previously invisible outcropping on the smooth metal gate.

"Thanks." I took it and followed Lance out the door, now fighting the battle of getting my purse back over my shoulder. I was so distracted that I nearly walked straight into the rescue center's board chair, Stan Oeschle, and his wife Gert. I glanced up from my purse and there were the Oeschles coming up the steps below me.

They didn't see us either, at first, because they were walking forwards and looking backwards, talking to Gert's granddaughter, Natasha. Fourteen with pale skin and heavily made-up eyes and lips, she walked a few steps behind them studying a white bandage on her hand. Stan was a good friend of Art's, and over the years, he had kicked in dollars to rescue us when the ends we were trying to stretch simply couldn't be made to meet one another.

Lance maneuvered me out of the way before a head-on collision as Stan looked up from Natasha and said, "Hello there, lovebirds!" Then, seeing the piece of paper still in Lance's hand, he added, "Don't tell me you put off the marriage license until *now.*"

When Stan spoke, Natasha immediately stepped down and to one side and engaged in a deep study of the concrete. Lance and I didn't answer and didn't look at each other. Instead, we both looked past the Oeschles and stared at Natasha, who didn't look up from the stairs. With her dark wavy hair, black outfit, and downcast eyes, she was a study in teenaged boredom. When she finished examining the steps, she looked closely at her hands, presumably studying her nail polish, which was shiny black except for the one index finger, which sported the bandage. I remembered being fifteen and worried about my appearance. A gauze strip to mess with my nails would have left me feeling seriously exposed.

After an awkward silence, Stan laughed out loud, and beside him, Gert blushed and smiled. Where Matt the clerk had treated our failure to prepare with something like contempt, the Oeshles thought it was funny.

Gert said, "Stan and I almost forgot to get the license entirely, didn't we?" Now I understood her slightly embarrassed reaction and his contagious amusement. I laughed, too, relieved that other couples made this mistake also and had been married for some time in spite of it.

"We have it now," Lance said, holding up the document we had paid forty-six dollars and thirty-five cents to receive. Then he went on, "You would not believe the morning we've had."

Ugh. This was not the time to make nice for the board. Now that my own wedding focus had been restored, I knew that if we didn't get to Mama's house soon, she would start calling my cell phone to harass us. But Lance was describing the orangutan to Stan, and I knew we would be on the steps a while longer.

I turned to Gert. "How have you been?" It seemed a safe enough question.

"Oh, you know," the older woman replied. Beside me, Lance waved a wild arm in imitation of the smack the ape dealt Art, and Stan boomed more laughter. Gert looked at the ground.

"Nervous?" I had an idea that they were here to visit the family judge.

"Well, I just want to see it finished."

Gert and Stan had been married nearly as long as the center had been in existence, but it was a second marriage for Gert nonetheless. By the time Gert met Stan, her daughter Linda was already a rebellious young woman. Linda's exploits had been the stuff of much late-night gossip with my mother when I came home on college breaks. Then, after her mother remarried, Linda quit high school, got pregnant, and ran away with the baby. Over the years, she let Gert and Stan see Natasha only sporadically, mostly when she needed money. Consensus (which meant my mother and grandmother) held that she made a living as a prostitute in Columbus. When Linda died from a drug overdose nearly a year ago, Natasha came to her grandmother and Stan permanently.

"Of course she's nervous," Natasha muttered. "She hasn't eaten a thing all day."

"Hush," Gert said.

"You have to eat," Natasha said. "How will you get . . ."

"Natasha," Gert said, "I'm going to be fine." Gert turned to me. "My stomach's been a little troublesome. I'm sure it will settle down once everything is finished here."

"And as soon as you can get out of town to take care of Aunt Gretchen."

"Natasha! I'm sure Noel doesn't need a rundown of our problems."

"You want me to tell the truth! All the time, you say, 'Tell the truth, no matter how bad.' But she asked how you've been, and you've answered . . ."

"There's a difference between dishonesty and observing social niceties."

Natasha sighed and looked back at her hands.

Lance had reached the part where Art was stabbing fruit and waving the knife like a pointer. I said to Gert, "I didn't know your sister was sick."

"Oh, she fell again." I suddenly remembered that Gretchen suffered from MS, and I looked away.

Gert looked to the men as Lance pantomimed my perfect shot at the cantaloupe. She caught Stan's eye, and he stepped toward her.

I found myself examining Natasha. This was probably the first time the young woman had any stability at all in her life. What Lance and I were offering each other was a small act of dedication compared to the courage and trust this girl had to be showing every day.

In an effort to derail my fiancé, who was now reenacting Olivia's flight to safety by running up and down the courthouse steps, I asked, "When is the adoption hearing?"

"Half an hour." Stan's rich baritone contrasted with Lance's nasal imitation of Olivia's voice. "I can't thank you enough for writing us a reference. I really wanted someone from a younger age bracket to tell social services we were fit for the job."

"You'll be wonderful. You *are* wonderful."

Stan moved to stand beside Natasha, who finally looked up and smiled at him. The smile softened her face and lifted the appearance of boredom from it. In spite of my own urgency, I couldn't help but see the beauty there. She sank quickly back into inspection of her nails and prodded the corner of one step with her toe. I had seen the moment of transformation, and I'd seen the dullness settle down around her again.

Even though it was her adoption under discussion, she was demonstrating studied indifference to the topic. Not so unusual for her age group, I supposed, but it made me doubly grateful for my own teenaged nieces, who had greeted my invitation to be bridesmaids with joyful cheers.

"Tasha's had a hard time of it these last couple of years," Gert said. Natasha looked up again, and the smile she exchanged with her grandmother was something wonderful. Her eyes softened, as well as her mouth. She walked away from Stan to hug Gert. She did not resume her study of the ground, but instead leaned into the older woman and closed her eyes.

I felt like a voyeur watching them, and

turned my head to Lance, who was looking at me. He had finally stopped talking apes. Natasha and Gert's relationship must have been complicated, but the love in their faces was obvious, and it made me feel like everything Lance and I had put into worrying about this wedding was trivial. Here we were fretting over a commitment that had been real for a decade, while these two were looking forward to a relationship they had only enjoyed for a comparatively little while.

Seeing them put my own wedding jitters in perspective. But Natasha and Gert's fretful exchange earlier had also increased my certainty that my own mother's worried state about tomorrow's ceremony would be approaching a high. If we didn't get to her lunch soon, she would very likely spend the first ten minutes of that lunch telling us off.

Lance wrapped his arm around my shoulders. I put mine around his waist and started edging him down the steps. He smelled good, like sweat, the barn, and an Ohio forest.

"Congratulations," I told the Oeschles. I tried to remember if I was supposed to give any kind of a toast tomorrow night. Surely, yes. I wondered how I could mention Natasha in it.

Lance allowed me to pull him along, and

we were about to turn away when Stan said, "Do you think Art needs any help out there? I'd be glad to lend some muscle if it would do any good."

"I don't think muscle is what he needs," I said, still tugging Lance away. I didn't add, *And your muscles are a little past their prime.*

Lance shook his head and added, "But if you get a chance to call him and tell him to stay out of trouble for us, it would really help."

"Glad to," Stan said. "I'll give him a ring before we go in here." He looked into the courthouse building as he spoke, like he thought they might miss their hearing time standing talking to us.

"Thanks," I said. "We won't delay you any longer."

"I hope it all goes smoothly," Lance added as I finally got his feet moving in the right direction.

"The problems are all behind us," Stan called after us. "It's smooth sailing from here on out."

Stan's problems might have all been behind him, but Lance's and mine were only beginning. "Drive fast," I said as we got into the truck. "Before Mama works herself up into a swivet."

Lance drove in silence for a few minutes.

74

Then he said, "There's something you should know."

"What? With Art?" My mind was already back at the center.

"No. With Bub and Mom."

"What?" I said again. I did not have time to worry about Alex and Sophia right now.

He said, "I was trying to tell you right when things went crazy this morning." Even as he spoke, he was flying down the road, guiding our pickup out of town and back toward my parents' house. "I meant to bring it up as soon as things calmed down, but they never really did, and I got preoccupied driving to get the license."

"Lance, what is it?" Wasn't it enough that Alex was here at all?

"Mom thinks the wedding is a bad idea," Lance told me.

I clucked my tongue against the roof of my mouth. "That's not new."

"She's decided it's cursed."

Okay. That *was* new. "Oh, no. I know she doesn't like me, but that's going a little far."

"It isn't you. Or she says not," Lance explained. "It's the location. She wants us to use our own house or go to a church. Now that she's been over to your folks' place, she swears it's got bad karma."

"Your mother wouldn't know bad karma

from bad lunchmeat!"

"I know, I know. I didn't say *I* think this."

But I wasn't finished. "She doesn't like it that my parents' house used to be a funeral home? It's a little late. If she wanted a say in it, she should have come and helped us pick a venue that suited her. What business does she have voicing an opinion about any of this now? We're getting married *tomorrow*. Couldn't she have spoken up sooner? And I don't know if . . ."

Lance interrupted me. "It gets worse."

"It what?" I stared holes into Lance's right ear while he went on speeding down the road.

"Gets worse," he repeated. "She called in Bub to throw the whole thing off."

"Oh, she did *not*! Lance Lakeland, they can both go . . . sleep in a hotel for all I care. How dare . . ." I suddenly thought I might cry.

"And I wouldn't know any of it if Bub hadn't warned me. He's not going to do it. Not going to mess us up. She called him yesterday and practically ordered him to come in. Fed him some line about her own stress level. But then when he got to our place this morning, she had some scheme to crash everything. She was going to blow up your parents' house."

Stunned, I started to ask, "How?" But I stopped myself. "You know what?" I said instead. "I don't care. Not even a little bit." The need to cry was even stronger now. "They can both go straight . . . home."

Lance blew air out his nose. "They can't and you know it," he said. "Or she can't, anyway."

"I know nothing of the *kind*," I shouted. My voice echoed around the pickup's little cab and I deliberately lowered it. "If she doesn't want to see us get married," I hissed, "she knows how to book a hotel room and airline ticket for herself. And as for him . . ."

"And he offered to leave, and I told him not to."

"Why?" Our rapid drive abruptly turned slow as Lance exited the bypass and we came up behind a giant combine. It stretched so far across the little two-lane highway that cars going the other way had to pull almost into the drainage ditch to avoid getting broadsided. There was nothing for us and the three cars ahead of us to do but slow down and follow until the combine reached either its destination or a pullout long and wide enough that it could let us pass.

"I wanted to tell you all this earlier, but

77

we got interrupted," Lance continued. "Alex sees the same things you and I have been talking about ever since Mom got here. She goes off on these irrational tangents about things nobody can understand. She isn't eating right, and she doesn't seem to really realize where she is half the time."

"Oh, no." My anger with Sophia turned suddenly to concern. I had interpreted all of the things Lance was describing as symptoms of my mother-in-law's dislike for me. "I thought when you and I agreed she made no sense, we were saying something different."

"What do you mean?"

"I thought we were saying her behavior was rude and inappropriate. I didn't think we were saying she might be ill."

"Not might," Lance quickly corrected me. "Alex thinks her meds are off."

"Her insulin?" A lifetime of obesity had left Sophia with diabetes, even though she was comparatively thin right now. She also took thyroid medication.

Lance nodded. "And . . . others," he said. "Bub's waiting for Dad's flight to get in, and they're going to get her to a doctor this afternoon. He offered to take off and let Dad handle it, because he knows how much of a problem it is for us to have him here right now."

"You mean because he doesn't want to deal with it. And what *others*? Do you mean her thyroid drug?"

The combine finally pulled off and we took our turn to pass it. Lance shook his head, but he didn't answer me.

"What others?" I demanded, my voice low.

Lance shook his head. "It's . . . a longer conversation than we have time for right now, OK? I'll tell you tonight."

I started reviewing every word Sophia had said in the last week with a new ear. Perhaps Alex could be useful in his stay after all, but I was skeptical. And I was still far more concerned right now with my own mother and her notoriously high stress level. I leaned against my window and let the topic of Alex and Sophia drop. We would deal with them later. "Right now, we have to talk my mother down from completely resewing my dress or having a crisis about center-pieces in the next twelve to twenty-four hours."

"Ah yes," Lance said. "The dress."

CHAPTER 6

Lance wasn't comfortable with my dress. He had only been introduced to it once, two weeks ago, and the meeting had not gone well. I had worn it downstairs into my parents' back parlor. Instead of gasping with amazement when I walked in the room, he said, "I don't like it." In an instant, I understood why brides traditionally kept their grooms in the dark about such decisions. But I wanted him to see this dress, wanted him to see me in it, wanted him to *approve,* and it wasn't working at all. It was yet another decision we had left until nearly too late, and his reaction had been anything but complacent.

My folks had a front parlor, a back parlor, and a room we had labeled the living room, though it had probably started life as yet another formal parlor area. I envisioned myself stumbling from room to room, posing in different lights so that Lance could evaluate me until he liked what he saw. The idea didn't make me happy, especially since Mama and Daddy had a *lot* of rooms to choose from.

He had studied me wearing it and said, "You look like a kid playing dress up. The arms are too long and it sags in the chest."

I tried to show him how it would appear when alterations were finished, twisting up a handful of fabric to get it pulled tight across my breasts. But the chiffon slipped out of my grasp, and the sleeves got in my way. Finally, I gave up and said, "It's what I *have,* Lance. And it was my grandmother's."

"Your grandmother is four inches taller than you and a whole lot . . ." He stopped himself.

"A whole lot what?" I demanded, though I knew what he was going to say.

"You know," he said, gesturing around his own chest. "Bigger."

By "bigger," he meant chestier. I barely graduated into a B cup, and it's hard for me to find clothes that don't erase my hard-won breast bump. In the normal course of things, I didn't think about it much. But formal occasions never failed to remind me that I lived in a C+ world. It didn't help that every other woman in my family except Mama suffers from boobs in excess, or that

81

my little sister actually had to have hers reduced to save herself from back problems. I did not appreciate Lance's mentioning it right then. "I'll be wearing a padded bra, and Mama will take that *in*," I snarled at him.

I had already seen myself in Mama's full-length mirrors in the sewing room upstairs, so I knew how I looked. Lance's description wasn't at all inaccurate. But from the way Mama had described the alterations she would make, I knew the dress would be perfect. I had hoped to paint a similar picture for Lance, but he wasn't even giving me a chance. Even the parlor's natural light wasn't adjusting my fiancé's opinion.

"But the sleeves," he went on. "And the . . . whatever you call the bottom."

"The train?" I asked.

"No," he said. "The part out in front."

"The hemline," I told him. "The hemline can be taken in, too." I crossed my arms. "Is your *only* problem with my grandmother's wedding dress that it doesn't fit?"

We eyed each other in our formal wear. Mama was adamant that I would wear my grandmother's gown. Lance had still lacked for a tux when I gave in, so Art supplied a loaner to keep the groom from having to visit a suit shop with the newly arrived

Sophia. Mama, being a matcher and balancer, had wanted at least photographs of Lance's selection to compare with my dress. We had stopped by Art's to take pictures, and he instead handed the suit bag over. Of course, Mama had made Lance put it on.

Where my dress was huge on me, Art's suit fit Lance almost perfectly. It was unexpected, since Art was a little shorter than Lance, but they had the same leg length, and the two inches Art needed to make room for what he termed his bulging biceps and shoulders also left room for Lance's added height. I still found the fit suspicious. I wouldn't have been surprised to find that Art had taken Lance's spare clothes out of his locker at the sanctuary and bought the suit entirely to fit its current wearer. Mama would need to take in a little in the jacket to make the arrangement work, but the length was perfect.

Thus, it wasn't too surprising that Lance had asked, "Not fitting seems like a pretty big problem, doesn't it?"

Unsurprising, but annoying. I had wished for my mother-in-law. If she had been present, Lance wouldn't have been able to argue with me. He would have been too busy keeping her bad behavior under control. But Sophia pled a migraine. Personally, I thought she had a hangover. She had flown in the night before, and after a quick dinner with my folks, had been picked up by some girlfriend from Columbus.

"Maybe if it were too *little*." I had twisted to follow his movements. He circled me in a half arc, stopping so he wouldn't have to dodge the dress's modest train. "But too big is really easy to fix." Why couldn't Sophia be here to irritate and distract her son? She liked to flit. She had friends from Lance and Alex's days at Ironweed and she was using her two weeks' stay to get together with several of them. She had arrived home early that morning and gone straight to bed. I was simply relieved she had stayed the night with her buddy rather than either of them driving home after whatever they drank the night before.

"Is that the *only* thing you don't like?"

"*I* don't know!" Lance suddenly flopped down on the sofa. "I want you to have a dress of your *own*. Don't you think we can afford that?" He made us sound like paupers. Our salaries at the sanctuary didn't leave much room for extras, but we were frugal, and the answer was that if I had wanted to buy a new gown, we could have covered it. But it was both an expense I didn't desire, and an argument with my mother I could safely avoid.

All in all, Mama was more fretful about the upcoming ceremony and about this dress in particular than either Lance or I. She had just wanted to get started pinning and measuring. In contrast, once I accepted the gown, I lost any interest the subject had held and wished Mama could use a dressmaker's doll as a stand-in for the living bride.

Growing up with a seamstress parent, *I* knew that if Mama felt she could perfect the dress in two weeks, then it would really only take one. She had made prom dresses for my sister Marguerite and me while running a successful sewing business out of the house I grew up in. Altering my grandmother's gown while enjoying semiretirement would be quite simple. Still, her peace of mind mattered to me, and I liked the gown.

I sat beside Lance, forcing him to jerk his legs out of my way. "Have you ever priced out a wedding dress?" I asked. Two could play the pauper game. "I'd rather have a nice reception. And I like this. It suits me."

"Don't you look like a pair of dolls," Mama had rounded the corner into the parlor. I supposed so, I in my then ill-fitting dress, Lance in Art's white tuxedo.

Lance and I sank deeper into the couch, holding hands. Without looking at Mama, Lance said, "It seems like the dress is so important in the wedding. I don't want you to have somebody's castoff."

"Just because Nana never got to use it, that does *not* make this dress a castoff," I snapped. When Bill Cox skipped town the same day of his wedding to my grandmother Franny, the town gossips had a field day speculating whether the two had ever wedded at all. They had not. Mama remained prudently silent. We contemplated these words for a little while before I added, "I think the dress looks fine. The dry cleaner can get out the yellow, and Mama can take in the seams. It's not like you aren't wearing somebody else's clothes, too." Probably a falsehood, but he hadn't worked that out yet. "The suit and dress will go together," I went on, "and that's all we needed to figure out today anyway. I'm not so far out of date, and you're not so very trendy that we clash, and neither one of us is horribly 'eggshell' with our white." Mama hated eggshell.

Lance had grunted and loosened his tie, which was black.

"You look adorable," Mama had said. "Now hop up and let's get you changed. I'll run it uptown to the cleaner's after lunch."

Mama never went downtown. She always went uptown. Downtown meant Columbus, which could have been in Europe to hear her talk about how far away it was. Uptown mean Ironweed.

Lance grunted again.

I told him, "When people have lived together as long as we have, different things matter. Maybe when I was thirty and fresh out of grad school, I'd have wanted everything to be new. But honestly, I don't think of our wedding like some testament to how pretty I look in lace."

"You *do* look pretty in lace," Lance offered, snuggling in closer on the couch, rather than getting up as Mama had suggested. He leaned around to put his arm around me and try for a kiss.

I let him peck me but squirmed loose before he could do anything to make Mama blush. "Not now." I flicked my mussed brown hair out of my face and held several strands up for scrutiny. "Ugh. More gray. Anyway, lots of brides wear family gowns."

"I like your gray."

"Watch it, or I'll start talking about your bald spot."

He reached up to rub the top of his head like he was checking for bruises, then hauled himself to standing and offered me a hand up. I was fighting my gray one dye bottle at a time, and Lance had long since given up the war against the empty patch in the middle of his head.

"Bleach it, then nobody will know the difference when you color," my mother advised. Mama's hair used to be brown, like mine, before the gray set in. Now she dyed it a shade of blonde so bright that I called it "way-off-canary-yellow" and wore it in a stylish pixie. On her, the horrible color and adorable cut emphasized her femininity. It would have made me look like a prepubescent boy.

I tucked the offending strands behind my ears and let Lance help me up. "Anyway," I said, "I'm more interested in the mortgage, the groceries, and trying to pay for this honeymoon. Spending a lot of money for a dress I'll only wear one time doesn't make sense to me."

"Don't let her kid you," Mama said. "You and I both know she wouldn't have invested money in a dress twelve years ago, either." She pulled out her cell to photograph us standing awkwardly in front of the sofa.

"Oh, Mama, put that thing *away*," I said. "We look absurd right now."

But Mama snapped two more shots before popping it back into her pocket, where it promptly started ringing.

"Oh!" Mama said, "Oh, oh! Smart-phones!" as if that explained something. Even though she had been dexterously tapping the screen a moment before to take pictures of us, she suddenly seemed all thumbs when forced to confront the same machine in another capacity. She juggled it from hand to hand, nearly dropping it while she tried to poke the right spot to answer.

"Mama," I said, "you have to tap and drag. It's . . ."

Before I could finish speaking, Mama's finger finally connected with the screen in the right pattern. "There," she said, then, "hello!" Moments after that, the chipper edge faded and she said, "Oh." She drifted back toward the kitchen, saying, "Yes, John, you *do* need to dispute the charges with a check card. It isn't the same as a credit card at all. It's a formality, dear."

"Honey, get me out of this thing," I had said to Lance. "I think it will work, and I feel like a ragdoll in it." I turned around to present my back so he could undo the row of tiny buttons around the neck.

As he started tugging, the front door opened, and a voice called, "Ding DONG!"

"We're in the back parlor, Nana," I said. Then, to Lance, I added, "Wait a minute. I want to see what she thinks."

Lance smiled, and I turned to face the hall again. I turned a full circle as Nana entered the room, tugging on the train to keep it from twining around my legs as I spun. While I was turning, Lance sucked in his breath.

"What?" I asked him.

He tried to explain. "It still hangs and sags" — he gestured to my arms and chest respectively — "but . . ." He trailed off, still circling his left hand like he expected it to conjure words out of thin air for him. Then he said suddenly, "I like it. I like it very much."

"But you said . . . ," I protested.

Nana cut me off. "No, dear. I agree with Lance. It looks nice. I'm glad someone will finally get some use out of it after all these years." And I realized he had spoken entirely for my grandmother's benefit. Whether Lance liked the dress or not, whether *I* liked it or not, Nana clearly loved it. All the memories and heartache, and she still loved her dress. She clasped her hands at her chest and quickly released them. Then she added, "Of course, in my day, the groom never saw the dress until the day of the wedding. I wonder what would have happened if I hadn't made Bill wait. Maybe this would be a second wearing instead of a first." At eighty, Nana still towered over me. Although she was stooped now and walked a little slowly, her green eyes shone with a joyful light, even in a wistful moment like this one, as she looked at me in her dress.

"What was it like for you," I asked, "raising Mama alone?" It wasn't a topic I had ever broached, but I suddenly couldn't imagine why. My grandmother had been a single parent in an age when girls were routinely sent away for nine convenient months in the event of an unexpected pregnancy.

Franny Cox had laughed as she paced around me, gathering fistfuls of fabric to pull the hem off the ground and putting them in my increasingly overburdened arms. Nana was not troubled about stepping over the train, and the chiffon didn't slip out of her grip, even while she was handing more of it to me. I resorted to tucking it under my elbows. When Nana was finished, I stood a little awkwardly, half clutching, half pinning the hem clear of the floor, while she stood behind me pinching the chest tight.

"It wasn't that long ago, really," Nana said at last, answering a question I had thought she might ignore. "Most people thought we'd eloped before Bill went off to Korea, and I let them lie to themselves. And I wasn't alone, really." Now she had moved on to the sleeves, tugging so they hung at my wrists, not down over the palms. No mean feat, especially considering that she did it one-handed without dislodging any of the tucked-up skirt or letting go of the back of the dress. She went on, "Mother was horrified, but she stood up in church for me. And that's not something you saw every day. She was a very formidable woman, my mother. Very formidable. Your sister is a lot like her." Last of all, Nana pulled the throat tight for a moment, then nodded once before letting it all go again.

"Yes," she said, talking about the dress now. "Lenore and I can sew that."

"Meaning *I* can sew that," Mama said, returning from her phone call, stuffing the device once more into her pocket. "Mother, you know your eyes aren't up to needlework."

"My eyes are fine," Nana snapped, pushing her glasses up her nose.

"You crochet," Mama said. "But we're talking about tiny stitches. When was the last time you even embroidered?"

"Stop it! Both of you!" I threw up my arms and dropped the cascades of fabric

Nana had tucked up for me. "Or I swear I'll get a tailor." The two of them cackled, like they thought I was making some kind of a joke. "Lance, get me out of this thing," I said, meaning it this time. I retreated upstairs to the sewing room as delicately as one can while trailing a wedding dress at least three sizes too large, and Mama, not Lance, followed.

CHAPTER 7

Now, two weeks later, that dress sat waiting for me on the dress form that actually had been a decent stand-in while Mama removed the skirt so she could raise the hemline and shorten the waist.

"Isn't it bad luck to have your wedding dress fitted too many times?" Lance asked. He parked behind my mother's car and we got out.

"Of course not," I told him. "It's very *good* luck, because it's less likely to fall off you walking down the aisle." I would have thought that Lance would be happier about my re-refitting. Waiting around one more time while Mama went over me with a pincushion looking for flaws put off the trip to find centerpieces. He started to grumble something else, and I added, "Anyway, it delays the trip to the craft store."

"There is that."

"After lunch, you get to tell my dad we'll

be back later to stay the night." I walked in ahead of him, denying him the chance to retort.

As I had expected, our lunch conversation centered around Mama's last-minute concerns. She was worried about the cake, because we had declined to go for a tasting sometime last month and had left the flavor entirely up to the baker.

"You didn't at least tell them marble or yellow?" she demanded.

"Or chocolate," Daddy added, sipping his coffee. "You might have ordered chocolate."

"I'm sure Ironweed Confections knows your favorite flavors and mine," I told them. "We've been getting Saturday cupcakes there I think since I was born." And I had so told them a flavor; they wouldn't take the order without it. But I wasn't releasing that detail for public consumption and debate.

Mama wasn't sure about the plastic tablecloths currently sitting in her basement. "Why don't we look at getting decent replacements today?" she wanted to know. "You got those other ones at some chain back in March."

"And at bargain basement prices," I added.

"Exactly. You have no idea what might be

wrong with them. Every one already has a hole for all we know."

"They're fine," I said. "It's quite enough that we have to have centerpieces," a detail I considered frivolous. "We can put any holes under those."

And that brought the conversation back to its origin, and Mama's real fussing point today. She was deciding between a central candle surrounded by ivy and a simple bowl with floating votives for each table. She wanted Lance and me to agree on one or the other. I didn't like either, but found the votives less kitschy. Lance wasn't much help. He sat with his arms crossed over his chest once he finished his sandwich. Then, whenever Mama asked a question, he waited for me to answer and agreed with me using monosyllables.

Mama said, "I'm sure the bowls should be clear glass, but they would need to be opaque to be sure we could hide holes in the tablecloths."

"Mama, there won't be holes."

"How can you be sure?"

Lance ventured, "Opaque bowls will look fine."

And Daddy backed him up, saying, "Exactly!" He was even more of a conscript than Lance and I at these festivities.

Everyone but Mama was finished eating by that time, and Lance and I started putting away the bread and condiments. "Go on upstairs, Noel," Mama said.

"Oh, leave them alone, Lenore," Daddy said. He got up. "I'm going back to my garden." We would be getting married in that garden tomorrow. He was far more concerned with making the roses beautiful. The back door banged behind him, and I heard a chorus of barking from my parents' dogs, who had been banned from the kitchen for the meal.

Lance and I got as far as taking the dishes to the sink before Mama finished her own meal. She waved to us and dusted some crumbs off her chin. "I'll get that later," she said. Then my Nana banged into the kitchen. "There you are!" Mama exclaimed. "I was worried something had happened to you."

"Please, I'm only eighty. I don't think we need to take away my car keys yet."

"Noel, get her a sandwich." Mama opened the refrigerator and pulled the ham back out.

"I ate before I came over."

"But you knew this was a planning lunch."

"Which is exactly why I ate first. Let's go fit that dress."

"You two get ready," I said. "Lance and I are just going to load the dishwasher and I'll be up."

Mama started to say something, but Nana shooed her on out of the kitchen. I was grateful that my grandmother recognized my need for a few minutes alone with my fiancé. I knew they would both be waiting with needles outpointed if I didn't hurry to join them. But I wanted just a few more minutes alone with Lance before the wedding madness ensued.

He frowned at their retreating figures, and I handed him a plate. Half of his problem was that he wanted to get the centerpiece search over with (if we had to have centerpieces at all), and the other half was that he didn't really want anything to do with the process. He was trying very hard to be a twenty-first-century groom, but we both knew he couldn't have cared less about the decorations. He stayed involved because he knew I didn't care either. Every time we came to detail tension, I threatened to make him elope and swore the entire ceremony was for the relatives.

Lance and I tucked the last of the dishes into the rack and loaded the machine with soap. I was thinking about my mother and grandmother. I said, "I don't understand those two. They snipe back and forth so much, but they don't even seem angry half the time."

"Who?" Lance asked. "Your parents?"

"No. Mama and Nana. But that's another thing. Why can't Daddy keep track of his cards? Mama whispered before you came in that he's had another card stolen because he left it somewhere. Your mom has issues and my dad's going senile. Crazy, isn't it?"

Lance turned and walked toward the door, heading for Daddy and the rose gardens. Then, quite suddenly, he said, "I think your mom and grandmother learned to get by that way. It probably goes back to Franny having to be a single parent in the nineteen fifties. She was joking about it with you when you asked, but we both know your nana didn't have things easy." I loved how Lance had made the leap to a two-week-old conversation, knowing I would be there, too. He continued, "I think she and your mom learned to put up with each other is all." Then he turned and went back out to make sure there was going to be room for us to stay here this evening.

As if that could possibly be a problem. Mama and Daddy had whole wings of the house to shut off in cold weather. Lance and I could have lived like the Mad Tea

Party and slept in a different room every night if we stayed here regularly. Even with Nana staying for the wedding *and* my sister and her family coming in tonight, they would have space for us. Still, it would have been rude not to give any warning at all, and Lance enjoyed spending time with Daddy, even if he pretended not to know anything at all about the flowers.

Mama and Daddy lived in a huge old Victorian house that had once belonged to the town mortician. It came with an overgrown English garden for them to rehabilitate. Sophia only learned the house's history when she came into town, and that was surely why she thought the place was cursed. I found her conclusion ridiculous.

In twenty-four years of living here, the closest my parents had come to a haunting was some mysterious attic scraping probably caused by squirrels. The building had been both funeral parlor and morgue, and Sophia most likely thought dead bodies last present seventy-odd years ago guaranteed lingering unhappy spirits. *Some of those people died gently in their sleep,* I fumed now as I mounted the steps to try on my dress one last time. *Quite a lot of them did.*

It seemed unlikely that Sophia was considering how commonplace a dwelling like this one would have been in the late 1800s. In the nineteenth century, it wasn't at all unusual for the local funeral home to double as the morgue and be operated out of a person's home. These buildings tended to be large to accommodate their dual role and allow for big wakes.

The town of Granton, however, burned in the 1930s, during the Depression. While this was one of the few homes and businesses to survive the fire unscathed, the funeral jobs had shifted when people drifted into the county seat of Ironweed only a few miles down the road, unable to rebuild in a time of need. By then, the county had a morgue of its own, and the funeral director simply moved his business out of his abode and set up an office in town.

When he died some years later, his home passed into other hands. Those hands all belonged to the same family for a few generations. My parents waited a long time for the house to come on the market. Daddy had his eye on the gardens. Mama had hers on the turrets.

Growing up in Ironweed, it had been one of those things I heard about for my entire childhood. We used to drive out to old Granton (which didn't even rate its own zip code) to look at "our" house and plan our futures in it. Mama even took the step of giving the widowed owner our phone number and telling her we were interested if she ever wanted to sell.

Nothing came of it until my first year of college. Then, one day, my little sister got home from school and the phone was ringing. It was Mrs. Johnson calling from the bank, ready to finish a deal she considered my mother to have initiated some six years previously.

Within a week my family was moving.

At that point, I was not attending Ironweed U. I completed my undergraduate work at Midwestern College, a couple of hours to the east. So I heard about the move while living in a dorm and came home at Thanksgiving to find all my old possessions at the new house. Over two decades later, many of those belongings still sat in boxes in a closet in a room Mama had labeled mine. She wouldn't throw them out, and I hadn't needed them since before they were relocated.

Still, I liked this house. I had grown up looking forward to living here, and it felt like home to me. I enjoyed its character and thought my parents had done an excellent job making it their own, with restoration work on the interior and much planting in the garden. I lived with them for a lot of graduate school, and I found the house as comfortable as if I *had* spent my childhood in it.

Upstairs, Mama said, "You've left so many important things until so *late.*"

"The only things left are little," I protested. "My dress, decorations, flowers, the caterer and the license. We got the license this morning, and I talked to the catering company last Wednesday. And I always knew the dress would be fine."

"And now you don't have flowers at all," Mama snapped.

"Oh for pity's sake, I have an entire rose garden full of them. Could anything in this whole world be more lovely than Daddy's flowers?"

Mama had to concede that point. "But the *caterer,*" she fussed, looking to Nana. "You call the caterer a 'little' detail. You can't expect much from a company you booked on a week's notice."

"They'll be fine," I said. "I know them." They supplied the food for all of the center's fund-raising events, and I didn't think it really mattered much what we served. Nobody remembers the food at a wedding. And we *booked* them back when we set the date. We finalized the menu a little on the tardy side. I didn't give Mama the satisfaction of knowing that the caterer shared her opinion about food chosen a week and a half in advance based largely on what was already on order.

"That's certainly true," Mama agreed. "I don't think there's one of these businesses that one of us doesn't know some way or another."

I was standing in a ridiculous corset and my panties while she fussed with the zipper that she had sewn under the buttons before she would let me pull on the dress. Then heavy footsteps sounded on the stairs and Lance's head appeared in the doorway, saving me from having to think up a response to something that hadn't been a question to begin with. "It's Bub," he said, without apologizing for barging in on me half naked. "He and Mom are having some kind of a catfight. I'm going to try to sort it out without dragging you in. I'll be back to get you later. You're going to have to cope with the centerpieces without me."

"Lance, if he's hurt your mother," I began. But I didn't know where to end the sentence.

"No," Lance said, "I don't think so. He's the one calling. I'll tell you when I know more." And he headed down to the truck

104

alone. Now, I regretted being trapped into a final fitting. I regretted his brother's unexpected arrival. And most of all, I regretted loaning my mother-in-law my car for the length of her stay, especially since she had only used it once. Mostly, her friends spirited her places. If Lance and I hadn't been riding together, I could have followed him over after I finished with this dress nonsense, and made Mama and Nana deal with the centerpieces after all.

"Hurry up," I said to my mother. "We haven't got all day for this."

Mama ignored me and actually set the dress down. "When were you planning to tell me that Alexander Lakeland is here?"

Thanks so much *honey,* I thought at Lance. *There was a* reason *I had you talking to Daddy about why we needed a room, and an even better reason why I had you doing it after the rest of us were upstairs.*

"I found out before the orangutan crisis, Mama, and Lance heard right before that." We had explained the morning's events briefly before Mama launched into wedding mode at lunch. "We invited Alex for Sophia's sake, and she made him come."

"Really," Mama said. "That's what he says? And you believe him?"

Nana said, "Let go of it, Lenore."

105

Mama rounded on her instead. "How am I supposed to let go of what he did?"

"If *I* can do it, then you can, Mama," I snapped, seizing the dress and jerking it on.

"Be *careful,*" Mama scolded, hurrying to help me get my arms and head through the right holes. She didn't raise the issue again, but the rest of the fitting was tense and unhappy as memories filled the room.

We headed out to buy centerpieces in a similar mood. We drove uptown to Ironweed, even though there was not one store in town that could possibly satisfy our needs. We got out on the town square and Mama said, "Now, I think we need to try Winkie's Trinkets first, then the Diamond Dovecote after that. They always have little things."

"Mama," I said. "Can't we be a little practical? There's nothing here for us. None of these shops will have more than a few of any one item in stock."

"I'm sorry to say it, but Noel is right," my grandmother chimed in.

"No you aren't," Mama argued. "You're not sorry at all. You've been taking her part since she was a toddler arguing with me over cookies."

While Nana tried to convince Mama that we needed to make do with the craft store on the edge of town, I made a quick escape into Hannah's Rags, owned and operated by my best friend Hannah Rice.

"I'll be a second," I chirped, and left them bickering on the town square. I believe Mama tried to call after me, but I ignored her.

I always loved to go into Hannah's. Her window displays were a study in contrasts, with sometimes a neat little girl's dress, complete with pinafore, hanging next to a dashiki, or a spiffy suit paired up with ripped jeans and time-faded shirts. Today, she had a funny little half jacket hanging above a pair of parachute pants. Staring at the storefront was enough to ease my tension with a sense of the whimsy she brought into everything.

Inside, there was Hannah along with two other friends, gossiping around the counter. If anything could have made that blasted afternoon feel better, it was these three. I'd known all of them for years, but Hannah the longest. We were best friends since first grade, back when hers was one of only a few black families in town. She went away to college someplace out east. Our undergraduate years predated the widespread use of the Internet and cell phones, so we lost touch for a little while.

Then when I was in grad school, she came back. She called out of the blue one afternoon, and it was like neither of us had ever been away. She came home to open her store, taking a bet that the nation's only social-justice-science-centered university could provide enough clientele to revitalize a downtown area that was lagging behind. She bet wisely, and soon her vintage store was joined by a dozen more shops. Today, she was sketching something that she swiped under the register as soon as she looked up and saw me at the door.

"Hello there! Were your ears burning?" asked Mina Tudor. Mina's daughter grabbed a phone out of her mother's purse and drifted away down the aisle. Mina and her daughter were carbon copies of each other, with green eyes and red hair styled into identical bobs. I went to high school with Mina. She stayed in town and completed her undergraduate degree at Ironweed. These days, she was a stay-at-home parent, and her preteen daughter lurked out of range of the group, pretending interest in the store's contents so she could send text messages without her mom and her mom's friends hanging over her shoulder.

"Only from my mother's scalding," I said. Jan Willoughby added, "You almost caught us talking about your big present." Jan was six feet tall and the only blonde in the group. She also had on a tie-dye shirt and one of those crinkly skirts designed to give off earth mother charm. Jan was anything but an earth mother. The clothing was absolutely a front.

"Very funny," I told her. Lance and I had been very clear that gifts were to go to the center, not us. "Anyway, why aren't you off in Columbus fighting for a bigger share of the pie?"

Jan was a corporate lawyer. She had moved to Ironweed because her therapist told her if she didn't get some relaxation, self-imposed stress would kill her before she turned fifty. She fired the therapist and moved out here. She claimed her commute was the calmest part of her day. When she wasn't wearing a suit and tie, she dressed like this. And she had an irresistible laugh, which she turned on now. "Even the Great White Shark needs a day off here and there."

I turned to Hannah. "You better not be getting me a personal gift," I warned.

"Scout's honor," she said.

"We dropped out of scouts together."

We all laughed again, and Hannah said, "You're about as prickly as a cactus today. What do you need, honey? Do you want Jan to file suit against your mom?" We laughed some more, especially since Jan, while she could eat somebody up at the office, in the courtroom, or on the basketball court, was otherwise pretty laid-back (one reason she fired the therapist).

"Sell me something. I ran away from the centerpiece committee out there, and I'd better have an excuse for it when I catch back up to them."

"OK, I'm on it," Hannah said.

She vanished into the back of the store and emerged less than two minutes later with a pair of antique hair combs she had gotten at an estate sale. My debit card suffered dearly for my few minutes of centerpiece-free living, but I was pretty sure Hannah sold them to me at cost. The combs were delicate mother-of-pearl, and they would look perfect with my veil. The interlude was worth every penny.

When I returned, Mama and Nana weren't by the car, they were prowling the aisles of Winkie's Trinkets, Mama bemoaning the fact that even if they *could* find the perfect thing on a day's notice, it wouldn't be available in the right quantity on time. I bit my tongue and did not say I had told her so. The boutique's owner, a good friend of Mama's, told her three times that she needed to go shopping out on the bypass. Mama glared daggers at me for failing to plan well enough to support the local economy.

But when I said, "Let's go face the box store," she came along without further complaint.

When we got to the craft store, Mama resumed the battle of what kind of centerpieces to use. She held up garland next to candles, wondering aloud, "Would it be too autumnal, do you think, to wrap the garland around a big candle? Or maybe that would be Christmas."

"I thought we were using the floating votives," I said, maneuvering our cart over to glassware. I thought I could get different kinds of bowls so the centerpieces weren't all identical. That would be more my style.

Then my phone rang. Lance. "Where are you?" he asked without preamble. I could tell he wasn't calling to tell me he had sorted out the family squabble.

"Craft shop," I said.

"Which one?"

I named it.

"On the bypass?"

"Yes."

"I'll be there in ten minutes tops. Meet me out front."

"What is it, Lance? Is your mom hurt?" It didn't matter that Alex had been the one calling him back at the house. I could still imagine any number of harms he could have caused his mother. I couldn't believe Lance and I had been wishing him on her a few hours ago.

"Mom and Bub are fine. Dad's here, and he can deal with them." *What, then?* But he didn't make me ask. "Honey, we've got trouble at the sanctuary."

He hung up before I could ask more.

"What happened?" Mama demanded at once. "Is Sophia . . ."

"Sophia's fine," I said in a dazed voice. "Something out at the center. I knew I shouldn't have left. I knew we should have gone back. I have to leave right *now.*"

We were standing beside a mixed display of vases. As carefully as I could, I started loading them into the cart. All of them. When Nana realized what I was doing, she hurried over for a second cart so I didn't stack them on top of one another. Mama stared at me the whole time, until I handed her my purse. "There," I said. "Those are my centerpieces. You can do whatever you want with them. Lance and I are planning to stay with you and Daddy tonight. I hope I'll see you at the rehearsal."

I started to walk out, but then had to return to get my phone out of the purse and transfer it to my pocket, all the while imagining all of my friends and employees trapped inside the sanctuary barn by a run-amok orangutan.

CHAPTER 8

Lance barely stopped long enough for me to get in, and if he had violated speed laws getting out to Mama's earlier, he now made them seem like outmoded suggestions. I didn't dare distract him by asking what crisis we were pelting toward, but rode instead clutching the grab bar, hoping he wasn't about to catapult us off the road at every curve. My fingers felt cold, and they were going numb by the time the center came into view. Then I heard a siren and saw an ambulance flying up behind us in the rearview mirror.

"Oh no," I said. "No, no."

Lance said quietly, "I think they found him."

"What?" But he didn't answer. We turned down the center's lane, and I craned my neck around to watch the approaching red lights.

"Found who?" I demanded as we reached

the tree line. The emergency vehicle, still out on the main road, disappeared from my view. Nonetheless, and especially since Lance still didn't answer me, I found myself whispering orders to it. "Keep going," I said. "There's someplace else you need to be." *Found who, indeed.* I knew who.

But the wailing didn't fade from my hearing, as it should have done if we were moving away from the ambulance down the lane and it was continuing up the road.

"No!" I told it. "You made a mistake!" The sirens got louder, and then it reappeared in my rearview. When we didn't accelerate fast enough, it blew its horn and drove right up on our tail.

Lance increased his speed, sending us forward at some forty miles per hour down our narrow service road. He reached for the clicker that would open our gate, but the gate swung inward before his hands touched the button. Darnell was waiting right there in the golf cart, ready to let the ambulance in. He didn't even seem concerned that the orangutan might be back here. I met his eyes as Lance and I sped past, and the chill that had started in my fingers spread all the way up my arms. Darnell's skin is black. Very black. But right then, his face was sallow.

Lance hurried on, heedless of the fauna that might, and often did, cross our road. My stomach ached with the certain knowledge that in the hours we had been absent, something had gone irreversibly wrong. Lance whipped out of the ambulance's way on the parking pad and screeched to a halt. Olivia and her fruit truck were gone, but the lunch crew was still present (far too late; they shouldn't have still been there), and several vehicles crouched where only Darnell, Trudy, and Art's cars had been parked before.

The barn doors sat wide open, and Lance and I pelted through them still ahead of the EMTs, who were running to catch up. In the seconds that it took my eyes to adjust to the dimmer barn light, I had time to see the silhouettes of our volunteers. They were arrayed near the lunch tables, almost as if things were normal. Almost like we might still find out things were fine. But then my vision cleared, and I saw a woman named Jen pointing wordlessly out the back door. I ran out back and halfway down to the enclosures, where Trudy knelt on the ground beside a bloody figure. Art. I threw myself down next to him and screamed his name. Back inside, I heard the EMTs clattering into the barn, calling for us to clear away.

Art lay still. Newly formed bruises covered his body, and blood trickled out of his smashed nose. His gray hair was stained red. He didn't look like the same person who we had left less than two hours ago. "Oh, Art," I moaned. There was nowhere I could touch him. Not an inch lay unbloodied. And he was covered in tufts of orange orangutan hair.

Beside me, Lance swore, and then, when that didn't improve the situation, let loose a string of curses that ended in a primal howl. The EMTs stopped their advance down the hill to stare at the madman storming around their patient. One said, "Sir, you need to step out of the way."

Suddenly, Art's eyes flew open. One of the pupils was fully dilated, staring straight at the sky, while the other swiveled unnervingly to focus on me. "Noel," he said thickly.

"Art!" I wanted to hold him, but there wasn't any part of his body where I dared to even put my hand.

"Security tapes," he said. Gurgled, really.

"Art, don't talk," I tried to tell him. But I was crying now, not at all able to speak properly myself.

"Watch the tapes," he said. "So smart."

117

His eyes were closing again. He was drifting. But he rallied one more time to say, "It tried to save me, Noel. That animal tried to save my life." And then his eyes closed again, and Lance pulled me away so the EMTs could do their jobs.

Before we left to follow the ambulance back to the hospital, I had time to notice one thing. The primates, who had been worked into a fervor this morning, were all quiet. I think that was when I knew Art would die.

CHAPTER 9

I sobbed all the way to the hospital, cursing myself for leaving him alone.

"He wasn't alone," Lance said. "Darnell and Trudy were there the whole time, and the lunch volunteers came in at noon."

"What happened?" I asked.

Lance explained. "When she called, Trudy said Art went out to the security shed to get the tapes and didn't come back. She wanted my OK to organize a search party."

"He doesn't need to get any tapes from the shed," I protested. "They download to his computer every night." Then, "I knew it, I knew it! He was going right back out there to look for it alone!"

"I don't know," Lance said. "Probably, yes."

"He wasn't out front," I pointed out. "He would have been out front if he'd been going up to the security shed."

"Probably," Lance said again. "But he was

telling you to look at the tapes."

"For God's sake, it's all digital!" I cried. Lance glanced over at me, not risking his eyes off the road for long at this speed. I shook my head and set aside the question of why Art would claim we were looking for tapes when everything was digital. The man had a head injury. It was impossible to know what he meant. I said, "OK, so he went out front, then what? How did he get out back? He said the orangutan tried to save his life. Do you think he meant spare?"

"No," Lance said. "I think he meant 'save.' "

"Why? You saw all that hair. It already hit him once this morning. He thought it was pulling its punches then. Maybe that was his warning. Maybe he found it again, and . . ."

"No," Lance said. "No. Darnell said Art came staggering up from the enclosures maybe five minutes after Trudy hung up with me. He was still talking then."

"What did he say?"

"Not much that made any sense. The only thing that Darnell got before Trudy sent him to make sure the gate was open for the ambulance was something along the lines of, "He would have clubbed me to death if it hadn't come along."

"He *who*?" I demanded, knowing that Lance had no better answer to that question than I did. "And which *it*?"

"I think the 'it' is the orangutan. But who would be back in our woods with a club?"

"Oh *God,*" I said. "And whoever he was, I think he *did* club Art to death."

"Me too," Lance said quietly. We were at the hospital now, arriving behind the ambulance, which roared up to the emergency entrance. Lance laced his hands over the steering wheel and rested his head on them for a minute. "I think he's already gone," he told me. "And before we go in there and find out, I need to know something."

"What?" I asked.

"Are you still ready to marry me tomorrow?"

"What?" How could he be thinking about the wedding right now?

"We're going to go into that emergency room, and it's going to be nuts. It will be hours before we find anything out, and we are going to be torn apart hoping we're wrong. We need to decide now, before all that happens, if we're going to celebrate anything tomorrow."

"Our families would be so disappointed if we didn't," I said.

"Our families can go *hang,*" Lance

snapped. "We're not getting married for them, are we?" When I didn't answer immediately, he prodded, "Are we?"

It was so hard to think. My feet wanted me to move inside. But I heard what Lance was saying, not only his words, but his meaning. He was asking if I had changed my mind. I wiped my face with my sleeve and, as much as I could, turned off my thoughts of Art. Instead, I breathed deeply and tried to think about my fiancé.

When Lance proposed to me last year over dinner, it was almost casual. I made Nana's prizewinning potato salad, and Lance raised the house's temperature baking our entrée. I couldn't remember what that main dish was. He probably could, but I wasn't about to admit that he'd shocked most of the meal clean out of my head. I remembered that it had a strong spicy smell, one that hung in my senses; I would forever associate it with our engagement. But whatever it was, Lance hadn't baked it one time since. Besides that aroma, what I remember is that we weren't ready to turn on the AC for the year, and the kitchen felt like the inside of the oven. So we moved dinner to the porch, where it was cooler.

Lance backed out of the house onto the porch, plates balanced in front of him, and no hands free. He said, "Get the door, will you please, Noel?" As if he needed to ask. I had already jumped up to shut the heat in the house. When I turned back to the table, he was sitting down to his food.

Our dishes are brown stoneware with a solid blue rim. But at my place, instead of a helping of whatever damned thing he'd heated up the house with, Lance had put a ring. The gold band and white diamond contrasted sharply with the plate. I made a low sound deep in my throat and held onto that doorknob like a lifeline.

Lance didn't look up. He studied his own plate instead, waiting for me. He had posed himself with a fork, like he was getting ready to dig in. But the fork didn't move toward the pungent food. It hovered in midair until it started shaking. And that was how I knew he was nervous.

"Lord, Lance," I said. "What brought this on?" I took myself over on rubbery legs and joined him at the table.

He looked up finally, but didn't say anything for a while. Then, "I've been thinking a lot. About you. About us." He had probably planned what to say, but the words still came to him slowly. I waited. At last, he continued. "And it's been nine years now. I'm not going to change my mind. I hope you aren't either."

I thought he might say more, but he went silent after that.

I laid a hand on his arm, the one he still hadn't lowered to the plate. I waited until he looked up at me. "No," I said. "I'm not. You're right, love. After nine years, I guess it's time."

We were both shaking too badly to get the ring on my finger.

His words came back to me now, sitting in the truck, heavy with the grief of what awaited us in the hospital. "I'm not going to change my mind," he'd said. But that was before Mama turned our quiet little ceremony into a spectacle with formal wear and dozens of guests. Yet he was the one asking me if I still wanted to marry him tomorrow. And he might have been asking if I wanted to postpone a celebration in the face of such tragedy, but I thought the question went much deeper.

Every last-minute decision had been solved by someone else's force. Never by mine. Certainly, there had been Mama and her chart propelling us forward. But also, Lance had been ready to talk to the caterer weeks ago, willing to visit the baker ages before I was. And completely upset that I wouldn't go pick out a wedding dress of my own. He was asking me if an idea that had sounded good back on our porch over a year ago had lost its appeal.

It had not.

So I turned Lance's own words on him. "I'm not going to change my mind," I told him now, as I opened my door and swung down onto the parking lot asphalt.

He got out of the truck and came around to join me. "Neither am I," he said. "And I don't think Art would have wanted us to stop now."

"No, he wouldn't." And then I started crying again because we were already speaking of our dearest friend in the past tense.

Lance and I sat out in the emergency room waiting area simultaneously hoping for and dreading news. Back when we left the center, I had left an urgent message for Art's nephew Rick. Without bothering to return the call, Rick came to the hospital, arriving shortly after we got inside.

His state of shock was far worse than ours. He had been on a job, and he kept saying, "I was so close by. Why didn't he call me?"

"He didn't call us either," Lance said. "I don't think he could."

We tried to explain exactly how bad Art's condition was, but Rick didn't seem to understand. Eventually, he said, "I was so close by," so many times that I realized what he meant by it. Rick owned a construction company, one of the few to survive the recession. He was "close by" because he was on the mall building site less than two miles away from the sanctuary.

"I didn't know your company was doing the mall," I told him, since our continued explanations about his uncle were having no impact whatsoever.

"Yeah," he told me, still sounding dazed. Then he added, "I'd have thought Darnell would have mentioned it." I shook my head and shrugged, not making the connection. "You know," he went on, seeing my confusion, "Darnell Marshall. Hasn't he been volunteering with you?"

"Yeah, but how do you know him?" I asked.

"Used to work for me," Rick said. "I've been hoping I could bring him back part-time. On the mall thing."

"Yeah," I said. "He's at the center right now."

Rick cocked his head quizzically at us and finally said, "Wonder why he didn't tell you." Before we could pursue the conversation further, a nurse appeared calling for Art's family. I thought we wouldn't be allowed back, but Rick lied smoothly for us, identifying me as his sister even though we had only really met him at Art's holiday parties until today.

I don't remember what was said, honestly. Only the expression on the doctor's face stayed with me, the way his eyes seemed wide and heavy, his mouth open and frowning at the same time. And I remember the smell. The same way that the spices of Lance's meal from our engagement stay with me, the antiseptic hospital stink will forever call to mind Art's death.

The next few hours of that day were a blur. Art was gone. His heart had stopped beating, and he had stopped breathing in the ambulance. No number of codes and doctors were able to save him.

"All the king's horses, and all the king's men," I murmured to Lance, who did not finish my nursery rhyme. We took turns sitting with him, Art's nephew still maintaining the pretext that I was his sibling.

At some point, Lance stepped out and placed some calls. Not long after, my mother and grandmother arrived with an entire pressure cooker full of soup. It had been intended for our meal after the rehearsal. Mama didn't say the word "centerpieces" even once. Instead, she dished me a bowl of vegetables and beef floating in a tomato base, then handed me a spoon and said, "Eat. Please, honey."

I ate. What else could I do?

Then I suddenly remembered that the primates would need food again this evening. I leapt to my feet, but Lance said, "I've got Trudy and Darnell taking care of things at the center."

"But are they *safe*?" I demanded.

"Everybody is moving in pairs, and I got the security company to send in a couple of extra guys. Plus, right now the place is swarming with cops."

Mama asked, "Will they shoot it?" and it was several long silent moments before I realized she meant the orangutan.

"Why would they shoot the orangutan?" I demanded. "It didn't do this!"

"How can you be sure?" Mama asked. "You said yourself that Art probably went out looking for it on his own."

Before I could answer, Lance cut in, "And he probably ran into poachers or trespassers. Somebody beat him with a branch. The police found that."

Mama couldn't let a point go, especially if it was something she didn't understand, until she'd hashed it over a dozen ways. So even though Lance's tone and body language should have been a deterrent, and even though I was standing right beside her heading for panicked hyperventilation, my mother said, "I don't understand why that makes the animal a less likely suspect."

"Primates don't use tools the way we do," Lance snapped, pushing away the bowl of soup she was offering him. It had been sitting so long that it had gotten cold anyway. "There's anecdotal evidence that a few chimps in the wild will beat each other with tools. But that's not orangutans. I guess it might have thrown a branch, but that's not what Art said. This kind of hurt, it's human." He looked up as he spoke, not at Mama, but at me.

"It has fingerprints," I added, my words running together as I hurried to get them out. "Surely the police can figure out if it touched the branch at all!"

"But," Mama protested, and then she stopped.

We were all thinking about the same thing now. Lance was forcing us to think about it. For a bitter moment, I wanted the orangutan to have beaten Art, because if it were an animal, then it would have been easier to avoid thinking about who had beaten me.

CHAPTER 10

I met Alex Lakeland halfway through my graduate program when he accompanied Lance to a rescue center function. I liked being a scientist with a social life, a smart girl who knew how to have a good time. Lance himself was a little too introverted to attract me, but his brother swept over in a button-down shirt and said, "I'm bored sick. Let's go dancing," and right away he had my attention.

I liked going to bars on Fridays. I could come home tipsy with a research insight at two a.m. and call Lance, certain that he would be awake and thinking along similar lines. Even then, we thought alike. But I was attracted to Alex.

Art's fantasies to the contrary aside, Lance and I didn't date until after things fell apart so spectacularly for Alex and me. I was following up a biology degree with work toward a doctorate in the same field when I picked up a research assistant position at the primate sanctuary. Art had a vision, and he was selling it to anyone listening. He liked to get a student or donor out behind the barn and say, like he hadn't courted a dozen others with the same words, "Primatologists with advanced degrees go into labs because that's where the money lies. Rescue work is haphazard and poorly funded." He swept an arm around as if to prove his point with the barely adequate facility surrounding him. "But look at these animals. They need us. And if we can convince those eggheads to get out of the laboratory and into the field, think about the changes we can make. For us. For them."

At that time, the center had about two dozen monkeys and two chimpanzees. Art was raising money for a more complete enclosure. The spiel continued, "Moreover, researchers, the people with doctorates, are so quick to generalize from a single experience. We need," and here his voice swelled to a rich crescendo, doubtless a tone cultivated to draw his Ironweed U donors in with repetition of the school's mission statement, "to put more social-justice-minded researchers into the *field*. Too few of the so-called experts are willing to listen to stories from keepers and trainers. We have a unique

131

opportunity with *this* sanctuary to bridge *that* divide, to establish research that will back up and explain the anecdotal evidence. That's how we can make rescue work a worthwhile scientific venture for a greater number of scientists." Like most of the students and potential donors who came into Art's domain, I was captivated by his unique ideas and rich baritone voice. Unless he was in a cage covered in hay and sweat, he dressed impeccably, and somehow made the hard work seem like a business venture that required the right team. I found myself drifting from laboratory biology into primatology.

Lance hailed from the Pacific Northwest. After travelling in Africa, he found himself following his little brother to college. He came to Ironweed on a football scholarship, following on the heels of the younger, more athletic Alex. But he was a quick hand at everything he tried, and Ironweed didn't field the best team. It wasn't hard for him to get his trip to Ohio paid for by the Ironweed athletics department. Ironweed loved him because his high GPA spoke well for the team.

Its coaches *had* to graduate their students, because those students didn't have futures in the pros. Its reputation was more for turning out good coaches, and most of the young men who suited up every Saturday in the fall did so with an eye to one day leading teams of their own.

And then there was Lance. He took the scholarship because he was a decent player and it would pay for his education, but he came to Ironweed for its science program. He did not take a degree in sports anything, but instead divided his time between the field and the lab. Even as an undergraduate, he worked at the sanctuary. Where I didn't find out about Art's venture so close to my own back door until I came home from my BA (and to my credit, the center was still in its infancy then), Lance came specifically to work with Art.

He had traveled to Africa as a young teen, and what he learned there about primates drew him toward a degree in that field. As soon as he graduated high school, he went back to Africa, only returning for his degree four years later because a research visa was hard to obtain without one. He wanted to work full-time in his chosen field. He heard about Art and his center from Alex and set his sights on attending Ironweed. He was Art's first real student after Art opened the sanctuary doors. I came along later.

Lance and I worked together at the center

throughout graduate school. We partnered on several research projects, writing grants and papers together, but never feeling any attraction. Or anyway, I didn't feel attraction. I found out later that Lance felt it, and strongly, but never acted, because I was always dating somebody else. And I did, too. I went around with several guys, all of them really the same guy with different names. I thought that since they were all I could pick up, they must be all Ironweed had to offer. I expected I would finish my degree and move away, that maybe the good guys were in larger cities.

I assumed Lance was planning to leave after he completed his degree, when I thought about it at all. He said as much, speaking of Africa with great nostalgia. It never crossed my mind that he had come to Ironweed meaning to stay. I didn't realize in those days that he was invested completely in Art's vision, and that he wanted to remain in rural Ohio so he could continue his research with his mentor. He loved the center and, like Art, he couldn't imagine himself anywhere else. And that was the state of affairs when Lance brought Alex to the center function, where he asked me to dance.

Even then, Alex was on the path to a

strong coaching career, like so many other Ironweed football graduates before him. He was an offensive coordinator for Toledo South's football team, and I don't know whether it was the cologne or his fondness for ten-gallon hats, but I liked him from that first moment of introduction.

The two brothers looked a lot alike. They both had black hair and gray eyes, angular jawlines, and in those days, they both wore close-cropped beards. But where Lance was reedy and tall, Alex was barrel-chested and somewhat shorter. He had probably been visiting Lance to dodge the shrapnel from a bad breakup, but I didn't know that at the time. He was also already completely sloshed when he came up to me at that function.

I *did* recognize the drunkenness, and I thought it was endearing. He said, "Let's *dance*," even though this was one of those coat and tie affairs where well-heeled donors circulated in the university's conference rooms politely sipping champagne while they waited for Art to show a video about the larger chimpanzee enclosure he was hoping to fund.

"No, I don't think we'll be dancing here," I said.

"Then come on with me," he said. "I

know exactly where we need to be. I'll even let you drive."

I stayed until after my part in the presentation, then let Alex lure me away. I drove him out to a nightclub, where we danced until two thirty in the morning. Within two months, we were spending every weekend together, and within three, he had asked me to marry him.

I couldn't say yes. It was too soon, too fast for someone like me, who did everything through planning and analysis. My refusal didn't end our relationship, but that was when things started to unravel. Three months and he owned my soul. But I didn't understand that. It was years of therapy before I realized how quickly I had given myself away. I did see that nearly every time I joined him or he joined me, Alex was drunk, but that described any of the guys I went around with. But after I declined that proposal, the loving hand he laid on my arm whenever we left a building became a pincer, the arm around my shoulder a vise grip.

And then he started hitting. I was an educated woman who understood the cycle of violence from an intellectual standpoint. I didn't know what it was like to love someone who terrorized me. At first, it was only when he was visibly drunk, and I blamed the alcohol, not the man drinking it. But even in those early days, I knew better than to tell him he had a problem. He had used the phrase, "if you know what's good for you" the first time he struck me, and I did know. Or I thought I did.

I shut up and took it, sure that Alex was a scientific riddle, ready for me to solve him. Instead of looking up domestic violence, I looked into changing myself. I accepted his marriage proposal, because I thought he was acting out the hurt I had caused him when I said "no" the first time.

Our relationship improved for a little while after that. He turned back into the merry dancer who had picked me up at the center's function. We made a whirlwind trip out west so I could meet Sophia and Alex's father, Wayne. His parents were distant, at best, and Sophia even said, "You'll be like the other ones," right to my face.

When we got home and I asked Alex which other ones Sophia had meant, he lit into me with a kitchen mug that shattered into a thousand pieces. In the emergency room, I told the doctor I fell through a glass door. He didn't believe me, and he even managed to get me away from Alex long enough for a nurse to ask if I had been abused, but I kept lying to cover for the man I thought I loved.

And so we went on for eleven more months. It wasn't all bad. We still lived in separate cities, and I saw him mainly on weekends. But he would appear at the center sometimes with roses, in the middle of the week. Or he would send candy through the mail. He threw me a surprise birthday party with all his friends at his apartment. And I stayed with him for those times. For the beautiful surprises and the moments of love.

But Alex was convinced that I had somebody on the side. Somebody named Lance. In reality, I had come to the realization that I wouldn't leave the center without finding another job. And I wasn't looking very hard for a job because I knew they didn't exist. I loved the animals at Art's sanctuary. And I spent a great deal of time that should have been devoted to my dissertation in developing new enrichment activities.

Alex couldn't leave *his* job. Not a rising star in the world of NCAA coaching. And in any case, his work paid better, and he thought that since I wasn't planning to use my doctorate to earn big bucks in a lab once I completed it, it must be largely for show. He started referring to it as my "M-R-S." A therapist later pointed out that he felt threatened to have a girlfriend with more education than he had.

He started spying on me, and became convinced I was cheating on him with his brother. I *was* frequently in Lance's company those days, as I had been throughout grad school. We were research partners and friends. Lance suspected the abuse before he was certain, as much because he knew his brother's history as because he knew me.

And then he knew for sure.

Even though I always wore long sleeves at work, the spider monkeys gave me away one day. I shut their enclosure gate and the mesh snagged on my sleeve at the elbow, jerking me forward and ripping the fabric. I stood regaining my bearings for a moment too long after I got disentangled from the metal. I didn't feel the tail that snuck in while I was staring straight at its owner. I turned to walk away from the enclosure, and I stepped straight out of my shirt. It was so surprising that I didn't do any of the things I might have done to stay dressed if I had seen it coming. But my shirt jerked once, I pulled my arms free to get untangled, and it popped off over my head. In an instant, I found myself exposed.

I squeaked and crossed my arms over my bra, but it was my arms that I should have been covering, and my stomach, and my back. I looked around to see how I might get back my clothing, since its new owner had pulled it close to the mesh and was working it through the two-inch-wide gaps with dexterous fingers. When I turned back, there was Lance, staring open-mouthed, a look on his face that could only be called heartbreak. I fled indoors and got a spare top out of my locker.

When I came out of the bathroom, clothed once more, Lance confronted me directly. He said, "I have a phone number for you."

"Leave me alone," I told him.

He said, "No."

"Leave me alone, Lance Lakeland. I have to take this kind of crap from Alex, but you've got no claim on me whatsoever."

"No you *don't,*" he told me. "You don't have to take *that* from anybody. Listen, Bub's been engaged twice already. I should have told you sooner, but I don't mess around in his life. And I didn't know for sure what was going on. But I know both women broke it off pretty quickly. And I know you're my friend. And I know he . . . I know he did that to you." Lance pointed to the top half of my body. I felt like it would never be protected despite the fresh shirt I wore. It was impossible to say which purpling or yellowish mass he meant, or whether he was referring to all of them together. He went on. "His last fiancée was named Nicole. She gave me her number to give to you."

"What are you talking about?"

Lance said, "I don't . . . she didn't mean you specifically, but right after they split, she gave me her number and said to give it to Alex's next . . . arm candy." He blushed at the term even more deeply than I had seen him blush at the sight of my bruises.

"Leave me *alone.*" I was trying not to cry, humiliated to have this part of my private life exposed.

"I didn't know why she gave it to me, or I wouldn't have held onto it this long," he began, but I left. It was more than I could stand to hear.

Since he couldn't get me to listen, he went behind my back and gave the number to my mother. Mama already knew. Arguments with her about Alex had led to me moving into the apartment. She tried to get the police involved, but since I wouldn't report any abuse, they didn't take an interest. When Lance brought Mama that phone number, *she* called Nicole, who agreed to call me.

I wasn't home, so she got the machine. She said, "Hi, my name's Nikki, and I hope you can call me back."

That was it. She didn't leave her number, and she even concealed her voice, tried to use a chipper lilt so nobody could recognize her. But Alex did. Checking up on me, he played the messages before I got home that day to hear them. I always checked my complex's lot for his car, because he was showing up more and more frequently without warning.

So I knew he was at my apartment before I went inside. I was braced for trouble. But delaying trouble with him made it worse in the long run. When I walked in, I knew at once by the collection of beer cans spilling out of my sink that he was drunk. I came inside and shut the door. Then I turned my face to the wood and leaned into it, drained from the days of listening to Lance and my mother say horrible things about Alex, things that were that much worse because they were true. Standing there, I heard Nicole's voice, and it confused me. "Hi, my name is Nikki, and I hope you can call me back." Click. Click. Understanding washed over me. The answering machine.

He would want to know who this was, this Nikki, and what would I tell him? "Hi, my name is Nikki and . . ." Click. Click. No. He didn't *want* to know. He *already knew.* Alex was rewinding the tape. Playing it over and over again. He had done this before with messages from Lance, searching innocent statements for signs of an affair.

"Hi, my name . . ." Click. Click. It wouldn't do any good to claim I didn't know her and couldn't imagine what she wanted. Lying, like putting it off, only made things worse. Mama had told me to expect the call. I had been fuming all the way home about her interference, her attempts to involve the police, and this ridiculous effort to drag in Alex's ex-girlfriend.

"Hi, my . . ." Click.

Click.

"Hi . . ." Click.

Click. He played the message repeatedly while I stood breathing, bracing, because I knew what was coming. If I tried to leave, he would be on top of me faster than I could open the door I was leaning against.

"Hi, my name is Nikki . . ." Click. Click.

Bang! The answering machine hit the door beside my head.

I flinched to the left and tried to explain. "No, please, Alex. You don't understand."

Another *bang,* this one on the other side of my head. The phone. Terrible choice of words. I knew better than to tell Alex he didn't understand something.

The next sound was a crunch. I turned from the door to see him coming toward me, spinning the phone base by its cord. The crunch was a picture splintering as the impromptu mace connected with it. Alex continued whipping the phone base around his head, coming at me with a look like murder in his eyes.

"Help me," I whispered. I shouted it, screamed it. "Help me! *Help me!*" But nobody answered, and I barely had time to drop to the ground and bury my head between my knees, trying to protect it from a man who wouldn't show me mercy.

It must have gotten worse and louder, because a neighbor called the cops. But I don't remember anything after that moment when I realized Alex didn't mean to let me escape my apartment alive. At the hospital, *this* hospital, Lance and Art sat vigil with my family until they sent me to Columbus in a helicopter.

Now, I couldn't stand being out in the waiting room, knowing that Art wasn't going to walk out the doors again. Lance and I had left Art's room to give Rick some time

144

alone. His mother was Art's sister, and Art was the only remaining sibling of three. Now Rick had no family left on that side. I didn't know about his father. Maybe Rick had no one left at all. I couldn't stand to be still, but I couldn't bear to invade Rick's space, and my anxiety sent me straight back into memory.

They thought for a while that I might die, and I still bore scars down my back from the electric cord's prongs. The neighbor's screams drove Alex out before the police arrived, and that saved my life. That and my dropping down face forward. My facial bones were broken in several places, but not destroyed. He went after my shoulders and spine, and he fled before he broke my neck. Through plea bargaining, he wound up in a rehab program instead of jail. To his credit, he had never tried to violate the restraining order. Had never tried to make contact.

It was only when I was recovering from being beaten half to death by his brother that I realized how much Lance cared for me. I could barely complete even basic tasks for myself when I was released from the hospital, so he helped my parents move me back home, into a downstairs room because I still had dizzy spells and couldn't manage stairs.

He brought me the results of the experiments we had completed, collected books and articles from scientific journals for me, then typed up dissertation chapters I wrote in shaky longhand because I couldn't lift either arm as high as a keyboard yet.

In the first six weeks, when it seemed like all I could really be grateful about was that the disorientation from the head trauma decreased the more I used my mind, Lance waited patiently for me to think through concepts that were my own to begin with and hid the frustration he must have felt when I simply couldn't remember. When physical therapy for my slowly healing left shoulder left me in tears, Lance put a pen in my right hand because he knew I craved work to overcome my thousand degrees of guilt and self-doubt. When my family watched me with pity as I limped around, and jumped in to help me with even the smallest tasks, Lance bought me space to do things on my own, no matter how long it took.

I resisted my growing emotions for him, frightened of walking into a rebound relationship that would only end in sorrow, but I slowly came to understand that I loved Lance deeply, more passionately than I had ever loved his brother. Our first real date followed the night I hobbled across the stage to collect my PhD a few minutes after he collected his.

In the years since we moved in together, Lance had resumed conversations with his brother, clipped discussions that rarely lasted more than a few minutes. They had never completely lost contact. But Alex did not call the house, only Lance's cell. And from what little I overheard, most of their talk centered around their parents.

Mostly, I left the room and tried not to think at all when Alex called. But now, his face was impossible to drive out of my mind.

CHAPTER 11

Mama turned on Lance. "That horrible brother of yours," she began. She clutched her ladle so hard her whole arm shook. And then Nana eased it out of her fingers so Mama could sit down.

I hastened to say, "But Alex wasn't anywhere near the center today, so don't worry."

"Yes he was," Lance cut in. He took my arm as he spoke, cradling and supporting it, holding on to me in case I fell.

"What?" I nearly spilled my own soup jerking my arm away.

"He came out to talk about Mom. He wanted to see me in person. I guess he got there right after we left, but Art put him to work."

"He was *there*?" I demanded. "He could have . . ."

"I don't *think* so." Lance was clearly choosing his words carefully. "Trudy says

Art swore her and Darnell to secrecy, then lied and told Alex we would be right back after we got the license. Art meant well. He couldn't possibly understand how serious this is with Mom. Anyway, Alex got sick of waiting, and after he'd helped with primate lunch, he went home. He was long gone from the sanctuary by the time Art went missing."

"He would have been furious when he found out we weren't coming back!" I said, backing further away from my fiancé. "What if he didn't leave at all? What if he drove down the lane and waited?"

Lance shook his head. "I don't think so," he said again. "But I guess we might see that on the security video. If he did wait, and Art stumbled around . . . it still doesn't make sense, though. I was *with* Bub at our place when Trudy called. And Bub's got other stuff on his mind right now. I don't think so."

"Where was the branch?" I demanded, trying now to concentrate on that. If I thought about the branch, then I wouldn't think about Alex. But instead of distracting me, thinking about the branch made it worse. Alex had always been one for using whatever was on hand.

"I don't know," Lance said.

"So has anybody actually seen it? How do they know?" What if it wasn't a branch? Had I looked the way Art had? So bloody that I was barely recognizable? Hard to say. Most of the damage had been done to my shoulder, back, and skull. Alex had purpled the left side of my face, but I'd managed to shield those bones from breakage.

"Trudy overheard the police radios," Lance said. Then he crossed his arms and sat back down to his own cold meal. Trudy was a dispatcher for the sheriff's office who volunteered at the sanctuary before Art charmed her away from that job with promises of an underpaid internship. He persuaded her to go back to school and get a completely different degree by offering her less money and the nosebleed insurance that Ironweed gave its grad students. She jumped at the chance. Never having liked police work, she wasn't a hard sell. But it probably wouldn't have mattered if she had loved it. Art could coax anybody. His love for his work made the listener want to share it. And it was good now that Trudy knew most of the force, a little bit of police procedure, and every single code that squawked out of the police radios.

If she said the police found a branch, and the police thought someone used the branch to beat Art, then what she said was certainly the case. "Oh God," I said. I wished I hadn't jerked away from Lance. I wished Mama hadn't sat down beside the soup. In spite of all my efforts, all I could think about was fists. Alex's fists. And the telephone base.

Lance might not think his brother had killed Art, but the coincidence seemed too great for me. It pulled me back a decade, and suddenly I couldn't stand up any longer as memory took away the strength in my legs and made me sit down. Lance moved nearer as I started crying again.

I leaned into my fiancé, trying to get myself under control. Lance pulled me in close, stroking my back and saying, "It's going to be OK," over and over, until my ragged tears wound down.

Almost as soon as I'd regained my composure, my phone rang. Trudy. "Damn, I meant to call Lance," she said. "I know you're distraught right now, Noel, but we've got trouble. These cops have no idea what to do with our primates. I had to take a gun away from the spiders."

"A what?"

"A service revolver. Spider monkey picked it straight up with its tail."

"Oh dear Lord, a gun!" I said, envisioning the harm *that* could cause.

"A gun what?" Mama asked.

At the same time, Lance exclaimed, "Who has a gun?"

"The spiders got one," I said.

"I got it back!" Trudy was quick to clarify. "And I don't think it could have fired. That's not our biggest problem, though."

"It isn't?"

"No," she said. "They don't understand that even if an orangutan *could* have taken a branch to Art like that, it *wouldn't* have done so. And they can't even be formally sure it was a branch that . . ." Her voice quavered, because she had as much trouble talking about what had happened as the rest of us.

Finally, she continued, "If they see the orangutan, they're going to shoot it on sight."

"We're coming," I said, and hung up.

There wasn't anything we could do in the hospital, and there wasn't any reason for us to malinger in the emergency waiting room, where we must have made a strange sight for the people coming in with broken arms and bloodied faces. There was a grieving room we could have gone to, but Rick's wife and children had arrived and were there with him. And he was Art's real family. All of it. He had been so kind to let us stay with him to say goodbye, but it seemed inappropriate to disturb such a sharp and private grief any further.

We didn't need to be taking up any more room out here. Trudy needed us back at the sanctuary to save the animal that Art insisted had tried to save him. "Can you tell . . . um . . . my brother that there's an emergency at the animal sanctuary?" I asked a nurse. "He wanted me to wait for him, but I can't."

It was true. Rick had said, "I think I need to talk to you," in a choked voice as his wife came in. But whatever he might have needed to talk to us about would keep. I was *not* going to call him when he needed to be with his family and when we needed to get back to work.

As we left, Mama said, "I guess I'll call the guests. Do you think Sophia could help me do that?"

Lance and I exchanged a glance. Mama thought the wedding was off. I embraced her tightly before I said a word. I was so grateful that she could recognize the depth of our tragedy, and that she was willing to throw over her perfect chart for a crisis. "Only the ones coming to the rehearsal dinner," I said. "Can the rest of you walk through it without us tonight? I think we probably have the simplest jobs tomorrow."

"Are you *sure*?" Mama asked.

It struck me, as it had when Lance asked me if I still wanted to marry him, that Mama wasn't asking the smaller question. She didn't only want to know if I wanted to get married tomorrow. She wanted to know if I wanted to get married at all. She remembered, still, every bit as painfully as I did, what happened the last time I was engaged.

"Yes," I said. It came out choked, like I was talking around tears again. But really, it was the first time since the craft store that I hadn't felt like crying.

She hugged me. "OK," she said. "We'll figure out something." And Lance and I were off again in a race to the center.

"He could have done it, Lance," I said, as we barreled along the same stretch of road for the third time in a day. I meant Alex, and Lance didn't waste time pretending otherwise.

"Could have," Lance said. "But I don't think so."

I began listing the strikes against Alex. "We have no idea when anybody decided Art was really missing in relation to when he left. Alex might have had time to . . ."

Lance interrupted me with a shake of his head. "I don't think so," he said yet again.

"It's not the timing. I'm with you there. But he's . . . he's not the same person we used to know, Noel. He's changed. Really changed." The truck wasn't eating up the road like it had been on our last trip this way, but I was still amazed we didn't find ourselves ticketed. Lance went on, "You'll have to see him before you really believe me. But that's not why I think he's innocent."

"What, then?" I tried to remember if I'd ever heard Lance actually defend his brother before. Ever. They hadn't formally split until Alex battered me to within an inch of my life, but I didn't think they were close before then. Other than the diminutive "Bub," Lance had never showed any affection for Alex that I could remember, nor had Alex for Lance.

Now, he cleared his throat. "The reason isn't a good thing." He spoke slowly, crafting his thoughts before each word. This was how Lance talked when he was working through a puzzle. Crosswords and primate research alike received this treatment. It irked me for Alex to get that same level of respect. Then Lance said, "Let's go about it this way. When did your dad's first credit card go missing?"

"What has that got to do with your

155

brother?"

"Work with me here," Lance said.

"OK." I tried to clear my mind and think, but it was nearly impossible. Finally, I said, "Months ago, I think."

"It happened once, months ago. I mean recently."

"Then I don't know. And I don't see why it matters."

"I think," he said, "and in retrospect I should have seen it, that it was the Friday after we picked up Mom from the airport and brought her to dinner at your folks' place. Right before your first dress fitting." He gave that a minute to sink in. "I'm pretty sure the excess charges started that night."

"Lance, what are you telling me?"

He took a deep breath and said, "My mother has been stealing your father's cards. Every time she sees him. And then she's been taking your car and driving into Columbus to run them up."

"She has *not*!" I said. "Her friends have been shuttling her. She's only taken my car on one trip when I begged her to get my oil changed because I'm past due. That's exactly the kind of ridiculous accusation Alex would make. I think he made this whole thing up, and the part about her wanting to wreck the house, too."

156

"Noel, she admits it," Lance told me.

"Of course she does," I snapped. "She's backing up her . . ."

"No!" he interrupted me. "She denied it until Alex showed me the odometer and the shopping bags. Unless the techs at the lube shop botched the distance to the next oil change, she's put close to three hundred fifty miles on the car she's claimed she wasn't driving. And the whole guest room closet is full of what she's bought."

I sank back against the seat, flabbergasted. "So your mother has been stealing *my* father's credit cards to do what? Why?"

Lance said, "Anything at all to drive the wedge. Anything at all."

"She really hates me that much?" I asked.

Lance said, "I don't know if it's directed at you, or if she's gone back around the crazy bend. Do you know what she bought?"

"No," I said. "What? At this point, I don't think anything would surprise me." Mama had confided in me that there were, between the four cards, close to five thousand dollars in unauthorized charges.

"Casserole dishes."

"And what else?"

"Nothing else," he said. "Two hundred ninety-two casserole dishes. I had to count them."

It was the final thing my brain couldn't process that day. Marriage licenses, centerpieces, Art's death, and my future mother-in-law plotting against me with casseroles. "My God, Lance. I wish I'd known this earlier. We could have floated some damned votives in those and skipped the whole centerpiece shopping trip." And then we both laughed so hard that Lance had to pull over to the side of the road with tears streaming down his face.

"OK," I finally said. "But how does that exonerate Alex? I will concede that she might have him distracted, but he's the only person I know capable of the kind of violence it would take to . . . to . . ." My hysterical laughter threatened to turn ugly again, as my mind flashed to Art's ruined face.

"It doesn't," Lance agreed. "Not entirely. But it makes me think we're still looking for someone. He didn't even stay at the center long enough for us to have gone out and returned. And I've got that from Trudy and Darnell both. He stayed for an hour, slogged around a couple of buckets, and left. He wanted to tell me about Mom in person, but he didn't dare leave her alone for much longer than that."

"That's what he says." I wasn't letting the

man who had nearly killed me off the hook so easily.

"It's what he says, and I believe him," Lance told me. "We need to see the security video."

Now *that* was something we could agree on.

It was heading on toward sunset on the most insane, horrible day ever when Lance and I arrived once more at the Midwest Primate Sanctuary. Even the sign out front brought Art to mind. He had envisioned interconnected sanctuaries, not merely accredited affiliated institutions, but a nation-wide primate rescue network. Midwest Primates was supposed to be the first, with five others to follow around the country. I didn't know if his dream would ever come to fruition now.

But we had other worries, like the police car drawn up across the lane, and the large sheriff's deputy standing outside the car, barring our entrance.

Lance pulled in, and the deputy was beside the truck before we could even open our doors. "Need to see some ID, folks," he said. Someone had clearly prepared him for our arrival, because we didn't get "Move along." Fumbling for my wallet, I produced the envelope with the marriage license instead, and handed it to Lance so I could root deeper in my purse. The cop whistled and I looked up.

Lance had handed the envelope to the officer, who, naturally enough, had opened it. "Oh for pity's sake." I leaned across Lance to pluck back the marriage license and hand the man my driver's license instead. "Why'd you give him that?" I asked Lance.

"You handed it to me," Lance protested.

"To *hold* so it wouldn't get messed up while I dug around in here."

"Sorry."

The cop said, "When's the wedding?" as he studied my driver's license and, apparently finding my own features similar enough to those of the woman in the picture, returned it.

"Tomorrow," I muttered. *Not that it's any of your business. And don't you dare ask me if the deceased was going to be the best man.* But why would he ask that? Of course he wouldn't. It was my own mind playing with my soul.

"Good luck," he said. "Be careful going back there. Drive slowly. Critters run right across that lane."

As if we didn't know already. "Thanks."

We had to get through another roadblock

at our gate. "Keep your eye out for that monkey. It's out there hollering in the trees now. We're trying to get a mess of dogs in to take care of it."

"You're *what*? It's . . ." Lance began.

"First of all, orangutans aren't monkeys," I interrupted him. "And second, you aren't bringing a bunch of dogs onto this property without . . ." Without what?

"A warrant!" Lance, the lover of crime shows, finished for me.

The deputy shrugged. "Just don't get killed."

In the barn, we found a sheriff's detective camped out in a folding chair, guarding Art's office. He had interviewed our volunteers, and after they delivered lunch to the enclosures, he had sent them all home. Only Trudy and Darnell remained, at their own insistence because Lance had largely put them in charge and because the police seemed to think our apes and monkeys were getting ready to swarm out of their cages at any moment.

"This one's over my head, folks," the detective, Andrew Carmichael, said to Lance's question about gaining access to Art's office. "That computer is part of a chain of evidence. At this point, I'm trying to secure the scene."

"What about dogs? The deputy out front said . . ."

The detective shook his head. "Garret's terrified of the mosquitoes. Nobody's said anything about dogs to me."

I felt some measure of relief, but on the topic of Art's office, he was polite but firm. We couldn't get anything out, and the places we could go on our own property were limited. It didn't help that in addition to all of the day's sounds and images floating through my mind, the theme from *The Andy Griffith Show* had started whistling around in my head as soon as Carmichael introduced himself. His pale brown police hat evoked the program for me, even though Andrew Carmichael was black. "What about the orangutan?" I asked. Lance added his explanation about primates' tool use, orangutans' in particular.

Detective Carmichael said, "There's a couple of things you aren't considering. First of all, I know Miss Trudy. Love her to death, but she's too quick to jump to conclusions from what she hears on our squawk boxes. We don't *know* or *not know* about a murder weapon until anything we *might* have found has been analyzed and compared with your friend's skin and clothing." At least he didn't call Art "the victim."

At the hospital, Art's name had almost immediately been subsumed under this new identity as "the victim." "Your friend" was much gentler.

"And from what little your people have told me, the animal could have killed your friend with its bare hands. Is that right?"

I nodded mutely, flashing back to this morning when the big ape smacked Art so casually across the road. Lance said, "Could have, but . . ."

Detective Carmichael went on. "So what if your friend tried to defend himself with a club? If there *was* a club, what if it had the ape's blood on it?"

"But he said it tried to save him," I protested.

"I hear you," Carmichael told me. "I'm trying to get you to see this through my lens. I know this is hard for you. But I'm not doing my job if I don't follow up on every single possibility. And right now, my best suspect is a pie-faced redhead who should really turn himself in for questioning."

The detective's attempt at humor fell flat. Lance said, "It can't do that if you shoot it on sight."

"No," Carmichael said. "But it also can't kill one of my officers or one of your people. Safety has to come first."

Lance started to argue something else, but an idea struck me. I said, "So, 'shoot' could have a pretty broad interpretation, right?"

"What do you mean?" Carmichael asked.

I said, "If we could arm your people with *dart* guns, they could neutralize it with one of those. There's no reason 'shoot on sight' has to mean 'kill on sight,' right? We're not advocating letting the thing run wild. It's in our best interests to see the orangutan contained."

"Wait a minute." The detective pulled out his cell phone, talked for a few minutes, then nodded, hanging up. "Maybe," he said. "But it's ultimately going to be my supervisor's call. He'll be back up to the barn pretty soon for you to ask him yourself."

I shrugged. I couldn't control that, much as I wanted to. When the animals were set loose from the private zoo in Michigan (and many of them wandered into Ohio), police had slaughtered them. Nearly fifty animals murdered because of a shoot-on-sight attitude. Lives lost because the police didn't know how to contain the animals appropriately. About time they got an education.

Lance said, "Noel, we've only got two dart guns."

"It's enough to start out with," I told him. "Damn shame if Art's orangutan died on our watch."

Somewhat reluctantly, Detective Carmichael let us into our own office, watching carefully while I looked up home numbers to beg help from the zookeepers I knew at the Ohio Zoo and elsewhere in the state. All four of them were willing to collect and deliver the dart guns in person. The mass execution of exotics saddened them as deeply as it did us. Our friends at the Ohio Zoo were particularly rent by the affair, since they and their staff had been scrambling to lure and contain the animals while the situation unfolded along the state border. But a scant six of the creatures freed into the wild had been rescued. They wanted to help us save the orangutan here. The others were equally passionate, but they were further away, both emotionally and physically. Still, they were coming.

They were coming, and I needed only to wait.

CHAPTER 12

At last, I had done something, and some of my feelings of helplessness faded. Now I could turn my attention to the animals we were already responsible for. Random officers posted in and around the enclosure area had our primates in a high state of excitement, and I could hear the racket inside the whole time I was making my calls. I wanted to get out there as soon as possible to minimize disruptions to their lives.

Lance booted up his computer.

"What are you doing?" I demanded.

"Getting the security videos," Lance said.

"Excuse me?" That was Detective Carmichael, eavesdropping on the conversation.

"I'm not planning to fool around in anybody's crime scene," Lance said. "The videos back up to Art's computer and to ours. You are welcome to sit down and join us watching." Lance braced himself in front of the machine, arms crossed like he thought he could actually stop the detective, or like he thought our computer wasn't now in the officer's provenance.

Carmichael seemed momentarily nonplussed. Trudy had, after all, and with our permission, given the police full control here. Detective Carmichael was, by his own description, the junior detective of two. The senior detective was still out on the grounds, at the place they had found by following Art's bloody trail back into the forest. Carmichael was up here to babysit us. He hadn't chosen the duty, but he was doing his best. Everybody else had been following his instructions pretty much to the letter. Our obstinacy clearly puzzled him.

For my part, while I didn't want the police disrupting our animals or, God forbid, shooting one, I wanted them here. We were all aware that whoever hurt Art might still be out in the woods. I scolded myself mentally for minimizing the violence. Art hadn't been hurt. He'd been killed. But I shied away from that knowledge to concentrate on the thing that had set me off on this train of thought. The police might believe he'd been attacked by an orangutan, but we knew he had not. There would no doubt be search warrants and the like to allow the cops full access in the future, and

167

even if not, we *wanted* them here, and we *needed* to cooperate with them.

That was why we had agreed with Trudy's willingness to give them full run of the place, even more than they would have needed. Even when Art was still alive. Maybe alive. Probably not. As I fished around in my mind to escape the cycle of Art's death and find a tactful way to tell Lance to back off and let the detective do his job, a human voice rose above the ape and monkey chatter out back. "Hey, give that *back.*"

Detective Carmichael groaned. "Not again," he muttered.

Instead of arguing with the man about our enclosures and office, his crime scene, and the boundaries of both, I jumped out of my chair. "Excuse me," I said, and brushed past him to find out what was wrong, Lance close on my heels.

Even from the top of the hill where we were, I could see the spider monkeys were at it again. They had a hat, and the unnerved officer to whom it belonged was standing under their cage, shouting. Trudy, who was already standing at the barn door looking down on things, groused, "I told him not to stand so close." Seeing us, she said, "Let me take care of it."

I said, "This one probably needs a team approach." She had been taking on the police as if they were her responsibility entirely, simply because she used to work dispatch, and I didn't think this fair to her. So I followed her down the hill, along with the detective. Behind us, Lance faded back into the barn.

The young cop should have been more wary, given that Trudy had already rescued a service weapon from this group of trouble-makers. But he was, as Carmichael con-firmed in the string of curses that followed us down the hill, a damned rookie. And maybe the young man thought he was far enough away from the spider monkeys. If so, he was wrong. He probably didn't even feel the tickly little tail encroaching on his head. I certainly hadn't felt the one that stole my shirt and exposed Alex's abuse so graphically to Lance.

We had to dodge yellow crime-scene tape and walk beside, rather than on, the worn footpath in the grass, as the police had care-fully marked off Art's trail. I found it hard to ignore the visceral reminder of his ab-sence, so I focused instead on the rookie deputy engaged in a battle of wills with an animal more cunning and stubborn than he could have imagined.

"Hey!" the officer shouted again.

"You're upsetting them. You'll make it worse," Trudy yelled. It was doubtful he heard her over the din.

The officer jumped up and made a swipe at the air, trying to retrieve his cap, but it was already miles above his head. He looked like a little kid in the middle of a game of keep-away. "Calm down!" Trudy called. "They'll never give it back if they know you want it."

He made another leap, and his fingers brushed the brim, but the monkey hoisted its tail higher.

"It's laughing at me!" he said accusingly, as Trudy, Detective Carmichael, and I drew nearer.

"Of course it is," I snapped. "You should have heard them the time they stole a shirt off of me. There I was in the middle of the yard half naked, and a bunch of nasty little monkeys laughing the whole time." I didn't know whether they were laughing or not. But I had seen Lance retreat toward our office, and I was looking for ways to buy him time.

"I need that hat!"

It was similar to Detective Carmichael's, with a flat brim and round bowl of a top. Maybe this was the same guy who would be filling out a very awkward report about the theft and return of his sidearm later tonight. I wondered how young he was, then how old I was that I was sizing up an officer of the law and casually labeling him a child.

I said, "Stay calm and we'll get it for you," then turned to Trudy. "I'll need your help to do this."

She and I were standing side by side, angled to face each other without losing sight of the monkey or cap. The hat's round top allowed the little monkey to balance it on its tail like a circus act with poles and spinning plates. On an inspiration, I panto-mimed flicking something to Trudy. She smiled her understanding.

"Do what?" Detective Carmichael eyed me warily. "Feed it? She did that by herself earlier." I half believed he was on to me. But then, maybe I was paranoid because I didn't know exactly what my monkeys and I were engaged in myself. The detective was accidentally right. The best way to get the hat back would be to barter with the animal. Trudy had done that earlier, trading the gun for a choice treat. I didn't want to succeed too soon, though.

"No sir," I improvised. "If we have to, we'll feed it, but that risks us being bitten. It's going to be aware that we've already tricked it once with snacks and might not be responsive to that."

"Then what? Deputy Greene needs his cap back."

"Spider monkeys are best at imitative behavior," Trudy piped up. "We need to show it what to do with its prize. Deputy Greene, stand back a little, and wait there, like you're getting ready to grab a disc. Detective, can we play catch with your crown?"

Detective Carmichael cocked an eyebrow, and I thought Trudy would get a lecture of some kind. But he pulled off his hat and flicked it to her in exactly in the style I had imagined. She caught it and threw it back, not to me, but to the detective. That wasn't what I had in mind, and I was already wondering how long I could maintain this charade or how long I would need to. To my surprise, he spun around and threw it to me from behind his back. I caught it and returned fire. Next he shot it overhand to Trudy. Then across his shoulder to me. Between his legs to Trudy. Seven times we threw his hat around between us, and I don't think he returned it to us the same way twice. Trudy looked like she could hold her own, but I was hard pressed on my end to keep it from hitting the ground.

Finally, he finished with a flourish and bowed. "Champion disc golfer," he said to me. "We play every Saturday down in Ironweed Park, and you ought to join back up, Miss Trudy. And bring your friend along. But what does that do toward getting yon deputy his hat back?"

By now, the other officers stationed around the enclosures were watching us, and when the detective bowed, they clapped appreciatively. Smoothly, Trudy said, "Look, it's getting ready to throw. Now that we've shown it what one *does* with these funny flat things, it may flip it over to Deputy Greene."

In fact, this was about the least likely thing to happen. The only thing I could say for sure was that we'd distracted the little animal from trying to eat the hat, as it had stared at us with a cocked head for most of the performance. It was still perched on its roost, waving the purloined item back and forth on the end of its tail. This evening was proving more interesting than any of the enrichment we could bury with its meals. And then another tail intervened and turned Trudy from liar to prophet.

"See!" Trudy said, as if she could have had any idea the hat would be stolen a second time. "They're making their own version of the game."

No. The second monkey came along and swiped the booty.

They couldn't run away without dropping their prize, thanks to the enclosure's mesh, and I was half afraid one or the other of them would pull the hat back to grab it with their fingers and direct it straight toward their sharp little teeth. Instead, they kept it up, stealing the hat back and forth with their tails in an apparent imitation of our throwing game.

"OK," I said. "This isn't how I imagined it, but they're very creative little critters." *No. Just very possessive ones.* "Officer Greene, there's a broom handle over there." We actually used it sometimes to hide objects under the hay at feeding time. "You need to poke it up and grab your hat exactly like they're doing with their tails."

To my complete surprise, it worked like a charm.

"Bravo," Detective Carmichael said, as Deputy Greene dusted off his cap and replaced it on his head. "Now stand *right there.*" The detective indicated a spot for the young deputy to place his feet, then waved off the rest of our police audience. "If that's everything, let's go back up that hill and see what your husband has found."

I wanted to say, *He's not my husband yet,* but I simply lacked the energy to argue. Then, while we were walking up the hill, the senior detective caught up to us, and it was some time before we got back to Lance and the computer. Until the unfamiliar human voice temporarily out-shrieked the rackety primates, I had hoped our dart guns could magically arrive from all parts of the state before Carmichael's possibly uncooperative supervisor returned from the woods. But a shout — "Wait for me, Andrew! Tell me more about these dart guns!" — quenched my hope.

Detective Carmichael introduced us. "Noel Rue, this is Detective Hugh Marsland." I nodded, then turned and walked toward the barn to buy myself thinking time. Detective Carmichael wanted to help us. Trudy had been buttering him up the whole time he was in the barn, and she had used coffee and her own time working as a dispatcher to build a marvelous rapport. He thought if the darts came in before his boss got back, he could maybe pass them off as the best option. Now that strategy was moot.

Lance came out when we entered the barn, as soon as he heard us talking. Then we spent the better part of forty-five minutes arguing back and forth about the merits of dart guns. Detective Carmichael proved to be a strong advocate in spite of his junior status. Even though I got the sense that he was uncomfortable with it, he argued successfully to get the zookeepers admitted to the premises, at least long enough to give *us* the dart guns.

When Christian Baker from the Ohio Zoo arrived, he prevailed upon Marsland to accept use of the nonlethal weapons. Christian was a burly man, tall with a massive chest, a graying beard, and a vaguely Scottish accent. "Look," he told the senior detective, "it was a public-relations nightmare when those poor critters had to be put down up north, wasn't it?" Christian managed to sound far more sympathetic than I would have done.

His voice even remained gentle when correcting Marsland, who was referring to the orangutan as an "orang." "That's offensive," Christian said. " 'Orang' means person. 'Orangutan' means 'person of the forest.' You don't want to be calling the orangutan the same thing as one of us." He said it like a kindly chiding schoolteacher. He sounded so disappointed in the ignorant detective who had said it that I thought now was a bad time to tell him I had forgotten that bit of college learning myself. Working in a sanctuary, it was easy to get caught up in the needs of the animals we served.

By the time Christian was through, the destruction of all those wild creatures up north sounded like an unfortunate accident, completely the fault of the fools who had freed them. And I agreed they bore responsibility there. But the laws that allowed a poorly staffed roadside zoo to collect so many wild animals in the first place carried an even greater burden. And the police, who reacted with violence instead of thinking through the situation, held the most immediate and public responsibility for the grim outcome.

At some level, Marsland must have felt the same way, because he eventually allowed Christian to approach pairs of officers and show them how to operate the guns. Christian said he would stay here until this was taken care of. We needed his help badly. We didn't even try to argue, and since he had our approval, the detectives didn't argue with his remaining, either. Trudy and Darnell were good. But she was an intern, and he was a volunteer. If Lance and I planned to get married tomorrow, they needed expert guidance in our absence.

Detective Marsland started phoning to

confirm that Art had been pronounced dead at the hospital so he could formally make the assault a death investigation. I couldn't imagine why it mattered.

Trudy was allowed to go off premises to make copies of our controlled drugs cabinet key, and Christian patiently taught the officers how to fill the darts if they ever needed to make one themselves. Now I at least knew the right cocktail for an orangutan. In the wake of their efficiency, Lance and I found ourselves once more sitting in front of his computer, looking at the program that backed up our security footage each night. After all, nobody had actually confiscated it yet.

While we were down tormenting the spiders into relinquishing Deputy Greene's cap, Lance had manually launched a backup. Now that it was complete, we had the files Art wanted us to look at. But before we could, Detective Carmichael appeared once more in the doorway.

"Why don't you go home, get some sleep tonight, and get married tomorrow?" he asked.

I didn't answer him.

Lance demanded, "Could *you* sleep?"

It was nine o'clock; the sun was finally setting. Christian, Trudy, and Darnell had worked out a sleep schedule that would allow them to rest and remain on the premises, and our overnight security had arrived in the form of a lumbering man named Jack and his equally burly partner Sam. Lance and I did not need to be here any longer. Yet the feeling remained that we could not go. The last time we left to go get married, someone died.

Detective Carmichael said, "I'm not the one giving orders. So it's a suggestion, but now you've got me wondering why your friend had to go out at all if these security files back up to your computers every night."

"My question exactly," Lance said.

Following their train of thought, I added, "Art may have *said* he was going out to look at the videos, but maybe he was really going out to look at whatever the videos showed."

"Does Miss Trudy know that?" Detective Carmichael demanded. "Because she and your volunteer were adamant . . ."

"I doubt they know it," I said. "And if they do, who thinks of such things in a crisis?"

Exhaustion and sadness sat heavily on me as the detective perched on a chair between Lance and me to watch with us and maybe see what we couldn't see. Maybe he was there because he wanted to keep us from deleting any files we might not have already launched. Or maybe he was simply being nice. Lance asked him, "Why don't *you* go home? If you're not the one giving orders, doesn't that mean you have to get back to the station and fill out reports?"

"It does," Carmichael said, glancing at Lance in a thin-lipped way. I wrapped my fingers under the chair's edges and wriggled my toes rhythmically in my shoes.

Then Carmichael's face relaxed. "The truth is," he went on, "I'm not personally as ready to let go of this as I am professionally. Muscogen County barely has the resources to solve a domestic violence case these days. But that doesn't mean I don't feel a sense of responsibility to my neighbors. And your friend Art had a knack for making people mad."

"What do you mean?" I asked, anger lifting some of the despondent fog. *How could anybody get* mad *at Art*?

"Ever since those animals up north got killed, he's been in my office once a week pointing out the same thing could happen right here. He was so sure we would shoot your monkeys if they ever got out. And now one has. And we're probably going to shoot it. Those dart guns are nice, but I don't think we'll see many cops on any force reach for one of them before they go for their service weapons. I'd be lying if I said I didn't feel bad about that."

"This one was never *in* to begin with," I snapped. "Somebody dumped him off outside our gates in a wooden crate, then scooted."

"And Art told us to look at the security footage," Lance added. Then he went on, "I think he saw something on there that made him go out to check the gate. I don't know why he didn't take any of the others with him, or why he said he was going out to check the video when he had surely already seen it. But whatever he saw could lead us to his killer."

"And if it *does*, I'm taking it straight to my boss," Detective Carmichael snapped. "Someone unfamiliar with the way your center operates could watch these for weeks and not see anything. You know the place, and you're more likely to recognize something unusual. But you are *not* to interfere with a police investigation."

"I'm not planning to. Anything we see goes straight to you cops. If that's why you're staying, you can feel safe now about *going.*"

The detective sighed, his angry mask eroding further into weariness. "No," he said, "I'm staying because I feel responsible. We didn't even give your friend the time of day when he was thinking about the future. None of us did. The captain shunted him off on animal control; animal control waved him over to Detective Marsland; Marsland sent him to me because I'm junior; and I brushed him off entirely. I kept asking him if he was planning to break all his cages open and see what we did. He said, 'Of course not' and I tuned him out. Maybe if I'd been listening, he could have called me first when that animal got into your property this morning, and maybe he'd still be alive right now."

Whatever his reasons, I was grateful for Detective Carmichael's presence when the footage started to play. Having an audience forced me to hold my pain in check. It was unbelievably difficult to watch Art get batted out of the way at any speed. Without a third party to keep us focused in the present, my emotions would have gotten the best of me again.

Lance had downloaded all of yesterday's recordings, from the areas surrounding the enclosures, the front gate, and even inside the barn, in addition to the footage from today. But we all agreed it was today's film we wanted to view, specifically this morning's adventure with the orangutan.

Our cameras were motion activated, and each new activity generated a new file. We didn't have to sit through periods of stillness. My heart constricted every time Art wandered into the field. I waited with tension each time Lance started a new file, hoping and dreading. *Will Art be in this one?* I wanted to reach into the screen and pull him out here to sit beside us and tell us what we were looking for.

The ape's arrival was fairly dramatic. The screen jumped to life with the image of a pickup truck hurtling down the lane. The detective drew in a breath, and I looked over to see him watching with wide eyes. He held his phone up like he was getting ready to dial it. In the back of the pickup, our orangutan was standing half out of his crate. The video didn't capture sound, so we could see, but not hear as he splintered a board and held it aloft as he clambered out on top. The truck stopped at the gate beside our "please honk horn" sign. Undoubtedly, that was exactly what the driver was doing. Lance and I had heard it a lifetime ago when our worst problem was Alex's unexpected arrival in town.

The orangutan jumped up on the cab and threw the crate out the side, then leaped out on top of it. The truck stayed around for a few seconds, then reversed out of the frame nearly as fast as it had arrived. We all watched the orangutan rip its crate apart for a little while. Then Art showed up and went into his ape whisperer routine.

"He's lucky he didn't get killed right *then*," Detective Carmichael said.

I bit my lips and tried not to cry.

After that little bit of activity, the tapes revealed nothing unexpected. We captured the retreating truck's front plate. "I have to call this one in," Carmichael said, and left the room. After a few minutes, he came back and said, "I ought to get back to the station." But he didn't leave. Another hour of viewing showed nothing worthwhile on the other files that could have prompted Art to claim he was checking the tapes. For that matter, Art himself never appeared on camera again, confirming Lance's point that he hadn't needed to go out front and check the tapes, and had never intended to do so.

My eyes had gone dry and my butt and feet were numb. Our office was too small for three people, and all of us were sweaty, even with the door open. My phone had vibrated twice on my hip while we watched, and I needed urgently to return the call. Then Lance said, "I'm going to go back to the truck and advance frame by frame through that one."

CHAPTER 13

I sank back down in the chair, resigned to several more hours of staring at a computer without blinking. The detective looked as frustrated by Lance's announcement as I felt. His expression asked *why*? Lance answered, "Maybe I saw something. It's nagging me. We'll leave after this, I promise. We've got good people here and we really are getting married tomorrow. Really." This last was directed to me.

I breathed in and out, letting go of my tension. "It's fine," I said. "I want to know as badly as you do."

"Thanks, honey," he said, and squeezed my hand.

He scrolled through the truck scene for a few seconds, then stopped as the truck rolled past our security shack. The shack partially obscured the truck from the camera, which was mounted on the gate. "There," Lance said.

At this slower speed, I could see what had caught his eye when the video was going much faster. "Ohh," I breathed. "Oh, no. Oh, *Art*."

"I don't see a thing," Detective Carmichael said.

"There," Lance repeated, jabbing a finger at the screen.

"Tell me." The detective was starting to sound angry again.

"Look." I grabbed a pen and pointed at the screen's fuzzy background. "Run back to the very first frame."

Lance had some trouble doing this, as the computer wasn't really set up to view this kind of recording at more than a cursory level. We were watching on a basic media player, and he was reversing and advancing by the click-and-drag-very-slowly method. But eventually, he got back to exactly the moment we were looking for.

"There, do you see that?" I used my pen to point at a blur.

Detective Carmichael asked, "What exactly am I looking at?"

I don't think he needed me to tell him. But I said it anyway. "That's a second animal. It rolls off the side of the truck and into the woods behind the shack too quickly. I can't tell what it is."

Again, we moved through the video, image by agonizing image. And finally, in a single frame, the film caught the second animal clearly.

We groaned in unison.

"Tell me that's not what I think it is," Carmichael said.

"I'm sorry," I answered him. "We're looking at another orangutan."

He groaned again and started dialing his phone. It looked like the animal was thrown from the speeding truck, though it was difficult to know whether it had fallen or jumped. But why didn't Art go out front to check it out? Shouldn't the video have shown Art later walking or driving past the security shack?

"Yes sir, I'm still here. Yes, sir, I did hear you the first time. I'm leaving now. Sir, they identified a second orangutan." The detective nodded to us and departed.

It was too much, there were too many questions, and I was exhausted. We alerted Christian, Trudy, and Darnell to the second animal's presence and finally made our way back to our own truck. "We should be the ones spending the night here," I said. The relief crew, as I had started thinking of our intern, volunteer, and Columbus import, said it was time for some watchful waiting.

Most of the police had already gone home, and the orangutan would be sleeping.

"Now might be the perfect time to try and find it," I argued.

"Possibly," Lance agreed. "But now might also be the perfect time to get killed. The orangutans are *not* the only dangerous creatures in our woods. And we need to trust our people. Christian knows more about orangutans than either one of us. He's already planning to move the bedding out of the trees tomorrow."

"Why move it?" Volunteers had been placing bedding the whole time Art was wandering in those woods. But nobody had seen or heard anything unusual.

"Art had them put it up high because orangutans are arboreal in the wild. But in captivity, they are as likely to look for it on the ground."

"OK. But shouldn't we be here?" The sentiment felt as halfhearted as my body felt exhausted. We got in the truck.

Lance said, "Trudy has been interning with us for almost two years now. And Darnell is one of the best volunteers we have. We are getting married. We *must* go." Lance started the engine, then added, "Art was a really good leader because he knew to trust his people. Right now, you and I are the leaders, and we have to do the same thing. They haven't let us down all day. And they know to call us if things get out of hand."

He was right. And I had been the one aching to leave not even a whole hour ago. It seemed like my desires yawed along with my grief for Art. Our lane was deserted, as the police had, after asserting control over the situation, left most of the actual investigation for the light of day. With nothing left to distract my attention, I reached for my phone to return the call that had buzzed back while Lance and I were sitting with Detective Carmichael. It was a call I dreaded.

I had left messages with Art's two most recent graduates, Gary and Sally, and it was Sally trying to return my call while I was inside. This time, she answered on the first ring. "What's up?" she asked. "You sounded all upset on my voice mail."

"Sally," I said, "I don't know how to tell you this. We've got really bad news here, and we wanted you to hear it from us first."

"OK, how bad are we talking? Did one of my chimps die? I was worried about Lolly's blood sugar."

"No, the chimps are fine. We got Lolly and Arrin both stabilized this past week. This is a lot worse."

190

"What is it?"

"Art," I said. And suddenly the rest of the words couldn't move from my throat to my mouth. My chest constricted, my jaw locked, and tears coursed down my face again. Lance took one hand off the wheel to rub my neck. Finally, I got back enough control of my emotions to say, "Art's been killed."

"Ohhhh." Sally made a sound like the wind had been let out of her. "That's really bad. What happened?"

Haltingly, I related the day's events, and by the time I finished, Sally and I were crying together. She asked, "What about Gary? Does he know yet?"

I said, "No, I haven't been able to get a hold of him. It could be days before he can call back from Africa."

"Haven't you heard? He didn't go," Sally said. "Or not yet. He's stuck with his mom in Philly until this Friday."

"What? No, I thought he took off right after graduation." This combined academic and practical approach to primatology was still relatively new, and Art's students remained the only ones in the field. Gary and Sally were both slated to complete postdoctoral field research starting almost immediately after they got their degrees in hand. Sally was working for the National Zoo, and Gary was supposed to be headed for fieldwork in Africa.

"No, no. His mom broke her hip again. I think she lay there a day or so before anybody found her. I mean, nobody thinks about a sixty-year-old woman getting hurt that badly, and she still won't tell her neighbors about the MS. Anyway, he's here until Friday. She got stable today. Maybe he's stuck in family mode. I'll text him and try to get him to call you." Sally knew how low the probability of my sending out an actual text was, let alone answering one from Gary. "Do you want me to tell him what happened if I talk to him first?"

"That might be good."

"Yeah. If he calls me first, I'll let you know."

I thought it more likely that he would call Sally than me. She was politely not saying that Gary felt Lance and I complicated his research by refusing, along with Art, to allow him to increase the number of interspecies enclosures and experiment with putting animals together that wouldn't have been near each other in the wild. "Thanks, Sally," I said. "I appreciate it."

After we'd hung up, I told Lance about Gary's mother and said, "I guess we should send him a card or something while he's still in the States this week."

"Yeah. I'm sorry to hear she got hurt. I can't imagine what it would have been like waiting for somebody to find her."

We talked about Sally and Gary and Gary's mother most of the rest of the way to my parents' house, to avoid thinking about the center. But they weren't topics we had any heart for, and we couldn't keep it up long enough to make it all the way home. We fell silent until we rounded the last curve, when we saw flashing red and white lights and a dull orange glow. Something at Mama and Daddy's was on fire.

CHAPTER 14

In days gone by, Granton grew up along a train line. The line was long since gone, and after most of the town burned in the Depression, the other buildings had been torn down over the years. So now, my parents' house sat alone at the end of a small wooded street. Because it wasn't nestled into other buildings, it had survived the fire that claimed the rest of the village. Unfortunately, that meant there was no possibility of this fire *not* being on their property. Would it now be destroyed by the element that had taken the rest of the town?

Wordlessly, Lance accelerated, as if our speedy arrival could somehow reduce the damage.

"Maybe we *are* cursed," I groaned.

"Surely Dad and Alex kept Mom out of there," Lance said at the same time.

"Oh, no! She wouldn't . . ."

"Yes," Lance said. "She would. She would.

Listen, Noel, after the wedding, you and I need to sit down. There's stuff I haven't ever told you about my mother. Stuff I should have brought up a long time ago. But I thought it was in the past, and it was a history I wanted to exorcise. If she's burned your parents' house, I'll never forgive myself."

But when we got there, my parents' house was not on fire. In fact, I was so focused on the building on the other side of the two fire engines that I initially didn't see the real source of the acrid, rubbery burning smell. Finally I found the flames and realized what was burning. It was sitting in the street under a couple of towering oaks. When I saw it, my eyes widened in recognition. I shrieked, "My car!" and threw myself out of the truck even before Lance could fully come to a stop.

I pelted forward at a run, blind to the danger ahead of me. I barely registered the sound of Lance's door slamming behind me. He seized me around the waist before one of the burly firefighters standing back by the trucks could run to intercept us. It *was* my car, visible in the flames and the glare of our headlamps. I lunged against Lance's arms in a futile effort to save my little blue Mazda.

Technically, the truck — the beat-up rust bucket that Lance and I had been rattling around in all week — was Lance's. It was the vehicle we used most, saving mine for distance trips or events where we needed to look presentable. The truck was scheduled to give out long before my little car. My car that I bought for myself brand-new, in the aftermath of my relationship with Alex. My car that I cleaned out weekly, took for timely routine maintenance, and splurged on custom seat covers for. My car that was burning in the street outside my parents' home, with flames shooting up so high I feared they would ignite the oaks and maples along the drive.

"My car," I sobbed over and over again. It was the final indignity to an impossible day, and when I stopped fighting Lance, I sank down onto the curb and bawled. He sat beside me, an arm around my shoulders, once again holding me while I fell apart. The reek of burning kept the car in the front of my mind and made it that much harder to stop crying.

At last, though, I realized that he and I weren't alone. In the collection of feet gathered around us in a protective half circle, I recognized Mama's pumps, Daddy's practical loafers, and even Nana's orthopedic clompers, the ones she called a pair of square Dutch barges. Another set of high heels could only belong to my sister, Marguerite, and the men's dress shoes beside her had to be her husband Dag's. On her other side, a pair of worn but expensive running shoes belonged to my niece Brenda, and behind Brenda, I saw my older niece Rachel's smooth flats, and my youngest niece Poppy's pink house slippers. A pair of little boy's sneakers indicated my nephew, Bryce. Standing with them, a little apart but still close by, I saw a pair of cowboy boots. Those could only belong to one person.

"You," I bellowed, leaping to my feet and charging toward Alex Lakeland. He backed quickly away. "Get away from my family," I shouted at him. "How dare you come back into my life and do *this* to me?" My throat felt raw already from the smoke and all the crying, and now my voice started squeaking as I advanced and he retreated.

"How *dare* you?" I demanded again. "How *dare you*?"

My father's voice cut through the fog of my rage. "Noel!" he called. "He didn't do it. He was inside with us when it happened."

"Don't you defend him," I snapped, rounding now on Daddy. "You have no idea what he might have done."

Rushing to Daddy's defense, Mama cried, "It was Sophia!"

"What?" I felt deflated, like a pumped-out bellows without any wind left.

"The police have already taken her away," Marguerite added. "Alexander is waiting for a cab to take him to his hotel."

Alex added, the first words he'd spoken to me in over ten years, "I rode here in your car with Mom and Pop or I'd already be gone."

Lance asked, "Where's Pop?" He wrapped his arm, which had been around my shoulders when I was sitting on the curb, around my waist instead.

"The police let him ride with them down to the station. I guess he's still sleeping at your place tonight."

"But, Mom?" Lance asked.

"She went kind of crazy," Alex said. "Crazier than she had been, anyway." Although he was answering Lance, Alex was looking at me. I hated for him, *him* of all people to see me this way, wretched and disheveled. My hands balled up into fists and I leaned hard into Lance.

Alex went on speaking, coming closer now, talking low, telling us what had happened between the time Lance left him and now. I barely heard him. Instead, I saw him. The closer he came, the better I could see. And by the time he reached us, I realized the only thing this Alex had in common with the man who had tried to kill me was those ostentatious boots and the ten-gallon hat that he wasn't even wearing but flipping around in his hands.

That Alex was brawny and ragged, with a drunk's sweaty sheen and scruffy hair. His eyes in those days had been perpetually dilated and his beard unkempt. Although he dressed nicely, it was always in loud colors. A bright red polo shirt and tight blue jeans with the inevitable hat. Tonight, his clothes could only be called conservative. A sooty white button-down shirt with gray pleated pants tucked into those boots. His beard was neatly trimmed, his body language subdued, and the sweat on his face seemed to be from exertion. Lance was right. His brother had changed. But how much?

I tried to pay attention to what Alex was saying. It was hard to tune into his voice now, when the last thing he had said to me, the last thing I could actually remember, was a week before he came after me with the phone base. He said, "See ya, babe." I couldn't remember him talking at all to me when he beat me that last time. Although those memories were hazy, and I preferred them that way, I now strained to call back a single word of his. But nothing came.

I said lots of things. I screamed for help and begged him to stop, and apologized for Nicole's call that I'd had no control over. But I don't think he said a word. Just grunted with the effort of holding me down while he beat me bloody. So the words he was saying now kept sliding back in time and sounding like other words, as I tried to remember something besides, "See ya, babe."

Finally, I grasped some of it. "We didn't want to make a big deal. Noel's folks don't know the half of what's been happening, and Pop and I didn't want to upset the apple cart. So I rode with them to keep an eye on her, but she seemed OK. She was . . . even when it was awkward with Noel's parents, with me being here and you not, she acted normal. Then she said she forgot her purse in the car. I got into a conversation with your sister-in-law's husband, and I guess too much time passed. I meant to keep an eye on her. I swear I did."

"But what happened?" I demanded.

Joining us, my father said, "We're not entirely sure. Those are my fuel cans there, for the bush hog." In the years since

Granton burned and disappeared, much of the former town had returned to farmland. My parents owned, along with the parcel that the house stood on, two additional fields. I didn't know what use they planned to make of them. Possibly they were an excuse for Daddy to buy a tractor and drive around mowing them.

Now that he mentioned it, I could see one of his big five-gallon plastic gas cans discarded some distance from the car.

Alex went on, "The next thing we knew, there was a bang, and Mom was running all over the yard screaming, *'Burn, baby!'* "

Daddy said, "Mama and I called for the fire department, and the police arrived not long after that."

Lance said softly, "Anything at all to drive a wedge."

Alex looked down and then away, toward the fire.

Long before the wreck that had been my car had finished burning, I went inside alone. I suppose since Alex wasn't staying at our house, I could have gone home, but I didn't want to face my guest room closet with five thousand dollars' worth of stolen casserole dishes or look at Lance's father, or at my driveway, where my little blue Mazda should have been sitting.

I went upstairs and got in the shower, only to have the door rattle open right behind me.

"Occupied!" I shouted to whichever member of my family *couldn't* hear the water running.

"It's me," Lance said. Couldn't he tell I was using the shower to get away?

And then he got in.

"What are you *doing*?" I demanded.

He didn't say anything. Instead, he pulled me close against him and held me while the water ran down over both of us. Eventually, before the water got cold or someone really did barge in, we got out and went to bed. But I didn't know whether either of us was really looking forward to tomorrow.

CHAPTER 15

"Aunt Noel? Are you awake?"

For a moment, I thought it was ten years ago and Rachel was spending the summer. She used to get me like this in the morning, whispering, concerned that she might be disturbing my slumber. Of course, she was. I never went to bed before midnight, and Rachel never got up after six. However, now, as then, I rejoiced in her gentle voice. What a glorious way to wake up on my wedding day.

"Yes," I said quietly, smiling as I opened my eyes, feeling like we really could move forward without Art, like we could get married without a best man. After the car debacle last night, Nana had come to my room to sit with Lance and me for a little while before she went on to bed herself. She called Art a great heart. She said his spirit would be with us, even if his body was elsewhere. Waking now, I thought *I hope so,*

Nana, before I returned my mind to the young woman who had come to get me like she used to when she was a child.

Rachel was not a child anymore. She was seventeen now, and Marguerite would not want her oldest in the room with Lance while they were both in pajamas. My sister read sex into everything her two oldest daughters did and said, fearful of becoming a grandmother too soon. It didn't matter that she wouldn't suspect Lance specifically of harboring intentions toward her children. She mistrusted *all* males where her slender dark-haired girls were concerned. Besides, I wanted to let Lance sleep. "Let's head down to the kitchen," I said.

Rachel didn't answer right away. I turned my head and saw her kneeling beside the bed. Once again, I was transported back to those summers when she stayed with us. Marguerite insisted she was too young the first summer. She said, "She'll be home before the first night is over," which would have been awkward since they were living in Schenectady, and Ohio to New York was no short drive.

But she needed the child care. Brenda, at three, was too young to send away, and the last months of that pregnancy with Poppy had gone very badly for my sister. Mama

204

went up to stay with the family, to cook, clean, and care for Marguerite. I came for a weekend, but I couldn't stay because I had a job. Moreover, I had only recently escaped my relationship with Alex and tentatively begun one with Lance. I didn't like to be away from work and home long. I offered to take Rachel home with me, promised to keep her a safe distance from the animal enclosures and generally protect her from harm. (Alex was safely locked away in a rehab program at the time.)

Although Mama and Marguerite never would have admitted it, two young children in the house with Marguerite overwrought and on bed rest would have been a strain. Which was why I got to keep the leggy, thoughtful Rachel at all. There had been one long tearful night when I thought Marguerite might be right, but the second morning Rachel had come to me like this, kneeling, serious, whispering me awake to ask, "Can we go meet the monkeys now, Aunt Noel?"

But this morning, my niece did not want to go see the monkeys. This morning, something was wrong. Her oblong, olive-skinned face was tear-streaked, and she was still sniffing a little. She turned her head, and our eyes met. "Help me," she whispered.

"Oh, honey." I sat up and pulled her into my arms. "What is it?"

She nuzzled against my shoulder. "I'm so sorry," she said in a choked whisper. "I wasn't thinking of the dress."

"The dress?"

My wedding gown was still upstairs on Mama's dressmaker's form, waiting for me to lift it up and put it on tonight. If one of the siblings had done something to it, I'd be more inclined to suspect the eight-year-old Bryce, with his fondness for stairs and boundless energy, not the cautious, responsible Rachel.

"I wasn't thinking," she repeated, "about the wedding. I was . . . it was after Mom tried to cancel senior prom." She looked at me in mute appeal, suddenly wary. Marguerite had lobbied the school board to halt the dance rather than allow a lesbian couple to attend. One of the girls was a close friend of Rachel's, and Rachel joined her friends in supporting the couple. After one horrible rally with mother and daughter hurling insults across a parking lot, Rachel simply picked up and moved out.

There had been a couple of rocky weeks when both my sister and my niece called me nightly expecting comfort and support. In the end, Marguerite relented, realizing that her relationship with her daughter was more important than a dance. Rachel had come home, but the damage Marguerite had caused was permanent, and now the two didn't talk much to one another, even though they shared a house again.

I patted the bed beside me, since it seemed we wouldn't be heading down for breakfast yet. Rachel climbed up and asked, "You've seen the dresses, right? Mom e-mailed pictures?"

Ah. The bridesmaids' dresses. Because I would have put this off also until late, Marguerite had simply taken the detail out of my hands. She demanded to know my colors back in January and assigned me some when I refused to pick. By March, she had her children perfectly outfitted in powder blue and sea foam green, and I had one less thing to worry about for June. And she *had* e-mailed pictures. I had never actually opened the attachment. Lance and I had instead allowed my sister to figure out the groomsmen's vintage colored lapels by working with my friend Hannah in her vintage store down in Ironweed.

Marguerite had been in her element coordinating Art, Xian, and Chesley to match Rachel, Brenda, and Poppy. Handy that she lived in Cleveland now, not all the way up in New York. The prom debacle was in late April, after the bridesmaids' dresses had been selected. I was getting a glimmer of what my niece might be talking about. Lance was awake now, perched up on his left elbow, stroking my back with his right hand. I turned my head and briefly met his eyes. He shrugged with his right arm, and I knew that whatever my niece had to say, he would be fine with it.

"I haven't seen them yet, love," I admitted to her.

"Oh." Rachel seemed to be thinking this over. Then she said, "They really are pretty. You know Mom. She'd never do anything gauche." She paused. "Here's the problem. Mine has spaghetti straps. And that was the last thing on my mind. And, oh Aunt Noel, I'm so sorry." It looked for a minute like she was going to cry, but she didn't. She also didn't say anything else. She lapsed into one of those Rachel-ian silences that indicated complete discomfort with a topic.

"Rachel," I said, "whatever it is, you know I support you. We support you."

She smiled at that and leaned heavily against me. Finally, she said, "I went and got a tattoo. And Mom hasn't got any idea at all, and I can't stand for her to find out." She hunched over to rest on my shoulder. She had gotten too tall to cuddle up to me comfortably, and I regretted it, because she needed holding. I did the best I could, wrapping my arms around her and pulling her into a tight hug.

Finally, I said, "A tattoo's not such a bad thing. Some are really nice. Let's see it."

"It really is. Nice, that is." She rolled up one of her nightgown's long sleeves. At the top, the tattoo covered her shoulder, then vanished into the nightgown's fabric. At the bottom, it extended a couple of inches toward her elbow. It featured a young woman's face in profile. The artist had captured Rachel's upturned nose and oblong eyes beautifully in ink. But instead of long dark tresses, the tattoo had rainbow hair. I stared at it for a little while, then said, "Honey, if you want this to show in the wedding, it is absolutely fine with us. Right, Lance?"

Lance was sitting all the way up now, studying Rachel's shoulder from behind me. "Yes," he said. "Absolutely."

"It's not you. It's Mom," Rachel reminded us.

"It's a little bit big to cover up with an adhesive bandage," I pointed out.

"I know. I even tried one of those big knee-sized ones, but the rainbow actually wraps up over my shoulder. Mom's no dummy. She'd ask questions."

"That she would," I said. "How did you even get it without some kind of parental consent?"

"Oh, you know," she said. "It was April, and I was living on Lisa's couch. And you know Cleveland's Pride community really . . ."

"I'm sorry, what?" Lance interrupted.

"Pride," Rachel said. "You know. Gay pride."

"Ah," he said. "Sorry. Not awake." Then he added, apparently thinking now about her sleeping on anybody's couch, "You could have come to us, you know."

"Little far to drive to school every day," Rachel said. "And we were pretty busy with the protests. But thanks, Uncle Lance." Then she suddenly burst out, "I wish I hadn't moved back in! It would have been better if I'd stayed away, but I didn't want . . . I mean, she's my mom, and I'm already . . ." Rachel's sentence trailed off. She didn't need to finish the statement. Her choice to attend college in the middle of the Arizona desert, about as far from her mother as she could manage without leaving the country altogether, was another sore spot for my sister.

"The tattoo," I said. "How did that come about?"

"Oh. Yeah. Lisa's uncle was pretty pissed . . . sorry . . . pretty furious with Mom." Rachel still blushed when she swore. Or anyway, when she did it around us. I was pretty sure that by her age I had been deliberately cursing in front of my parents entirely to enjoy their reactions. It was strange that a girl brave enough to stand up to her mother at a rally still got embarrassed over mildly bad words in front of her aunt. Rachel continued, "Lisa and I have been friends since grade school, and Lisa went through so much crap when she came out, and to have her best friend's mom try to turn her into an untouchable over prom . . ." My niece dissolved into silence again, and it took several minutes of back patting to bring her back around.

Finally, she continued. "It was awful. Not only that half the community didn't want Lisa and Nancy at prom, but that it should be *my* mom leading the pack. Anyway, Lisa's uncle does tats. A couple of the organizers helped me come up with this one and he inked it. But when Mom backed down, I didn't want to throw it in her face

211

so much. If I can get to August, I'll be gone, and when she sees me on holidays she'll think I did it at school."

"Which means," I said, "that we have" — I paused to check the clock — "a little under twelve hours to do something about those spaghetti straps."

"Less than that," Rachel said, "because Brenda and I are helping with the decorations as soon as the tables and chairs get here."

"Right," I said. "Whatever I do to your dress, I've got to double for Brenda's."

"No." Rachel shook her head. "The dresses aren't alike. I'm kind of lucky I don't have Bren's. Hers has off-the-shoulder sleeves that . . . there isn't much I'd be able to do if I had it." She looked at the ground and flushed even more deeply than when the not-quite-curse had popped out earlier.

"Honey, we can do this," I told her.

"Absolutely," Lance said.

I wanted to ask him, *How would you know?* But Rachel's face relaxed, and instead I tried to think. If we could work out a wedding without a best man, surely Rachel's dress would be a cinch. Six fifteen in the a.m. Mama could maybe whip together a couple of puff sleeves between now and then, but those might not be long enough and might still leave Rachel's shoulder blade exposed. And it would mean letting Mama see the tattoo for fittings, and, while I was sure she wouldn't want it visible in this evening's ceremony, I couldn't imagine that she would want to keep secrets from Marguerite. Maybe a wrap of some kind, carefully draped?

"OK, coffee," I said. "And let's get you out of this bedroom before your mom decides something inappropriate is happening between you and Lance."

"Oh, God," Rachel said. "She's going to drive me nuts, Aunt Noel."

"Me too, honey," I told her. "And she's been my sister a lot longer than she's been your mother."

In the hall, we met Marguerite coming down for breakfast. She glanced at the three of us suspiciously, as if she could sense that we were plotting against her. Truthfully, she probably *could* tell something was up. She had a sixth sense for trouble that she had been using against me since our own teenaged years. "Good morning," she said rather stiffly.

"Morning, Mom."

Forcing joviality I didn't feel at all, I seized Marguerite by the arm and all but dragged her downstairs to the kitchen with me.

"Let's get this going," I said to her. "After everything that went wrong yesterday, I'm going to need your help more than ever."

My sister seemed surprised. She stopped between steps and studied me for a moment with a skeptical eyebrow cocked. *Am I laying this on too thick?* I wondered.

Then her natural tendency to organize and direct kicked in, and she continued her descent. She said, "Breakfast first."

As soon as I got some caffeine in my system, the beginnings of a plan came to me. It was simple, really. I had to add a jacket to Rachel's dress. There was no other way to ensure that her shoulders would remain covered for the entire ceremony. We wouldn't be making one of those in twelve hours (now closer to eleven), though. It would have to be purchased. And I would have to do it without hurting Marguerite's feelings too badly or tipping her off about Rachel's arm. Yeah. Simple.

Chapter 16

Once we had eaten, Bryce dashing around the table helicopter-like until Mama sent him out back to exercise the dogs, I said to Marguerite, "Let's see these bridesmaids' dresses you put so much effort into finding."

Marguerite smiled suddenly. "All right," she said. "Let's. Do you want the girls to model?"

"No," I said hastily. "I want to see them laid out in front of Nana's gown. I know you had to work without knowing what my dress would be, and I want to make sure they all look right together."

"Not much we can do now if they don't," Marguerite said.

"Oh, you know," I said. "*We* can always do something." Calling on her sense of team play. It worked, because she didn't protest my reasoning again as we trooped up the stairs together.

The dresses stunned me. The only direction I had given was that I didn't want three identical bridesmaids. I wanted dresses that matched each girl's personality. This was an adult wedding, and I didn't want the ceremony to look like I was playing dollies. Quite frankly, I still expected matchy-matchy copies of the same gown in different sizes. Rachel's comment that her sleeves differed from Brenda's had been the first hint that my sister had actually followed my request. Now, when she let me into Mama's workroom with the girls' gowns laid out in front of Nana's dress, I could see that she hadn't merely done what I asked. She had intuited things I couldn't have guessed I would want and worked them into the selections.

Marguerite had not sewn these, but she had spent a lot of time and money finding them. "Oh, Margie," I said, using her childhood nickname without thinking. "They're amazing." If she had been anyone else, in that moment I would have reneged on my plan for adding a jacket to Rachel's gown. Tattoo be damned, I didn't want to alter a thing about any of these.

Marguerite had alternated colors, so that Rachel and Poppy, the oldest and youngest, were wearing sea foam green and Brenda, in the middle, had powder blue. Bryce's ring bearer suit matched Brenda's blue dress. And the dresses were none of them alike.

Poppy said, "Oh please, let me put mine on, Aunt Noel. I'll take it off after a minute."

"All right," I said. "But only a minute."

"Now Poppy," Marguerite said. "We already discussed . . ."

Brenda stomped her mother's toe. "I'm so sorry!" she said, even though it had looked pretty deliberate.

Marguerite threw her daughter a look that I couldn't understand and said, "We already discussed how soon before the ceremony to put on . . ."

"Oh *please*," Poppy begged.

"It's fine," I said.

"We didn't know Auntie Noel would want to *see* them!" Poppy said.

"Be careful," Marguerite said. "I don't want anything to happen to it before the ceremony." Poppy seized her dress and dashed to the other side of the room with Marguerite chasing rapidly after her. At ten, Poppy was the most energetic of my nieces. Rachel was thoughtful, and Brenda was athletic, but Poppy had earned the nickname "our little dynamo" early in her life and showed no signs of shedding it. Although Bryce was more boisterous, Poppy had her mother's nonstop energy. Also, of all four children, she was the only one whose features favored Marguerite's. Where Rachel, Brenda, and Bryce all had their father's hair, almost black, Poppy's locks were more of a mousy brown like their mother's. Like mine, for that matter. Poppy also had her mother's round face with its rosebud lips and incongruously lengthy nose, which seemed too sharp to hold the glasses the child was forever pushing back up.

"What was *that*?" I asked Brenda.

Brenda rolled her eyes. "Mom's never going to listen to what anybody else wants," she muttered.

It didn't seem like much of an excuse to go trampling Marguerite's feet.

Poppy flashed me her best smile as she spun back across the room in her ensemble. She wore a simple A-line that came to her calves. Mama would call it tea-length. Its flared sleeves almost reached Poppy's wrists at their longest point. Although the dress itself was sea foam green, a powder-blue sash tied at her hip. Flowers stitched around the hem in a slightly darker shade emphasized the skirt's simplicity and brought out Poppy's dark green eyes. The top boasted a rounded neckline that showed off an ivory cameo necklace Marguerite had probably coordinated with my jewelry by magic. Poppy would have wrist-length gloves that matched the flower stitching and a bow in the back of her bobbed hair later tonight, in addition to the pair of modest heels she had already put on.

Since we were down a man, Poppy would be walking in with Bryce. It was difficult to tell whether he had been upgraded to junior groomsman from ring bearer or Poppy had been downgraded from full to junior bridesmaid or both, but they liked the change. Poppy had told me at breakfast, "I felt funny walking in with a guy, you know? And Bryce didn't want to come in first all by himself."

Yes, I did know. Or I should have. Even though Xian was only slightly taller than I was, he was still over a foot higher than Poppy, and we hadn't considered the pairings at all when I selected young family members for bridesmaids but Lance chose adult friends for groomsmen. Now, Xian would walk with Brenda, who was actually a little taller than he was, and Chesley would accompany Rachel. Only Lance would be alone, waiting for me at the front of the garden, while we both tried not to think about who *should* have been walking with Rachel.

Poppy spun a less-than-perfect circle on her heel, drawing me back to the present and the dresses. She lost her balance at the end and fell back into Marguerite, reminding me why I wanted the gown back off of her as quickly as possible. All that energy didn't come with quite enough coordination for a fancy wedding if she got dressed much more than an hour early. Eleven hours? Disaster writ large. "You look beautiful," I told her. "Let's get you out of it until later."

Marguerite stepped behind Mama's changing screens with her. I turned my attention to Brenda's dress, the only blue one. It looked like it would be a little shorter on Brenda than Poppy's was on her. The layered skirt was probably knee length. It had an asymmetrical waist, and the top ran up to a sweetheart neckline in silky pleats. Like Poppy's dress, Brenda's had flared sleeves, though Poppy's looked a bit longer. "Polyester," Brenda told me when I bent down to touch the fabric. "Can you believe that?" At five foot three, Brenda was taller than I was, but not nearly by so much as Rachel. She wore her curly hair short for running. It was quite a bit longer than Mama's pixie, but not as long as even

Poppy's bob. The dress suited her perfectly.

"Taffeta," Marguerite corrected as she returned with Poppy's dress draped carefully over her arm. Poppy herself could be heard jumping down the stairs with noisy thuds that shook the walls.

Brenda ignored her mother and continued, "Mom totally had to show me on the Internet, because I was dead sure it was silk. Doesn't it feel like silk to you?" I nodded without speaking, touching the beadwork that ran under the neckline. "Isn't that *amazing* detail?" Brenda went on. "And there's more in the hem. I swear they look like they're held on with air." She continued talking, though her voice had turned into background noise. "I will absolutely *die* if one of those invisible strings breaks. You know, one did in the store. The first one I tried on was too tight across the chest, and it went 'pop' when I pulled it over my head, and there were little blue beads all over the boutique floor."

"Margie," I said, looking up at my sister while Brenda rattled on about the dress, "these are amazing. They're perfect." With an effort, I lowered my voice and went on, "There's only one problem . . ."

"What is it?" Marguerite said fast, holding Poppy's dress a little closer. "What's wrong?"

I sighed. Oh, it felt *bad* to pretend like there was something wrong. "Look at Rachel's," I said.

Rachel's dress was the most beautiful of the three. It was a narrow sheath with spaghetti straps and fabric that seemed made to drape. "Charmeuse," Brenda supplied without being asked. "They told me that at the store, because I knew it was different from mine, but I didn't know how, and I still thought mine was silk." Still talking, she wasn't watching my sister and I stare at each other.

"Hold it up," I directed Rachel.

Against her body, it looked even prettier, even over the nightgown. The sea foam green wasn't quite the same shade as Poppy's, or else the shine made Rachel's seem brighter, more sophisticated. As a seamstress's daughter, I had a good idea of how a formfitting dress like this one would look on Rachel's slender frame, and as an aunt, I had to applaud my sister for letting her daughter wear something so sensual.

"Brenda, hold yours up, too," I said, to give my other niece something to do besides talk. I wondered if I had brought this on by criticizing her behavior. Rachel was holding hers against her chest. Brenda did the same, flipping the sleeves up around her neck a little to get them out of her way. "Now hand me Poppy's," I told Marguerite. She handed me the third dress with great reluctance. I displayed it alongside the other two. "Now stand back and look," I said.

Rachel, Brenda, and I were arrayed around the dressmaker's form. We displayed the three gowns for an inspection that would have taken place months ago if I hadn't been such a lazy bride. Lucky for Rachel that I was, or I never would have found fault with Marguerite's choices.

Now I let my sister study us without speaking, willing her to see. Brenda was still talking, explaining the differences between charmeuse, taffeta, and a variety of other silky fabrics. "And you can make taffeta out of silk," she wound up, "but it's less expensive with polyester, and a lot easier to clean."

Come on, sis, I thought.

Then Brenda blurted out, "It's the *sleeves,* Mom. Everybody but Rachel has sleeves. Auntie Noel has those long sleeves, and Poppy and I have flares. But Rachel has those little spaghetti straps. It makes her the odd one out."

"Oh no!" Marguerite said. "Brenda, you're right." In an appreciative tone, she added, "Honey, you should really go into fashion."

223

I wasn't sure if I could have been so polite to a child who had just deliberately planted her foot on mine. Then she was quiet for a minute before she continued, half under her breath. "Why didn't I think of that before? I knew you were going to be in Nana's dress, Noel. I'm so sorry. I should have . . ."

"It's okay!" I cut her off. "It's fine. And I wasn't sure about Nana's dress until a couple of weeks ago. All three of them are beautiful. But . . ."

"I should have been thinking more like a bride," Marguerite went on. "I got so caught up in matching the girls without really *matching* them, you know . . . but now, OK. Rachel, we're going to have to sew sleeves on that thing. I'll get Mama and Nana on it right now."

"What about a cape?" Now that Brenda's expertise had been complimented, she had moved to stand by Marguerite. It was a little funny to see Brenda still holding her own dress up in front of her while offering her opinion of Rachel's gown to her mother.

"Honey, they can't sew a cape that fast. We need something in a couple of hours, and I bet they could come up with sleeves that go with . . ."

"Actually, I think Brenda's onto something," I said.

My middle niece's face broke into a broad grin.

"How so?" Marguerite asked.

Brenda almost shouted, "Vintage shop! That lady you've been e-mailing with. I saw her store coming into town. It was fancy stuff, too, not like junk."

"Yup." I nodded. "Hannah can fix this. She sold me a lot of my jewelry, and I think I saw a little jacket yesterday that would be perfect if it's still there." I moved to join Brenda and Marguerite, so that all of us could examine Rachel's dress. Rachel herself craned her neck to stare down at her own pajama-clad chest.

"It can't be green," Marguerite said, thoughtful now as we mulled the options. "Unless it's magically coordinating, and I'm not holding my breath there. But maybe if they had . . . would it be too much to hope for blue?"

"Ivory, actually," I said. "If it fits Rachel . . ."

"Or even if it's too big, we could put in darts," Marguerite mused.

"Right," I said. "It's a half jacket, really."

Marguerite worried, "But would the contrast be too much? I know you don't want these to be typical bridesmaid's things, but really, formal dresses aren't meant to have a lot of different colors going on."

"We don't even know if it fits her yet," I said.

"True," my sister agreed. "One thing at a time." Marguerite seemed to suddenly realize that Rachel had been silent throughout this whole exchange, because she said, "Oh, lord. Rachel, I'm sorry. None of us asked what *you* thought. I really don't want to minimize your perspective . . ."

"Oh no, Mom," Rachel said. "It's Auntie Noel's wedding. I want everything exactly the way she wants it." Her voice sounded strained, like it was an effort to grant this point. I thought the strain came from her fears about the tattoo, but it certainly would give Marguerite the impression that this was anybody *but* Rachel's idea, which wasn't an entirely bad thing.

"Are you sure?" Marguerite asked her.

"Absolutely," Rachel said solemnly. Then, she suddenly beamed. "Besides. Retail therapy is always good, right?"

I turned to go down and put on some clothes. Dressed, I stepped out of my room. I heard Brenda mutter, "Sorry about the foot thing."

I didn't hear Marguerite's response. A moment later, my sister was behind me. "Hurry up. I see Nana coming in from the

226

flower beds."

"So?" Not that I wasn't hurrying anyway.

"She'll put the kibosh on us for sure."

"Hurry," I agreed. She might be eighty, but Franny Cox took Marguerite and I regularly to task.

We scuttled downstairs and through the kitchen. Marguerite made it outside, but I was next in line, and Nana cut me off in the doorway. Bryce chugged along behind her, loaded down with the majority of the flowers they were bringing in to put in my hastily purchased vases. "Hi Mom," he said to Marguerite, then added, " 'scuse me" as he brushed past her without looking up. He edged around Nana and I into the house. The dogs he had been exercising earlier were now cordoned off in their outdoor run, barking madly, and I thought apologies in their direction for the boring day we were about to inflict upon them.

We all let Bryce through, since Nana had loaded him up with no fewer than five one-pound coffee cans holding freshly cut roses. He had two under each arm, pinned tightly against his chest, with the fifth held gingerly out in front. He smelled glorious. My parents' roses were the stuff of legend. They could have easily supplied a florist in season. When they bought this home, the old rose

227

garden had all gone wild. Mama and Daddy dug up and replanted. Now they grew ground-cover, hedge, climbing, and long- and short-stemmed varieties and spent hours a day caring for their plants. When Mama had a sewing job, as she had with my dress these last two weeks, the bulk of this tending fell to Daddy, who accepted only limited help from Nana. He was still out back, filling up more of the metal coffee cans with long stems. Peering around Nana, I caught a glimpse of him with his snips. It made me smile.

Retirement had been very good for my father, and I knew that even when Mama wasn't tied up with a project, those roses were more his than hers. The coffee cans entering the kitchen in a steady parade were his wedding gift to me today. The tables would have centerpieces. Exquisite center-pieces. And what more appropriate for a June wedding than roses?

I stopped Bryce for a moment to smell the collection of pink-tipped white ones he held before I let him unload on the kitchen counter. While Bryce hurried past to get in, my grandmother stared at Marguerite, Ra-chel, Brenda and me like we were a lot of guilty criminals. I remembered that look so well from my childhood. Marguerite and I would think we had pulled something over on our parents, only to be confronted by Nana's withering gaze that said, *You maybe confused those people in there, but there isn't any fooling Franny Cox.* "Where are you all going together?"

"Shopping," I said.

At the same time, Marguerite said, "Fashion crisis."

My sister and I glanced at each other, and she giggled like she used to when Nana caught us out.

Although Nana's expression asked if we weren't a bit old for these kinds of tricks, she said instead, "Now what kind of fashion crisis are we talking about here? Because if something needs to be fixed on one of those dresses, your mama and I can fix it, Noel." She was appealing to me like I, as the bride, had the final authority over such decisions. She didn't seem to realize my authority had been usurped yesterday by an ape and a killer.

I told her, "It's a long story, Nana."

"You can't leave!" she said. "The tents are coming in an hour, Poppy is turning the gazebo into something that would make Georgia O'Keefe fall over dead, and your father wants you over there to tell him if he needs to cut back the Sea Foams or if you think they don't overhang the path too badly." Let it never be said that old age had addled my grandmother's mind. These were clearly but three in a long list of vexations she had been saving for me.

"The Sea Foams?" I said, since my mind was still on Rachel's sea foam *green* dress and not on the Sea Foam *white* shrub roses lining part of the route I would walk through the garden this evening.

Lance rescued me. He swept around the corner of the house and somehow wormed between Nana and me before she could say another word.

"Darling," I told him. "Can you answer a flower question for my dad?"

"I'll try," he said. "But I would rather sweep you off your feet." He wrapped an arm around my shoulders and steered me back inside, forcing everyone behind me back too, and slowing down Bryce as he tried to get back outside to collect more flowers from Daddy.

When Bryce had passed, Lance said, "I need the car keys." He didn't seem interested in where *I* was headed, and probably had a pretty good idea anyway based on our early morning conversation with Rachel.

"You had them last, but they're on the dresser upstairs. Where are you off to?"

Instead of answering, he pulled me into a bear hug.

"Honey . . . ," I started to protest.

He released me, then kissed me hard on the mouth. It wasn't in any way chaste, and I felt a flush creeping up my cheeks even as he let me go again. He whispered, "I'll find the keys. I wanted to tell you I have to go out to the center. I'll be back by two, I swear, but Trudy says the cops gave us permission to place more food and bedding for lures. Listen, the cops seem willing to set up surveillance and dart the things for us. No bullets. Trudy thinks they mean it. I have to try to catch those orangutans one more time. If Art were there . . ."

He stopped suddenly, his own face reddening, and I knew he was close to tears. I knew that he meant if Art were there, the orangutans probably would have already been caught. But I also knew he meant that if Art were there, nobody would think one or both of the apes was a killer, and finding them wouldn't have so much urgency. "I know," I told him, suddenly fighting not to cry myself. "I know. Do what you need to, honey. I wish I could go with you."

We kissed again, less intensely this time, and he moved to go down the hall.

Maybe we thought we had been speaking

only to each other, but my family had heard every word. I turned away from Lance's retreating body to see them staring at us. Then Nana spun the cold water tap on the kitchen sink and loudly plunked her coffee can into the basin. Marguerite shooed Rachel and Brenda out the door with far too much gusto, though she herself remained behind; only Bryce, who had returned with another load of flowers, made no effort to stop eavesdropping. Instead, Bryce left Nana at the sink with the flowers and came over to us. "Are you talking about the orangutan that killed your friend?"

"The orangutans didn't hurt anyone," Lance said, turning back to the kitchen. "Some horrible person killed our friend, and . . ." Lance *was* crying. He swiped at his face a couple of times, but it wasn't enough to keep me from seeing. The sight of his damp, pinched face brought on my own tears. The kitchen felt too long, and my feet wouldn't cross to him. I swallowed and cleared my throat, trying to find words to fill the void between him and my eight-year-old nephew.

"And I'll thank you not to introduce the topic to my son again," Marguerite cut in, shooting Lance a dark look as she turned back from ushering Rachel and Brenda out to take hold of Bryce's shoulders and steer him toward the sink.

"Sorry," Lance said. He might have been speaking more to Bryce than his mother, but Lance was looking at me, and I finally found my voice to answer him.

"Don't worry about it," I told him, dabbing my own eyes with a shirt sleeve. "Go. See if a day of living on Ohio foliage has convinced the animals that the humans and their fruit trucks are worth their time. They're somewhere on the center's property. I'm sure of it."

"Thanks, honey." He came back and kissed me again, a peck this time, and turned away once more, asking, "Did you say the dresser?"

"Yes!" I called to him. Then I snapped, "Marguerite, come on. We've got to hurry up if we're going to have time for this."

"Oh no, you don't!" Nana had been pretending to work with the roses, but as soon as she saw Marguerite and me headed for the back door again, she turned off the sink and ignored a can of stems being extended by the startled Bryce. She marched toward us, hands on her hips. "You two are not sneaking off on some lengthy, unrealistic search when we have a wedding to put together."

"I don't have time to argue about this," Marguerite told her. "If you don't want us going off alone, then come along to chaperone."

She and Nana glared at each other for a long moment, and then Nana said, "I do believe I will." She took off her apron and hung it over a chair back with a snap before following Rachel and Brenda to the minivan. "And someone round up Poppy before she starts making plans to decorate the guests when they arrive."

Marguerite turned to me. "Are you coming?" she asked, advancing across the room.

"Yes," I told her. But more than anything, I wanted to be getting in the truck with Lance, to try and find the animals running loose at the primate center. Marguerite gave me a tissue she had acquired from the table. "I'm beginning to think my in-laws are right," I said to my sister.

"What do you mean?" she asked.

"I'm beginning to think this whole wedding is cursed."

CHAPTER 17

"Nonsense," Marguerite said. "Your mother-in-law *is* a curse, and I don't even know what to think about Alexander anymore. Now hurry up and let's see what we can do about getting Rachel some sleeves," and she preceded me out the kitchen door.

In the car, I blew my nose several times and wiped my eyes. Nana had taken the van's passenger seat, and Rachel and Brenda had the middle bench. I scooted all the way over in the third row and buckled in. Poppy catapulted in beside her sisters just before her mother shut the door.

I tried not to look at the scorched hulk of my former car as we pulled out, but it was hard to avoid, parked as it was on the street outside the house. Daddy would have it removed before the ceremony started, but for now it squatted there, homeless and ugly.

It was a silent ride, and I tried to lose myself in the scenery, but it was hard. This part of Ohio is all flatland. Corn and soy-beans, soybeans and corn, with a little hay sown here and there for variety. Fields and fields of green at this time of the year. The corn wasn't quite knee-high yet, and the soybeans still grew in orderly leafy rows. By late summer, the corn would be tasseled out and the soybeans dry and brown, ready for harvest, the hay ready for baling. But it was early June, and the earth was fresh and abundant. I felt like the fields were talking to me, saying, *See, here is life as it should be.* Lance would tease me for such a senti-ment. But Art would have understood. Art, who was no longer here to understand.

My melancholy increased at the edge of town, where it was impossible not to pass Ironweed U's campus. The town was named for the university, after all, and the two had risen up together in the early twentieth century. Graduation had come and gone, and most of the students had left for the summer. It looked as though they had never been here. We passed the dorms, where the neat green landscaping and absence of activity made me think of Art even more strongly.

On a Saturday morning in June, Art would have been in his office in the biological sci-ences building, writing grant proposals, or over at the library, irritating the staff with outlandish interlibrary loan requests. On *this* Saturday morning, he also would have been getting ready for the wedding. He would not have changed his routine at all, but he would have been thinking about us, calling us and jollying us through the stress. Because that was how Art acted when things got difficult.

Where had he been going yesterday? As crazy as the orangutan's arrival had been, it wasn't like Art to forget one of our most important protocols and head off alone into the bush when dealing with animals we knew we couldn't house. I sank against my window as we passed through the university's main entrance, wishing Art was alive so I could ask him. *What were you doing, Art? Where were you going that was so important? What weren't you telling us?* And, *Who did you piss off?* Rachel reached back over the seat and took my hand. She didn't say anything, but she squeezed my fingers. I squeezed back. It was good to have family.

We reached the town of Ironweed's shopping district, several blocks of stores ranging from herbal remedies to a franchise pharmacy sandwiched into an old-fashioned building. There were a lot of cars parked this morning, in spite of a conspicuous absence of nine-o'clock shoppers walking the streets. Commencement was last week, so I wondered if maybe the locals were starting to resurface for the summer. I thought Marguerite would have trouble squeezing her big van into the free lot that served as a partition down the middle of Main Street, especially if she wanted a slot close to Hannah's. There looked to be a dozen or more empty slots at the other end of the lot, but she drove over an orange cone blocking a newly painted space and jumped out. "Come on," she ordered us.

"Marguerite!" I said, following her out of the car. "You drove over a cone." Her front tire was on the "wet paint" sign. The pressure of having Nana unspeaking beside her in the front seat must have affected her thinking.

"Had to," she said. "We don't have a lot of time."

Nana got down and slammed her door, nodding as if the strategy made perfect sense. Nobody was behaving like they ought to today. Brenda stomping all over her mother, Marguerite parking over an orange cone, and my sensible grandmother nodding approval.

"But it says wet paint, right there," I protested. "You'll . . ." But Margie had buzzed across the street already.

The rest of us hurried after her across Main and down to Hannah's. Today, the window that had been so eye-catching yesterday was empty. A sign proclaimed: *Closed for renovation.*

"What?" I was so shocked that I verbalized the sentiment. "I was in here yesterday! Hannah can't be remodeling *now*. She's coming to the wedding."

I threw my gaze to Rachel, who met my eyes with a grim smile on her face. "Figures," she said.

"But I don't understand!" I wailed.

"I'm going in to ask," said my conservative sister. Urgency must have made her bold; she yanked on the door as if she expected it to fly open because she had demanded entrance.

It did.

The shop door popped right open, and I was torn between relief and horror. If it opened, Hannah had to be inside. But if she was closed for renovations, she must have spent all of last night packing up her goods, and the little white jacket we wanted was unlikely to be anywhere that Hannah could lay hands on it.

"Come on," Marguerite said, and she headed in, Nana following like they invited themselves into closed stores every day.

Brenda went next, and then Rachel, holding Poppy's hand, and I finally followed.

They rounded on me as soon as I crossed the threshold, all four of them. Nana and Marguerite grabbed one arm and Brenda and Rachel the other. "What?" I said. "What are you doing?"

"Surprise!"

I couldn't process what was happening. My sister, grandmother, and nieces caught me as I stumbled back. Where Hannah's racks had stood not a full day before, there were now tables, chairs, and *people*. My family, the people I trusted, had deceived me. All of them.

"Surprise what?" I yelled back. But of course I knew. My mind flashed to Hannah yesterday, as she slid that drawing under the register. To Brenda's foot and Marguerite's guilty giggle when Nana lit into us at Mama's kitchen door.

It looked like I was getting a bridal shower after all. I regained my balance soon enough, but it was longer than that before I got hold of my slightly hysterical bursts of laughter.

"You're so hard to do something *nice* for." That was Hannah, snickering at my discomfort.

"This morning?" I looked for my nieces and sister in the crowd as Hannah, Jan, and Mina came forward to lead me to a seat at one of the round tables erected where her racks should have been.

"Total setup," said Brenda, who, it turned out, had never let go of my left elbow. "Everybody but you, Uncle Lance, and Bryce was scripted. We had to scramble after we found out you would be with us at Grandmama's. And Bryce can't keep a secret for anything, so we knew he'd tell you if we let him in on it."

"You threw us for a loop coming to Mama and Daddy's house," Marguerite admitted. "But then Rachel figured out how to work you in and . . . it was *so hard* not to laugh!"

"But . . . but?" My eyes found Rachel's, and I pantomimed to my own shoulder.

"Oh, I know about the tattoo," Marguerite said. She rolled her eyes. "And don't you worry. Rachel has a jacket to go with that dress already. We left it in the dress bag and didn't show you."

"But she was so upset!" I said.

"That wasn't too hard," Rachel told me. "I don't even like to *think* about April, still. That prom was a nightmare from start to finish. Lisa and I felt like we *had* to go because of the whole stink, but half the school didn't want us, and . . ." She suddenly snapped her jaw shut.

"Hang on," I said. "You . . . I thought Nancy . . ."

"I made Nancy up for Mom's sake," Rachel said softly. Her face was already reddening, and I could see that this morning's dismay had at least been honest. She went on, "I never thought . . . once she put it together that there was no such person and I was really the other girl she was keeping out of prom . . . can we talk about this later?" Her words had fallen into a lull in the babble of conversation that had greeted our arrival, and I wondered if I had accidentally outed her to the whole room putting the scheme together for myself.

But the conversations around us all picked up again as if nothing had happened over at our table, and I hugged my niece as tightly as I could. "If you don't want to wear a jacket with that dress," I told her, "you don't even think twice about it." It was all I could think of to say.

Then I turned to my oldest friend and asked her, "Hannah, how did you do this?"

"At first it was easy," she told me. "Your mom was in shopping, complaining because you wouldn't let her have a shower. This was a whole year ago, right after you and

Lance got formally engaged. Anyway, she and I sort of put our heads together. We figured you would never expect it on the morning of your wedding."

"Plus that was the only time any of us could be sure you wouldn't suddenly go off to work!" Mama added, materializing at the edge of my vision.

Hannah continued, "We started decorating yesterday afternoon, and you barged right in on Mina, Jan, and I while we were planning." She was laughing as she spoke, not a hint of frustration in her voice, though I now knew she must have been hiding one of Mama's impossible charts under the register when I burst in.

"You even fixed the parking spot!" I told her.

She and Marguerite exchanged an amused glance. "We completely plotted it against you," Hannah said. "Now are you going to enjoy yourself or not?"

"Yes," I said. "Absolutely." I spoke into another lull, and this time I was sure the whole room heard me, because they cheered and toasted.

"I'm glad," Hannah said more softly. "I was afraid we might be doing the wrong thing after . . . that awful . . ."

"No," I said. "Art would have been heartsick if he had anything to do with stopping this wedding or anything about it." For the first time since Lance and I had started saying that to each other yesterday, it felt true. Art, the everlasting romantic, wanted to see us wed.

The party was wonderful. I could not help but enjoy myself when I realized exactly how much work and love had gone into the effort. Besides Hannah, Jan, and Mina, Mama had captured two of my old college roommates, half a dozen local friends, and at least twice that number of family members. I talked with cousins and aunts I hadn't spoken to in years. I got to see people in Lance's family who had always regarded me as a sort of curiosity, the never-ending girlfriend, before now.

Although I had to field several questions about my parents' house, these relatives had the grace not to say they thought it was cursed because it used to be a funeral home. None of them seemed to know what Sophia had done, and I hoped they wouldn't find out. A couple of them asked where she was, and Mama said, "Dinner didn't agree with her last night. She's indisposed this morning." They seemed pleased to know me in my new role as fiancée, and I forced myself not to think about their former judgmental attitudes when they were all being so pleasant today. I *had* been with Alex before Lance, and I doubted that Sophia had told them why Alex and I broke up. Or perhaps she had done so and cast me as a liar. Given that potential, maybe a little of their skepticism was warranted. All of them had to travel in for the affair, after all. I'd never even met most of them when I was dating the younger Lakeland.

As the shower wound down and they began making their way out the door in twos and threes, the last of my wedding jitters finally went away. Lance and I had decided to get married in a formal ceremony to please other people. These people. And up until now, everything I had done had been with them in mind. I had feared that formalizing our status in such a public way might actually drive a wedge between Lance and me, bring an end to something wonderful and comfortable. But seeing how the people we had been trying to please also wanted to please *us* eased my fears.

I still didn't think it fair that some of these guests would only find our relationship legitimate upon the advent of marriage. But as the party wound down a couple of hours later, I forced myself to think instead of the people who had always supported us, Hannah, Mama, Nana, and even Marguerite. "And every one of you lied to me!"

"You're not getting past that are you?" Brenda said with a smile. She was peeling up a white plastic tablecloth to be thrown away. I had been forced back to my seat every time I tried to help in the cleanup effort. So instead, I sat in a bewildering mountain of gifts, beaming at them all, marveling at their ability to connive. I picked up a flower-shaped dish that purported to be a romantic floating candle display.

Complete kit. Just add water and fire, the box assured me.

"It's what you get for not having a registry," Hannah pointed out as I put down the candle and picked up a silver First Christmas ornament. *Really? Our first one was a while ago.*

"But I *do* have a registry," I said. "We asked in the invitation for people to donate to the center instead of giving us gifts."

"Maybe they will for the wedding," Mama suggested.

"Or maybe," Marguerite said, "they feel like that's pretty impersonal and they want to give you something you can keep."

"I already *have* most of these things," I protested. And I didn't *need* quite a few others, but I didn't tell Marguerite that.

"Oh *can* it already," my sister said. "OK, so you are one of those unmaterialistic people who can go through life with few possessions and lots of love. Let people give you gifts, Noel. And if you turn around and donate them to a shelter, keep it to yourself."

"Oh blast, I'm sorry, Margie," I said, watching her attack the floor with a broom. "I didn't mean it to sound ungrateful. The whole thing took me completely by surprise. I was sitting there thinking about how much work went into this, and how much you all kept under your hats, and how hard it must have been, and how much I appreciate it."

"Congratulations," she snapped, murdering several cake crumbs and a dust bunny. "That was exactly the message you conveyed."

"I'm sorry, Marguerite. Really . . . really . . . sorry." My voice slowed down on that last apology, because my mind was suddenly elsewhere. I realized that I knew the answer to one of my own questions about Art. "Oh, God, I have to call Lance," I said.

I tried to stand up, but my knees were as jellified as they had been when I realized my whole family was lying about Rachel and her jacket. Only the shock in that case had changed quickly to pleasure. I wasn't feeling any pleasure right now as I fumbled through my pockets for my phone.

"Aunt Noel, what's wrong?" Rachel said.

"I have to call Lance," I repeated. "Oh, God. Art didn't . . ."

"Slow *down,*" Marguerite said. "Nobody can understand what you're saying."

"I'm trying to say Art was *expecting* those orangutans, Margie!" I shouted. "And he was up to something dreadful in the name of what he thought was good."

CHAPTER 18

When Lance answered, I said without preamble, "Do you remember, when we finally got Art into Darnell's car yesterday, how he kept saying we'd come too soon?"

"Um, I'm setting a bait pad with Trudy," he said. "What's this about?"

"Art was expecting that orangutan. *Do you* remember when he said . . ."

"Oh," Lance said, understanding in his voice. "He didn't mean *we* had come too soon, did he?"

"No. It was the orangutan. I'm sure he was expecting that animal, only not right then. Meet me at home." He barely gave his assent before I hung up.

Marguerite took me out to my own house reluctantly. "Shouldn't you pass your tip along to the police?" she asked.

"The people who think the orangutan is a man killer?" Last night, Lance and I went to sleep talking about how the police's misguided belief that an orangutan had killed Art was clearly dominating their investigation entirely too much. Although Christian and Detective Carmichael had lobbied for the animal all night, I still had only limited faith that the officers wouldn't shoot Art's orangutans. "Even if I particularly trusted them here, which I don't, I don't want to send them off on some other goose chase. They took his computer; they have his phone; I'm sure they'll figure it out themselves."

"And you're so sure you're right."

"No, I'm not. And that's another reason for me to keep my mouth shut. As soon as I'm sure, I'll get in touch with them. But I *know* Art, Margie. Everything he did yesterday was all wrong. He was being secretive, lying to people, *lying* to them, Margie. Lying to *us.* He was always the worst liar I ever knew. He couldn't even conceal it for ten minutes when a grant got approved or rejected. Something this big? He must have been going nuts with the suspense. If Lance and I hadn't been all caught up in the wedding, we would have realized sooner how off he was acting."

Marguerite asked, "Didn't you say you'd hardly seen him in the last few weeks?"

"Because of Sally and Gary's graduating.

Oh, I see. Maybe he was staying away on purpose."

"It's a thought," she said.

"He may have known something about the animals to make him think he could walk up to the one. Although that's still colossally stupid."

Marguerite seemed to be more of the cops' mind. She let me bounce ideas off of her all the way to my house, but she kept making me promise to take anything I figured out from my home office back to the police. Then, as she pulled into my driveway, she scolded, "Now we could hold the rehearsal without you last night. Lance's college friends and the minister were very gracious about that, by the way. But you will *not* be married by proxy. The wedding is at six. You *must* be at Mama's by five to shower, get your hair done, and get your dress on. Sooner is better."

"All right," I told her. "Thank you." Then I hugged her quickly and got out of the van, before she could change her mind and speed away without dropping me off.

I'd hardly let myself in the front door before the crunch of Lance's tires announced that he had arrived to join me. "Hey, you eat yet?" he greeted me.

I was still reasonably full from the shower,

but I joined him while he put together a sandwich out of the refrigerator. I asked, "Did my parents ever tell you what they were up to?"

"You mean the shower? Yeah, when I went out to talk to your dad about the roses on my way out, he clued me in. So I guess we've got a bunch more stuff coming this way."

"Yeah. Margie's van is loaded up with it. They'll bring it over tomorrow. She's all on wedding setup today."

"Anything useful?"

I said, "I don't know. Some of it is nice. Mama and Daddy got us more of our plates and those stoneware mugs. And Marguerite framed us a fantastic print of chimps in the wild. But a lot of it . . . I don't know what we'll do with a Tiffany lamp or an expensive vase."

"We could put flowers in it," Lance said.

"How you get these ideas. I never would have thought that through."

"And don't forget we have five thousand dollars in casserole dishes to return."

"Stolen casserole dishes."

"Do you want to see them?"

"No. How were things out at the center this morning?" It felt abnormal. Here we were sitting at the table as if we didn't have a wedding to attend in four hours or as if Art hadn't been killed last night.

"The traps are all laid. Christian was right there helping us lay out additional pads this morning. Actually, he didn't think I needed to be there at all."

The hope was that the orangutans, who were clearly used to humans, would expect us to provide their meals. Even if they weren't willing to come right up to the barn, they might settle down for an evening someplace easy for us to dart them. The big fellow had hitched a ride on Olivia's fruit truck. He either knew or smelled that it meant food. So it was probable they would look for the sources of bedding humans might provide rather than trying to make their own.

It hadn't worked last night, but nothing had been down on the ground then. Trudy and Darnell had rallied some of our most trusted volunteers to form a round-the-clock on-site crew, and they all went around in pairs. Nobody worked alone, and all of them, according to Lance, felt adamantly that we needed to be off getting married.

All we could do was hope the animals would get interested in the piles of fruit and blankets and come in. But other than that glimpse on video, nobody had heard a peep out of the second orangutan. Although the first one had sounded off several distinctive longcalls after its successful truck raid, it hadn't been heard or seen for nearly a full day now. We would absolutely have known if the animal was still making longcalls. The sound is like a cross between a pig's squeal and a man's groan, and it carries for miles. There really was nothing left to do but wait and see whether we found them first or the police did. If it was us, Christian Baker was still on hand to make sure things ran smoothly. If it was the police, I didn't hold out much hope that the animals would live.

Christian was a good man to have at the helm, and everyone was glad to see Lance off. They wouldn't have been happy to know what he was going off to do. There wasn't anything for us in Art's office at the sanctuary. His computer hard drive had been claimed by the cops, and his files, which we knew by heart anyway, held no answers. We knew how to hack his e-mail, but doing so from the center seemed terribly unwise, and there was a chance that he had left us a clue in our own basement.

While Lance and I were talking, I realized someone had left me a voice mail at some point in the morning. I checked it briefly. The message said, "Hey, it's Rick, Art's nephew. I think . . . can you call me when you get a chance?" The message time was seven fifteen. Sometime during the breakfast-dress chaos, then.

I tried to return the call but landed in *his* voice mail and continued the game of telephone tag with, "I got your message. Give me a ring when you get a chance." Of course, I said that as I headed down into our basement, the original cell phone dead zone. There were ten text messages that I did not check. Probably Rick as well. Anybody who knows me knows I don't text. If it's important, they call.

It might have stymied our cell phones, but the basement was fine for our computers. Our router worked pretty much anywhere in the house, and we kept the grant work in our home office. There was always something happening at the sanctuary, and our offices were right there in the barns, making administrative activities difficult. Art had joked for years about adding an admin building so we could get some paperwork done without driving ten miles away. But we ran on a shoestring. An administration building was not in our budget. So the ongoing and funded grant projects were in our basement and the rejected ones were in Art's office at the college. If he'd left his records at the college, or if it wasn't in e-mail, we weren't likely to find anything. But we had to try.

We knew all of Art's passwords, because they were all variations on the same thing: Pr1mat3. He used it at the center, at home, and at school, with sticky notes on the monitor to remind himself how many threes to put at the end and whether he was using a lowercase i or the number one that month. Only insecure if you knew the basic password or understood what "i, two threes in login" or "one, four threes in e-mail" might mean.

We did know, and we exploited it. But even before Lance navigated to Art's e-mail, I found a file marked *Orangutan* in the big cabinet labeled *Research.* He wasn't trying to hide anything at all, if one knew where to look and had time to bother. Which was much more like the man I knew than the one I'd seen yesterday. Marguerite really had a point about him staying away from us for more than the graduation. We had come here so many times when Art was alive. I couldn't count the number of Saturdays we had spent working out grant proposals in the basement while something cooked up in the Crock-Pot. I spread the file out on the computer-free side of my desk, half waiting for the man himself to come clomping down the stairs with gourmet coffee and junk food to sustain us. But he did not come, and he never would again.

I tried not to think about this as I pored over pages of rejected grant proposals, all composed in the last nine months, all of them completely new to me. I had never seen any of this before, and here it sat in my own house. Art had been working on this for three quarters of a year without our knowledge, smuggling the paperwork into *our* file cabinet because we kept the open research files. We *could* have stumbled onto it at any time. But Art liked to joke what a paper suck our research really was. Other than the three or four files in current use, we rarely got into the back files.

Eight months. An unheard-of length of time for him to keep an idea to himself. Although Art was perpetually engaged in fund-raising for us (and I tried not to think that Lance and I would have to do that alone now, or worse, that the board might find someone to replace Art and put that stranger in charge of our sanctuary), these proposals all related to an orangutan enclosure Art wanted to build. I tried to think. Had he been particularly cagey about his files? I didn't think so. Unusually organized, yes. But closed off? Never. Not Art. For most of the last year, Lance and I would arrive home to find he had everything sitting out on the table ready for us. He had been planning this very quietly indeed. Except Art couldn't ever be quiet. He would have told someone.

But who? Gary and Sally, perhaps? I made a mental note to call Sally back and see if she had any knowledge. Surely she would have mentioned it last night if Art had been talking to her about anything orangutan-related. But then, I'd delivered a piece of horrible news. Orangutans and grants might not have been at the forefront of her mind.

There wasn't anything in the papers from the filing cabinet to suggest where the orangutans running around the sanctuary's property might have come from, and I didn't see anything to suggest a grant had come through. "Do you think he was making general plans but hadn't gotten down to specifics yet?" I asked.

"No," Lance said. He didn't elaborate. We had been here nearly two hours, and I wasn't sure how much longer we could spend on the project today. We still needed to get married, after all.

I looked up from the files strewn across our desk. Lance was scrolling down an e-mail message, one hand on the mouse and the other hand cupping his chin. "Damn," he said. "Look at this. *Look at this.*" He jumped up out of the chair and stomped out into the hall. Faced with a choice between following him and finding out what had infuriated him, I opted for the latter.

I had to scroll around to read the message from the bottom up, in the order it had developed. When I did, I understood why Lance was steaming in the corridor. The chain started on an abrupt note, as if it were really the middle of a conversation, maybe a continuation of a phone call. And it suggested exactly what I had feared.

From: Aldiss Carmichael
  [mailto:acarmi@rrohio.net]
To: Hooper, Arthur J.
Sent: March 18, 6:00 p.m.
Subject: Help

Sir I am sorry we have not met, but I need your help. I am sure you understand why I cannot take these animals to the zoo.

v/r
Ace

From: "Hooper, Arthur J."
   <arthur.hooper@ironweed.edu>
To: Aldiss Carmichael
   <acarmi@rrohio.net>
Sent: March 23, 8:00 a.m.
Subject: RE: Help

Ace,
   I am sorry I did not reply at once. I see my sanctuary e-mails sooner, and you should contact me there. At the present time the Ohio Zoo is best equipped to help you in your situation. I repeat that I do not think they would arrest you, as you were uninvolved in the original crime. We do not yet have an enclosure to house orangutans, although I am steadily working toward that goal. I hope to be ready soon.

From: Aldiss Carmichael
   [mailto:acarmi@rrohio.net]
To: Hooper, Arthur J.
Sent: March 23, 6:00 p.m.
Subject: RE: RE: Help

   Respectfully sir what is your sanctuary address so I can send you mail there? I have done all I can. But the big guy is getting bored which is not good and the

260

female may be pregnant I cannot tell. I can no longer afford for their upkeep and such and I beg you to help me. I cannot have an arrest on my record. I have done my best but the animals are neglected they need a better home and they will arrest me. If you cannot take them I do not know what I can do.

v/r
Ace

From: "Hooper, Arthur J."
  <arthur.hooper@ironweed.edu>
To: Aldiss Carmichael
  <acarmi@rrohio.net>
Sent: March 26, 8:00 a.m.
Subject: RE: RE: RE: Help

Ace,
What makes you think the female is pregnant? Does she have labial swelling? My academic duties are extremely consuming at this time. Boredom is not a good thing in a great ape, but it is not necessarily a sign of neglect. Can you wait until the middle of June? I will arrange for you to donate the animals anonymously to the primate sanctuary and secure their safe transport to Columbus myself.

From: Aldiss Carmichael
  [mailto:acarmi@rrohio.net]
To: Hooper, Arthur J.
Sent: March 26, 6:00 p.m.
Subject: RE: RE: RE: RE: Help

Sir,
   I will try to hang on. Please send your sanctuary email address.

v/r
Ace

I pulled myself away from the computer, breathless. "My *God,* he knew!" I said to Lance, who was still storming back and forth outside the door. "He *did* know."

"How did *you* know," Lance asked me, coming back to the doorway.

"It was after the shower. I was thinking about how my whole family duped me, and how even the people you know best will turn around and surprise you. And that made me think about how much Art liked surprises. And then I flashed on his face, when we all jumped into Darnell's jeep."

"Yeah," Lance said. "I follow."

"He didn't look upset in the least. He looked exhilarated. And him saying, 'You came too soon,' " I went on.

"Right," Lance agreed. "I was furious that

he thought our help was a bad thing, but now I get it."

"It was such a strange thing to say. And it stuck with me. But he wasn't talking to us."

"No," Lance said. "He was talking to this Aldiss guy." On the phone, we had both thought it was the orangutan, but now I agreed with Lance. Art was saying that Ace had come too soon. Did it really matter? It meant Art, gentle Art, was complicit in a crime.

I surrendered the computer chair as Lance returned to try to find the rest of the conversation chain in Art's center e-mail. That search petered out quickly, and it became clear that Art either had never provided the sanctuary e-mail address or that he had continued the conversation by phone.

The best we could find was a series of urgent and mysterious e-mails between Art and Stan that broke off around the time the orangutans arrived Friday morning. Stan was upset about missing "the big reveal" because Gary had not yet left the country due to his mother's fall. Stan thought he and Gert might need to leave Natasha alone immediately after the adoption hearing to stay with Gert's sister.

"I didn't know Gary was Stan's nephew,"

I said. "I knew they were related, but I didn't realize his mom was Gert's sister."

"Me neither." Lance shook his head. "We should have, though, if we'd thought about Gary's mom and Gert's sister both having MS. Stan's not even related to Gary, and it would have been an odd sort of coincidence for two people in his life to have it. I think it's relatively rare."

"Yeah. Gary never talked about his mother much, though."

"True. Or not to us, anyway."

"Yeah." We both got along better with Sally. "Funny Stan didn't say anything about it when we saw him at the court-house."

Lance shrugged. "I want to know what this 'big reveal' was."

"I bet either Stan or Rick knows," I said.

"Art's nephew? Why?"

"When Art can't find a grant, where does he turn, every time?" I didn't wait for Lance to answer. "Stan. And when has Stan ever said no. He's building an enclosure, Lance, and Rick's always been his go-to builder."

"Was. He *was* building an enclosure."

I sighed and bit my bottom lip so I wouldn't cry. I tried to remember if Stan had acted in any way in the know about the orangutan when we mentioned it to him yesterday morning.

Stan could be fairly disinterested in the center. He and Art went way back, and he willingly funded our work, but in fact, we were just one of the only local millionaire's projects. He liked to play philanthropist, and any number of charities and even businesses could thank Stan Oeschle for saving them with money. Ironweed U had an Oeschle Building that he had been the largest donor for constructing. When no bank wanted a part in Hannah's Rags, thanks to the state of downtown Ironweed at that time, she had gone to Stan for a start-up loan. He darted from interest to interest, enjoying each as it suited his pleasure. So he might not have known much about progress after he signed the check.

I remembered last year when we acted as intermediaries between the roadside zoo in Indianapolis and the Ohio Zoo. In that case, the orangutan turned out to be an illegally smuggled animal, part of a small network of illegally traded exotics. Art had enthused to everyone for *days* about our role in shutting down what he termed a primate mill, even though several species of animals were involved. Stan's praise had been lukewarm at best until one afternoon he saw footage about it on the news and suddenly realized the importance of what Art had done. I wondered if this wasn't a similar case, where Art's tendency to wax eloquent had simply caused the man to stop listening. I hoped not. Or he would surely be feeling terribly responsible right now.

"The board!" I said. "We haven't called the board!" We hadn't spoken to Stan at all since yesterday. What a mistake. I needed to call him now, or we were sure to wind up discussing Art's death at the wedding. And even if Stan and Gert were taking care of Gert's sister, other board members would be coming.

"It's OK," he said. "I talked to Gert Oeschle last night while you were getting that deputy's hat back from the spiders. She was distracted, but she said she'd talk to Stan. I'm sure that's all we can do."

Lance shifted out of e-mail and instead tried to hunt up anything relevant about Aldiss Carmichael. Returning to the paperwork on the desk, I said, "None of this explains why Art told people he was going out front yesterday, when he was clearly going out back. And why was June so relevant? Because Gary and Sally would be graduated and the semester over? Surely that wouldn't keep Art from taking care of an animal. It's unethical, Lance. It's *unethical* what Art did." The words made me want to cry again. "Why would he leave a couple of animals, *suffering* animals, and not call the authorities?"

"Noel, June is relevant because of the wedding. Art planned . . . whatever this was . . . for us."

"That makes it *worse*!"

"Look. What if he thought they had decent conditions? All the e-mails said was that the male was bored, not that it was filthy."

"Why would Art think that? This guy is talking about getting arrested! Art would have known why he was afraid of that."

"People don't get arrested for animal neglect," Lance said. "They get fined. They get arrested for theft." He pointed me once more to the computer screen. "I knew I'd heard the name before," he said.

I looked up at the screen and saw a headline: EARLY REPORTS OF ORANGS IN-CORRECT.

As I started to read, Lance added, as if the computer could hear him and correct the words on the monitor, "The word is 'orangutan.' "

Earlier this week News Nine told you about the Michigan animal sabotage. New information in the case has now come to light. At this time, most animals are accounted for, having been put down by Michigan or Ohio police or captured by staff from the Ohio Zoo. This newspaper has also learned that there are not orangutans unaccounted for as was previously reported. Caretaker Aldiss Carmichael confirms that there were never orangutans in the collection.

I stopped reading. "Okay," I said, "so he lied and there were orangutans after all?"

"Exactly."

"So Art might have thought Ace had a place to keep them and got tired of doing it."

"That's what I'm thinking," Lance said.

At the very least, I preferred this image of Art to the one that suggested he would leave an animal suffering because of his academic duties or some secret grand plan. The Art I knew would have abandoned everything to save a primate in danger. But I wondered how much I really knew about Art anymore. If he thought the animals were stable, then yes, he might have done it exactly that way, delaying the situation until he could give it his full attention and pull off something flashy. Especially with Gary and Sally's graduation to consume him. And double especially if he meant to surprise us.

"OK, then let's go down the library and see if we can get a phone book and hope Aldiss Carmichael has a listed number," I said.

"I don't think we need to go about it quite that way," Lance said.

"What do you mean? You can't think we can drive to Michigan today. That's at least two hours away. It's already noon. Two hours both ways, plus trying to find the guy? We'd miss the wedding, and Marguerite would be furious."

Lance smiled and shook his head. "Is she the only one?"

"No, of course not. Mama, and Daddy, and Nana would feel terrible. And there would be all the people we'd let down . . ." I trailed off. Lance's smile broadened as he kept shaking his head.

"Do you know," he said, "that the first time I saw you, you were having some kind of an argument with an undergraduate?"

"No," I said. "But I don't understand what that has to do with anything."

"I think you were a teaching assistant. It may have been one of your students. You were making your point like that, listing detail after detail, all circling around a central idea."

"Oh-kay?" I couldn't understand how this got us any closer to finding Aldiss Carmichael. I was pretty sure I'd never had him in any class of mine.

"I thought you were beautiful." He took my hand. "And I remember when Bub did *that* to you." Lance fell momentarily silent and pulled me over to him by the hand he had taken. He put his lips to my knuckles and wrapped his free arm around my waist. "I was alone with you in the hospital. You know, I was afraid your family would pull in around you. That they wouldn't let me come near. Especially since it was *my* brother who had put you there." He was rubbing my hand back and forth across his upper lip, making me realize he hadn't even had time to shave before he took off for the center in the morning.

"But they didn't," he continued. I couldn't follow his train of thinking, but I couldn't interrupt him either. "They wanted me to be there. They saw me as your research partner and someone who had tried to help you. And I was alone with you when you came around."

I remembered that. Lance was the first person I saw when I opened my swollen eyes two days after Alex battered them shut. (Technically, I got the broken nose because my head was getting pounded against my knees from the back.) At the time, I felt as mortified as I had when the spider monkeys stole my shirt. But now, I thought that if anyone had to be present in my life in that moment, I wanted it to be Lance. My parents spilled into the room soon after, but I would never forget his wide, sad eyes looking at me, unaware for a moment that I was looking back. "How does that put us in touch with Aldiss Carmichael?" I asked.

"It doesn't," he said. "I'm saying that all those people you listed aren't the only ones who would be unhappy if we didn't get married. *I* would be heartbroken."

"Oh, Lance." I let him hold me now, tugging my hand loose from his to wrap both arms around his neck and lean into his chest. "I'd be so sad, too."

"Good," he said. "Then we won't go to Michigan. But that wasn't what I meant anyway."

"Then what did you mean?" I asked without lifting my head off his chest.

"Come on," he said, reaching behind me for the car keys he had tossed onto the desk. "We have a police detective to interrogate."

CHAPTER 19

"Just because Ace has the same last name as Detective Carmichael, you can't assume they're related. For all we know, Ace is a white guy."

"No," Lance said. "The first thing I found when I searched 'Ace Carmichael Ohio' was his social networking profile, including a picture. And he's got a brother named Drew."

Detective Carmichael was Andrew. That significantly increased the possibility that the two men were related. "But Lance, that doesn't prove *anything,*" I said. We left the office and headed up the stairs. The finished basement was a definite plus of our small house.

"No," he agreed. "It doesn't prove a thing. And Drew didn't have a picture on his own social networking profile, plus he had privacy settings turned a lot stronger than Ace. But Detective Carmichael said yesterday that Art had been in driving *him* crazy ever since last October, right? Why?" We left the building and hurried to the truck. "We both knew he'd been lobbying the sheriff's department to develop a program for the appropriate sedation of exotic animals. But isn't it unusual that he picked the department's junior detective?"

"Detective Carmichael said Art got shunted to him."

"I don't think that was a coincidence. Last night, why else did Carmichael stay so much longer than any of the other police? Everybody but him was gone within an hour. I think he stayed from a sense of personal responsibility."

"He said as much."

"I think his sense of responsibility is a lot greater than we imagined."

It made sense, but I couldn't decide whether I wanted him to be right or wrong as we rode to the sheriff's building. And I feared that the personal responsibility might extend beyond dropping the orangutans. What if Ace Carmichael had killed Art?

We found Detective Carmichael in his office. He invited us in without asking for an explanation.

Lance began, "Do you by chance have a brother named Aldiss?"

The detective didn't ask us to leave. He didn't ask how he could help us, either. In fact, he didn't say anything. We sat in hard folding chairs across from his desk while he remained standing on the other side. We all looked at each other without speaking. That was how I knew Lance was right. Perhaps it was how Lance himself knew it.

The detective began with a question. "Do you have any idea how hard it is to hand your brother's name to your supervisor? I'm off this investigation, have been ever since I recognized that truck in your video last night. I can push paper, but not much else, because my brother represents a conflict of interest."

Without hesitation, Lance said, "Do you know how hard it is to go looking through your brother's apartment for the bloody evidence?"

"Excuse me?" Carmichael raised an eyebrow.

"What?" That was me, but I knew what Lance meant. After Alex attacked me, prosecutors had forced him to a plea bargain in the criminal case by presenting evidence of his abusive tendencies. They had a shirt with blood on it. Not mine. Not even Nicole's. The blood was from Alex's first fiancée. I never knew until now how they got the shirt, but the woman who owned it was more than willing to attest that it had belonged to her. I had never seen it myself, though I learned later that Alex kept it on a closet shelf.

I had wanted him to deny it. And at the same time, I wanted it to sink him. But the woman hadn't pressed charges at the time. It wasn't really salient to my case. Rather, it was good emotional leverage to keep the whole thing from going to trial. Alex swore he kept the shirt as a reminder of his own capacity to do harm. I thought it was a trophy.

Now I knew Lance was the one who went and got it. "How did you know about it?"

"Nicole told me. She found it when she was living with him."

"I'm sorry?" Detective Carmichael had raised both eyebrows.

Lance briefly explained what had happened. The detective whistled. "That's about seven kinds of trespassing on your part."

"I had the key. Alex asked me to get him some clothes. I found the shirt."

"Ah."

"So to answer your question, I know what it feels like to turn your brother in. But you're the cop. Not us."

"Exactly," Carmichael said. "And I know precisely why my boss needs to know my brother's name, but I'm not sure why *you* do. I don't even know where he lives. I see him at my dad's a couple of times a year, and we don't talk on the phone. I knew he worked for the zoo, and I knew he'd been caring for a couple of the apes, but I didn't know he was involved in any of this until I saw your security video yesterday."

After a little while of sitting in silence, Lance said, "We need to talk to your brother if we're going to have a chance of saving those apes."

"You think there's some *good* he can do?" Carmichael asked, slowly sitting down.

I let out a breath I didn't know I had been holding. Until that moment, I was still unsure. I had known it when we all looked at each other, but I only felt certain right then. "A great deal of good," I said. "He knows more about those animals than anybody else right now."

"Look at it this way," Lance said. "When you're trying to find a criminal . . ."

"A suspect," the detective said.

"Right," Lance said. "You interview members of the family first, don't you? Friends, people the suspect knows. And you're not only looking for somebody who might be hiding the guy."

"How do you know so much about it?"

Lance looked over the detective's shoulder at the cluttered wall behind him. "Watched a lot of TV," he muttered. "All wrong?"

"No," Carmichael said. "You're right. We're looking for people who would know his habits and behaviors."

I had to bite my tongue on an irrational urge to add *"or her!"* Instead, I said, "An animal like an orangutan is no different. We need to talk to your brother because he was these animals' keeper. He'll know what foods they like best, what beddings they like to nest with, anything at all that we could use to attract them to us."

"Last time I knew for sure, he was living back home, and he's long since moved away." Still moving slowly, without showing any sign of our urgency or expressing any curiosity about how we knew to ask *him,* the detective pulled his cell phone off of his belt clip. He stared at the phone, but said to us, "You know, he was in Iraq. Hasn't been the same since he came home. I guess it's PTSD. Maybe he's got it under control. Whatever it is, he got picked up for marijuana a while back. I reckon he's still on probation." Carmichael shook his head. "Well, anyway. I'll start with Dad." He dialed. Presently, he asked, "Is Mom there? Good. Naw, I didn't want to talk to her anyway."

We could only hear the detective's end of the conversation, but it sounded like he was having a difficult time. "I need Ace's number, Dad." After a pause, where we could hear his father speaking but couldn't understand his words, Carmichael said, "Yeah, I know it's been a long time. No, I don't see him and me mending any fences. About the closest we're liable to get is online." He rubbed the bridge of his nose and rested his elbows on the desk. He said, "I won't lie to you, I think he's in a lot of trouble." Another pause. "No, he's gone and done something stupid, Dad. No, I can't talk about it. But I think there's a chance for him to make some of it right before he gets run in."

He leaned back in his chair and shifted his hand so he was massaging his own temples with one hand. "Dad, I can't talk about it. I need his number. He's going to have cops at his door as soon as we get through some jurisdictional stuff . . . Yes. I know he's been doing so well these last few years. I know how much progress he's made. It's not drug related, Dad. I can tell you that. Ace is going to have police at his door soon, if they aren't there already. Dad,

I need that number."

And finally, "Thank you."

When he hung up, he gave a long sigh before he wrote down the phone number and then picked up his desk phone. "Hey, Hugh. I got Ace's number." He recited the digits, hung up, and dialed out on his cell again, without ever looking at us. Lance and I held our breaths to try and hear the other end of this conversation. What if nobody answered? What if Aldiss had his brother's number blocked? What if he simply wasn't near the phone? Then Detective Carmichael said, "Ace, it's Drew. Yeah, *that* Drew. You know any other ones? How you doing, man? No. No, it's never something good when I'm the one on the line, is it? Listen, I've got some people here who need to talk to you." Evidently, his brother tried to say something, but Carmichael went on quickly. "They're going to call you back in a couple of minutes, and you better answer them right."

He hung up and pushed the phone number across to Lance. "I'd rather know as little as I can. I am not formally a part of this investigation. But you ought to phone him now, before he gets preoccupied with something else."

Armed with the number, we returned to

our truck. Lance put his cell on speaker and dialed.

"What do you want?" Ace demanded.

Lance snapped, "Art Hooper."

"What?" Ace said.

Lance repeated, "Art Hooper. You've been e-mailing with Art Hooper at Midwest Primates. He's my boss. He's . . ." I thought Lance might say "dead," but instead he changed the direction of the conversation. "Listen to me, we need to know everything you can tell us about the orangutans running around our property right now."

Aldiss started, "I don't know what . . ."

This time, I was the one who cut him off midsentence. "No, there isn't time. You took those apes to save them, am I right?"

After a long silence, Aldiss said, "Yeah. I picked them up right at the start, when those boys turned all our animals loose. I didn't know who to give them to. And then I couldn't give them to anybody."

"You saved them. You did. But now you've put them right back in harm's way. And if you can't tell us the truth about what to do with them, that's all going to be a waste, because the police are going to shoot them."

"I guess Mr. Art would know better than me," Aldiss said.

"Art Hooper is dead, and if you don't help

280

us find those animals, they're likely to be shot for killing him."

"No!" Aldiss cried out. "Chuck and Lucy aren't like that. They're wild animals, for sure, but they wouldn't . . . he's dead? Who *can* take care of them?"

I wanted to say *not us.* Instead, I asked, "Why did you dump them like that?"

He groaned. Finally he said, "Look. I never meant that to happen. I couldn't keep them any longer. Chuck knew how to get out of the shed . . ."

"The *shed,*" Lance interrupted. "Like a *garden shed.*"

"I tried to tell Mr. Art I didn't have anyplace worthwhile to keep them animals. He thought because there's a run attached to it . . ."

Again, Lance interrupted. "What do you mean, a run?"

"Like a dog run," Ace said. "It's maybe six by six feet. But that male, Chuck, he was all the time bending the wire. And then he started letting himself out of the shed at night. I woke up Thursday morning, and he was hanging upside down off the roof outside my window looking at me, and that was the last thing. I thought, 'Next time, it won't be *me* he's looking in on.'

"So I played the radio to get him to go

back in the shed and I spent the rest of Thursday making up a couple of crates out of some two-by-fours and those skids they use for stacking boxes. And then come Friday, I turned up my truck radio real loud and opened up the shed. They always did like to go for car rides, so they climbed on up and got right in my little boxes. Even let me bang lids on them.

"And they almost made it all the way there to Mr. Art's place. But I guess they was getting bored, because I looked back, and they were busting out of my little crates like I'd built them out of paper plates or something."

I interrupted him to ask, "You didn't *hear* them breaking out?"

"No. I left the radio up so they could hear it. But they didn't want to listen, I don't guess, because I don't think I'd hardly pulled in Mr. Art's little road when Lucy jumped right off the side." Lucy. The female was Lucy. Ace went on, "And then Chuck came busting out of his crate, and he didn't act none too happy, so I hightailed it out of there." Chuck. Lucy and Chuck. It felt good to know the animals' names.

Now that Ace had finally started talking, he had a lot more to say to us. He went on, "I done all I can. And Mr. Art said he wasn't going to report me to . . ."

"Art Hooper is *dead*," Lance repeated. "And if you want those primates to live, we need to know as much about their habits as you can tell us. Like, is the female pregnant?"

"Yeah, I think so," Ace said. "Her junk's all messed up anyway."

I didn't want to hear that, and Lance didn't either by the sound of his expelled breath. We had gone from one uninvited orangutan to two and a half in a very short time span. "*How* pregnant," I asked.

"Um, they get together the same as you and me," Ace began.

"We know how they mate. How *long* has she been pregnant," I clarified.

"Oh. I guess if she wasn't already when she came to my house, then not that long after."

I did the math in my head from the animals' escape last October to the present circumstances this June. I knew chimpanzees' gestational period was roughly eight to nine months. Not that different from a human's. Like any responsible rescue, we don't breed. We manage our animals' fertility with birth control pills and careful monitoring. But Lance and I both had seen animals through pregnancies, as several of them had come to us pregnant. If an orang-utan fell into the same category as a chimp, and I had no reason to believe it didn't, we would soon have three lives in our hands, if we didn't already.

"You said they come to music," I pressed. "What kind do they like?"

"Oh, you know. The older stuff. Ciara, Li'l Wayne. They don't mind the newer ones like by Kanye and stuff. But it's the crunk they want most of the time."

I didn't have a chance to argue with him that my idea of "older stuff" didn't include anything produced in this millennium, because my own phone started chirping in my pocket.

I glanced at the caller ID, planning to answer only if the sanctuary was on the other end. But the name on the LCD screen was Olivia Johnstone, and I found myself climbing out to say, "Hello?" I hoped her fruit truck hadn't sustained any permanent damage from Chuck's assault on the back door the day before, and I hoped her peace of mind had returned.

As soon as she started talking, I knew I wasn't about to get so lucky. "I'm sorry I'm calling you at your wedding, but they don't answer at your center, and you have to help me!" she squealed, in a voice so panicked that I had an idea of what had happened even before she launched into her breathless explanation. "I heard the door slide up and down when I hit the speed bump on my way out yesterday. But I thought . . . I wanted to think it was because I don't have a way to lock it right now. That it was loose in the tracks and banging on its own. And I didn't want to stop and tie it until I was off your land, so I kept going. And then the door didn't do anything again, and I kind of forgot it, and everything was fine. I got home and tried to forget the whole thing.

"I took the kids down to the park this morning, and when we got back, that door was open again, so I figured neighborhood kids had been messing with it when we were out. But then I went to put my youngest down for her nap today, and I looked out the window, and there's an orangutan swinging around on my big boy's jungle gym, and Noel, here's the worst part. *It's a different animal.*"

She kept talking, but I didn't hear her. I held the phone away from my ear and shouted back into the truck. "Something's *right* in the world for once. Lance, we've found Lucy! Let's go before she moves on."

"What?" At the same time as Lance popped out the door of the pickup, Detective Carmichael's head emerged from the front of the sheriff's building. Seemed he wanted to know a little more than he let on if he was standing inside the front door watching us.

I was torn between fear that telling someone in the sheriff's department would be an invitation to getting my orangutan shot and an even greater fear that I needed the man's help. And when, I wondered, did it turn into "my" orangutan? Was this how Art had felt? I didn't have time to dither. "Olivia, we're coming. Stay inside and call your neighbors to warn them."

I hung up without waiting for more information from her.

"Detective," I said. "Did you wind up with any of Christian's dart guns?"

He shook his head. "All those went to the cops on the ground. I'm no longer . . ."

I didn't let him finish. "I was afraid of that." I paused, wasting in thought moments I needed for action. I knew where Olivia lived. It was a residential area some ten minutes from the sheriff's office and nearly twenty minutes from the sanctuary. We didn't have twenty minutes for Christian to get out to Olivia with a crate and dart gun. And Olivia said they weren't answering at the center. We didn't even really have ten minutes for Lance and I to get there ourselves. And without reinforcements, Lance and I were limited in what we could do.

I glanced quickly at Lance, who nodded. He was thinking along the same lines I was. "I think," I finally went on, "that we need a police escort, Detective. And I wonder if we might borrow your animal control van."

"Dunno about that. But we've got the paddy wagon right here. That do for one of those big apes?"

CHAPTER 20

Crowded into the detective's squad car like a couple of criminals, Lance and I tried to brainstorm. "We've got to make the truck appealing," I said.

"Detective, wait, stop at the grocery," Lance called out as we swung around a corner and sped past Hannah's shop and the other businesses on Main.

"I don't think we have time to be tourists," Detective Carmichael argued.

"We need bait," I said. "We've got to make the inside of that vehicle attractive."

So the detective swung into Grocery on the Go with his lights blazing and siren wailing. Because it was following us, the paddy wagon swung in behind. "Hurry up," the detective shouted, jumping out and throwing open our door.

Lance leaped up and smacked his head on the ceiling. I scooted past him and ran into the store. By the time I reached the produce section he had caught up, still rubbing his sore scalp. I elbowed past Mrs. Jane Eggers, one of Nana's canasta buddies, without so much as an apology. I had seen her at the wedding shower this morning, and now she wheeled around and stared at me with wide eyes. "Sorry, emergency," I said.

She said, "But . . ." and then fell silent.

Lance said, "Produce crisis."

I seized two pineapples and threw them into the cart, while Lance added a giant watermelon. Then I whipped around to head for the checkout. Beside me, Lance had one hand on his head. Trailing behind, the police detective had grabbed a cantaloupe. I cut into the checkout line, threw a random credit card on the counter, and called out, "I'll pick it up after the wedding."

"Police business," Detective Carmichael added.

As we exited the store, without waiting for anyone to bag up our purchases, I heard the cashier ask, "What kind of a police emergency needs *fruit*?"

We tumbled back into the car, and Carmichael screeched out to the edge of the parking lot. Before he could swing into traffic, a black car shot through the intersection. The detective hit his brakes and swore.

Craning from the backseat, I saw a gray head behind the wheel. "I would swear that's Gert Oeschle," I said to Lance. "I think that's Stan's car."

"I didn't think Gert drove," Lance said.

"I'd still swear that was Stan's car."

Carmichael pulled out behind it. I craned my neck to catch the plates. Stan's custom tags said DONR. But the car was too far ahead, and it cut out at the turn for the hospital. Then we rushed through that intersection ourselves, and Lance and I resumed our discussion of the problem at hand.

The police cruiser had an engine that our primate mobile could only dream of, and it made our speeding dashes of the day before feel like cozy trolley rides. Including our stop at the grocery store, it took ten minutes from the time we left the sheriff's office until we reached Olivia's street.

"Now what?" Carmichael asked as he pulled up on the curb.

"Now we place the fruit, open the door, and stay as far back as we can," Lance said. "Christian will come with a dart gun once I can raise him on the phone, but maybe we can get this hungry lady quarantined before that becomes necessary."

"I don't suppose either of these vehicles

has a radio?" I added. When Carmichael indicated his cruiser's two-way radio, I said, "No, like a radio-radio. One that picks up stations."

Before I could pursue that avenue further, we saw Lucy. She was, as Olivia said, playing on her son's jungle gym. While we all stood staring, she brachiated arm over arm across the monkey bars, covering the distance in two giant swings, then turning around without ever dismounting and going back the other way.

She was as filthy as Chuck, her hair matted with encrusted feces. She was too far away to smell, but I couldn't imagine the odor was much better than Chuck's had been. While we stood staring, she noticed us. With a huffing noise, she stopped midswing and dangled for a moment by one arm. For a few moments, she hung like that, looking at me with liquid brown eyes under her filthy orange hair. If she hadn't been my orangutan before, then she certainly was now. How could I possibly let her get killed when I was so close to saving her?

I eyed the police around me, all of whom had hands on their sidearms, although no weapons had yet been drawn. We didn't have any margin for error.

We had the answer to our pregnancy question, too. Lucy had labial swellings. Or, as Ace had put it, "her junk's all messed up." A human pregnancy showed in the stomach. An orangutan pregnancy showed in the bottom. Since Lucy was naked, she was quite literally hanging out all over the place. However, she didn't act like she was about to drop a baby on the spot, so we had some time to get her contained.

"Do you reckon she has any idea how to parent?" I asked Lance.

"Doubt it," he said. "Ace said she was hand-reared."

There wasn't anything to say to that. I turned my attention to our human companions. "She almost certainly associates guns with being darted," I told Detective Carmichael. "If you draw on her, she's not going to stick around to see what happens. Please, keep those things holstered." Slowly, the detective moved his arm away from his gun. His companions followed suit.

Lucy resumed her swinging. She was too far away to hear us, but she recognized the relaxed body language and responded in kind. Then she extended off the end of the gym and, instead of turning around, she grabbed the rope ladder and used it to fly out away from the jungle gym exactly like a kid would do.

Maybe it was the fact that she was so clearly playing. Possibly it was because Lance, who was *finally* on the phone to Christian, said very loudly, "She's *pregnant.*" Or maybe it was because all down the street, especially at Olivia's house, there were kids hanging out the windows to watch. But the cops only even considered their guns one other time.

"OK," Lance said, flipping his phone shut. "Christian's coming, but I think we'd all like to get her into the van before he can get here. We need to bust up the fruit a little, make it smell stronger, so it might get her attention. And I wish we had a radio."

"Surely *somebody*'s got a radio," I said. "You work on the fruit."

I headed to Olivia's house. "I'm sorry I panicked on the phone," she said when she came to the door. It looked like *her* baby wouldn't be getting a nap, because it was wide awake sitting up on Olivia's hip in a sling. Her house opened into the living room, and every room fanned right off of that. I could see a row of doors to the right, and the kitchen was clearly visible behind the TV. In a word, the house was tiny. Like every other home in the neighborhood, it made even Lance's and my small home look capacious.

Unlike the other houses in the neighborhood, though, Lance and I had helped build this one. I knew its layout intimately because I was here when they laid the foundation, and we had helped do everything but the plumbing and electricity. Olivia and her mother lived here with the children, and we had been part of her sweat-equity team helping a local housing program erect the building. The jungle gym was a surprise from Olivia's church. It was popular with the neighborhood kids. Also, it seemed, with visiting orangutans.

Olivia's baby started beating on her mother's chest and pointing back toward the little bedroom on the end of the living room where they and a crew of six or seven boys had been watching the action out the window.

"Miss Noel, can I pet it?" Olivia's son demanded, running up behind his mother.

A search through my memory failed to produce the child's name. I had met him. Once. Kids couldn't really be on a build site, but when the home was almost finished, Olivia's mother brought him by to see. Olivia was pregnant then. Her son was probably five years old now, and he didn't bear much resemblance to the little boy I remembered meeting. He had grown fast.

So I was relieved when Olivia said, "Shush, Randy. No."

"Please?" Randy asked. He was clearly talking to me.

"No, honey," I said. "She's a wild animal. She doesn't know her own strength. She could really hurt you without even meaning to." A collective groan met my statement. It seemed the kids had been waiting for me to referee this question and had held hopes I would rule in their favor.

"I'm sorry," Olivia repeated.

"Don't sweat it," I said.

Randy ignored her. "What's going to happen to it?"

"She'll go to the Ohio Zoo. The zoo can take care of her." Another groan from the bedroom suggested that this was the wrong answer, too. Did they think I was going to put up a fence and house her in the backyard?

"Those policemen won't hurt it?" Randy persisted. Oh, good lord. How much did this kid know about what happened up north?

"No," I assured him, with more confidence than I felt. It looked like he had a string of questions to follow up, and I didn't have time to answer them. Olivia kept trying to shoo him back into the other room, but he clearly planned to stay out and talk to me. "Honey," I told him, wondering as I spoke if he knew what I was talking about, "I have to go help catch that orangutan right now, and I need to talk to your mom. But if we get through this without anybody getting hurt, I absolutely promise that I'll invite you and your friends to come visit us at the monkey sanctuary before summer's out."

"Ohhh," he said. Clearly he *did* know what I was talking about. "Mama says you don't allow visitors out there."

I said, "These are extraordinary circumstances. I'll make an exception."

Round-eyed, he backed away to the bedroom with his friends, without looking away from me. He didn't even ask what "extraordinary" meant.

I refused to think about the chaos I had offered to unleash in a climate that was *not* a zoo or anything like it. But it bought me the peace I needed. Finally, I could talk to Olivia. "Have you got a radio I could borrow?"

Olivia looked over her shoulder at her entertainment center, where the radio was pretty much built in with the cable box and DVD player. She looked back at me and wordlessly shook her head.

"I got one!" Randy was back, hauling

something red. It took me a minute to re-alize it was a CD player and boom box, probably a prized possession.

"I forgot all about that thing," Olivia said. "The CD player's busted, but I guess the radio still works if the batteries aren't dead."

Solemnly, Randy turned the machine on. It blasted us with static, but that was fine. I could worry about tuning it later. Suddenly, I didn't regret promising this little kid and his buddies a tour of our facility. In fact, I felt pretty good.

As I returned to the curb, Lance threw down the watermelon with a good deal of drama, smashing it open before he picked it up and tossed it in the paddy wagon. "Check it out," I said, holding up the radio.

Lance countered, "Look at *this.*" The paddy wagon had blankets. I saw them as soon as Lance stood aside from tossing in the melon. He had arranged them so they showed out the door.

"How'd that happen?" I asked.

Detective Carmichael answered me. "I heard you all talking about what kind of traps you'd been setting up, and I had them grab us some blankets down at the jail-house."

"I could kiss you," I told him.

He chuckled. "What do you plan to do

with the radio?"

"Your brother said the orangutans come to music. I'm hoping to put the radio up on the roof and play something she likes." We already had Lucy's attention. She had stopped brachiating and rope-flying and was now perched on top of the monkey bars watching us intently, opening and closing all four of her great hands.

"All right, did he say what kind?" Carmichael asked, taking Randy's red radio out of my hands. "What station you think I ought to turn on?"

At first, I couldn't answer him, because it seemed so ridiculous. Here we were standing around on the curb urbanely talking about an orangutan's favorite tunes. "Crunk," I finally said. "But he seemed to think any rap would be OK."

"All righty. One-oh-four-point-three, then, coming up." Carmichael tuned the radio to a Columbus station that was initially on commercial break. Then he got in his squad car and talked on the two-way radio. "Edie," he said to the woman running dispatch. "We need a favor down here. Can you get a call through to a radio station in Columbus?"

While I had been getting the radio, police cars had arrived quietly at either end of the street, sealing the neighborhood off from traffic. I didn't feel like telling them it wouldn't do much good if Lucy took off across the yards. If I had, they probably would have started trying to evacuate the houses.

The station cycled through a commercial for a used-car lot, an ambulance-chaser lawyer, and a chiropractor. Lucy largely ignored us. She resumed the jungle gym games, climbing up the ladder now without using the rungs. Instead, she gripped the posts with her massive hands and shimmied up to dangle by the arms from the T-bar across the equipment's top. Then she pulled up and hung suspended by all four hands for a minute before she suddenly dropped to the ground, flipping upright along the way.

"Oh!" I jumped back. Even knowing how primates play, with a lot of physicality and sudden descents, the maneuver startled me. All of the cops went for their pieces, except for Detective Carmichael, who was still in the car on the two-way with Edie. But nobody drew and Lucy, completely unaware of her peril, began shimmying up the poles once more.

"She's going to do it again," I quietly warned the company on the sidewalks and around the cars. "They like repetition."

"Tell me about it." Deputy Greene was among the assembled forces, and he reached up to check his hat as he spoke.

Carmichael got out of the car and turned the FM radio up so that the tail end of the chiropractor's commercial blasted across the lawn. With a little help, he placed the radio on top of the paddy wagon, then led all the cops around the other side, out of Lucy's line of sight. Lance and I also stood back, though we remained in view. If she wasn't intimidated by us now, she wasn't likely to be. We stood close together, tightly holding hands while we waited for the ape to notice the change.

At first, she did not. The chiropractor wound into a public service announcement of some kind, and she dropped and climbed up the poles again. Sweet-smelling watermelon and tempting blankets had nothing on the playground equipment for an animal who had been living in boring confinement for the most recent months of her life. She surely recognized the paddy wagon for what it was, and the question wasn't whether we could trick her to come inside, but whether we could convince her that the confinement had more benefits than the kind of freedom she had been enjoying. And so we waited.

The PSA ended, and the DJ came on.

"Welcome back to one-oh-four-point-three, hip-hop and *more*. I am High-T and I aim to keep you pumping through the weekend. Now the all request lunch-power-hour is purely a weekday event, and it happens around noon, as I'm sure you all know, not the middle of the afternoon. How*ever*, I have a special request right now from Detective Andrew Carmichael of the Muscogen County Sheriff's Office." Behind the paddy wagon, the detective was shifting from foot to foot, looking anywhere but at the rest of the force. Which was difficult, since they were all crowded together in the vehicle's shadow.

The DJ continued, "Hello to all of you out there in the boondocks. Are you sure this is *from* the officer and not *for* him?" He laughed at his own joke, a deep, rich sound. Where the commercials had failed completely to engage Lucy's attention, that laugh got her to look. She had started brachiating again, and she suddenly swung over the top to stand on the monkey bars, holding on with all four hands. Finally, the DJ stopped laughing and continued. "Officer Carmichael would like to hear Public Enemy's '911 Is a Joke'. All right, Officer. This one is for you."

Even before the lyrics began, even before

the drums and backing bass guitar revved up, Lucy started heading our way. It's hard to say whether she was coming to the song or the DJ's voice, which she might have heard at Ace's home, if he could pull in Columbus stations from wherever he lived. Behind the paddy wagon, Carmichael was squirming under the amused expressions of his subordinates. In front of it, Lucy started loping across the lawn.

This was a tricky spot. We hadn't talked about what to do if it actually worked, whether we should get undercover or suggest that the officers do the same, and suddenly, we didn't have time to form a plan. The cops on the blind side of the vehicle weren't in a good place if Lucy overshot the goal, and Lance and I weren't in a good place if she veered away from it.

But she came so quickly, when — oh mercy — we hadn't expected her to come at all, that all we could do was stand still and watch. She only slowed for a moment in her approach to the paddy wagon, to pick up the blankets the detective had strewn. These, she tossed casually in the open door. Then, using the door for traction, she vaulted onto the top of the vehicle as easily as she had climbed up the monkey bars.

Detective Carmichael and all the police

surrounding him looked up to find Lucy standing above them, staring down.

"Get back," I whispered. "Back away."

Before any of them had moved, Lucy uttered a single huff, turned her back on them, and gave her attention instead to the red radio. She picked it up and cradled it, then sat on top of the paddy wagon, holding it close, rocking it against her body until the song came to an end and the DJ came back on the air.

"Officer, I hope that lured your suspect out to you." More laughter, as if the DJ couldn't believe the enormity of the prank that was clearly being played on some ignorant cop. "But in case he's still holed up, I'm going to give you another one for free. Here's a little bit of Ice-T from High-T on a Saturday afternoon. I'm going to play you a little 'Cop Killer.' Seriously, people, this guy's *murdering* me."

We were all watching Lucy. It didn't really matter what played at this point. We were so close to having her where we needed her. But, as my grandmother would have cheerfully pointed out if she hadn't been on the other side of town getting ready for my wedding, "A near miss is as good as a mile." Lucy on top of the paddy wagon was as much of a loss to us as Lucy over on the swing set.

Before we could regroup and adjust our plan, Lucy stood up and swung down from the roof, using the door to help herself in much in the same way she'd used it to get up. She didn't put down the radio until she landed, and then she carefully added it to the stash she had started making when she casually threw in the bedding Lance had taken out. After that, she collected some of the watermelon that had gotten left behind when Lance smashed the big fruit open on the sidewalk.

Then, with a very careful look toward Lance and I, she walked into the paddy wagon and closed the door behind herself.

The detective rushed around to make sure it locked, and then we all stood there gape-jawed while Ice-T continued his muffled one-man protest, presumably from the arms of a great ape.

Finally, Lance said, "My God, we *owe* you," to Detective Carmichael.

And he said, "No. If I'd done what I should have in the first place, maybe none of this ever would have happened. I owe *you* for giving me a chance to set some of it right."

"It *worked,*" said Deputy Greene, who stayed a sufficient distance from the van.

"How are we going to get that radio back?" I asked.

"You can't throw that like a disc," the young deputy said. Then he repeated, "It *worked.* If I live to be ninety-nine years old, I'm never going to see anything like that again in my life. That was *something.*"

Yes. It was. It was something. The sense of hope I had felt when I first answered Olivia's call blossomed into joy. I stood beside Lance, smiling madly. It *worked.* Something really was right with the world.

I got to enjoy that feeling for a little less than five minutes.

CHAPTER 21

I turned my attention to the radio. How to get it out. While I was contemplating some way to arrange an exchange with Lucy, the police barrier opened up to admit Christian.

"Why didn't you wait for me?" he demanded. His face was red, and he kept clenching and unclenching his big fists.

Lance said, "What?"

"The cops," he said, "wouldn't know. But *you*! *You should have waited.*"

"We couldn't exactly hold off," I said. "There was no way to know if she was going to run away or . . ."

"If she didn't take off when you came roaring up with half the police force in the county, do you really think she was going to go anywhere before I could get here to help you?" It was an amazing transformation from the calm of the night before. Where was the Christian who had persuaded an

306

agitated detective to carry dart guns when Art's six-month campaign on the same topic had produced no results? I was facing an enraged bull of a man who clearly thought we had handled Lucy's capture all wrong.

"Christian," I said. "We didn't know. We couldn't know. What if she got bored swinging and left?"

"Then you could have followed her," he snarled.

"Look," I said. "It worked out. She's contained. She's safe."

"And now you've got an orangutan with a radio," he snapped.

I said, "Yeah, we need to get the radio back."

"Orangutans are *curious,*" he said. "They take things apart. That thing has *batteries.* Do you ever put *batteries* into an enclosure?"

"Christian. I'm sorry," I said. He expected me, perhaps to back down. Hard to say. But I had learned the hard way that cringing away from an angry man was no way to solve a problem. I often wondered how different things might have been if, the first time Alex lifted a hand to me, I had stomped on his foot and left. Christian hadn't raised his hands, but he was right down in my face. I leaned into him, and we stood nose to nose. His awkward stance gave me an automatic advantage should things come to blows.

The police were all gathered in their own enclave around Detective Carmichael's car. They looked like a mini-football huddle. They weren't watching our confrontation at all. But I stood still, meeting Christian's eyes, waiting. I felt, rather than saw, Lance step to the left and come in behind me. The comfort that small motion brought almost made me smile. Almost.

Lance asked, "What's wrong with you?"

Christian looked above my head to Lance, but instead of continuing his tirade, he deflated. "I'm sorry," he said, relaxing against the paddy wagon. "I'm sorry. This has nothing to do with her." He pointed aimlessly at the vehicle that was holding Lucy. "I'm sure you handled it the best you could in the circumstances." He looked over at the police, then walked a little bit away from us and folded up his enormous frame to sit down on the curb in front of the truck.

In my experience, big people don't typically sit down where they won't have leverage to get back up again easily. "Are you all right?" I asked.

Christian shook his head. "No. I'm not. I didn't mean to come blasting in here like a cannonball. My God, you got one of them! You saved her. We'll get her to your quarantine pens and hope she hasn't taken apart the radio before we can trade out for it. She's going to be fine. Probably. But so much has happened since you left, and one of us should have been calling you, but we haven't had the time."

I suddenly remembered that Olivia had tried to call the sanctuary before she dialed my cell, and that Lance himself had been hard-pressed to get them to pick up. "What's wrong?"

Now that his face wasn't so red, Christian actually looked quite pale. The bags under his eyes stood out dark against his white skin, and he tucked his knees up to rest his elbows on them.

Lance said, "What is it?"

Christian wasn't answering. Lance and I glanced at each other, then sat with him on the curb, one on either side. Together, we waited. My euphoria at having rescued Lucy was completely gone, and in its place I felt only the knot of fear and tension that had been hurting my gut since Chuck arrived yesterday morning.

"I have bad news for you," Christian said.

I asked, "How bad?"

"The worst."

"Oh, no. Oh, that poor animal."

"No!" Christian said. "Not that. We still haven't found him. We heard another long-call right before things got crazy, but nobody could really follow up on that."

"That's some good, anyway," I said.

At the same time, Lance asked, "What, then?"

The big man nodded. "I really don't know where to start," he went on. He sat still a little while longer, then blew out a breath and said, "After you left, a couple more of those cops came driving up in a hustle. They wanted one of you, but were willing to talk to me after a bit." Again, Christian stopped. "I don't know how to tell you this," he repeated.

"I think we may know some of it," Lance said.

"Excuse me?" Christian said.

I explained. "We . . . ah . . . opened some of Art's e-mail."

"Then you know that he was expecting these creatures." Lance and I nodded. "That he knew they were in pretty bad shape, that the female might be carrying."

"She is."

"Lance told me on the phone. Dear God, what was he thinking?" Christian demanded, some of the earlier color returning to his cheeks. "Why would he ever let an animal suffer? He only would have needed to call. I would have gotten them myself, and maybe we wouldn't be having this conversation."

"We think," Lance said, "that Art believed they were living in humane, if cramped, quarters with a trained keeper."

"Why?" Christian asked. So Lance explained the chain of e-mails we had found, and told him about our phone conversation with Ace. Christian agreed. "It could have come about like that." But then he continued, "But that's not the worst of it. Not by half."

My stomach muscles (which I had thought could not get any tighter) clenched, and I reached around Christian's large back. I was trying for Lance, but when my hand got there, I found him also searching blindly for me. After we connected, we looped our clasped arms behind Christian's neck, holding onto him while we held onto each other.

Christian went on, "The cops are acting pretty cagey. They don't like to let out information. I had to pry pretty hard to get out that Art knew about the orangutans, and I think that's something they wouldn't have told one of you. They seemed to view me as sideways to the whole thing since I was in Columbus until sunset yesterday. The one thing they will tell me is they no longer suspect the orangutans of Art's murder."

"That's wonderful," I said. "What changed their minds?"

"They aren't saying. Only that we should keep it quiet and continue our rescue efforts." I nodded. Again, Christian said, "I don't know how to tell you this."

I wanted to scream, *"OUT with it already!"* But my stomach wanted me never to find out. It wanted me to take Lance's hand and walk away to get married.

Finally, Christian went on. "The troopers wanted to know a lot of information about your enclosures, where each one was in relationship to the others, and if there were others off-site."

"We think there might be," I said. "Art was . . . planning a surprise."

"Then they asked a lot of questions about the head of your board."

"Stan Oeschle?"

"The same."

"Why?" Lance wanted to know.

Christian shrugged. "Their questions weren't nice."

"What then?"

"They wanted to know if Stan and Art had any kind of falling-out recently. I said you would know that better than me, since I'm a visitor."

I shook my head. "Not that I know of," I said. The e-mail between the two of *them* that Lance and I found sounded perfectly normal.

Christian nodded, filing that information away. "Then they wanted to know whether there were any places in the buildings where Dr. Oeschle could have hidden something."

"*Hidden* something?" I said. "Like what?"

Christian said, "They didn't say. Actually, they said 'stored an item discreetly,' but it amounts to the same thing. I let them look around the place. I assume you don't mind. I don't guess they found anything, because after that, they wanted to walk the grounds some more, and they started back along the same path you showed me this morning, Lance."

"The one Art followed in last night," Lance said.

"Yeah," Christian said. "I was going to call you, but almost as soon as they went back there, one of them came sprinting back out shouting at his two-way radio. That rattled pretty much everybody. He stopped by the barn long enough to tell us all to stay put, not to leave the barn for any reason. Then he got in his car. We could see him parked there, talking on his radio for a while."

When Christian once more fell silent, Lance prompted, "What happened?"

"A lot of things all at once. About a dozen more emergency personnel showed up. More police and an ambulance. Trudy didn't have much patience with the lot of them, and she went off to go tell them our volunteers needed to go home and that we didn't appreciate being stuck in the barn when we should be caring for the primates. Then the ambulance crew took off down that same path with a stretcher, and when they came out, they were carrying somebody. I didn't get much of a look, but Trudy did."

"Who was it?" Lance asked.

At the same time, I said, "Was it an alive somebody, or a dead one?"

"Trudy says it was Dr. Oeschle. She doesn't think he was dead."

"What do you mean, Dr. Oeschle?" I demanded, pulling away from Lance and Christian both. Suddenly, I was the angry one, Christian the victim of anger that had nothing to do with him.

Lance said, "We saw Stan yesterday down at the courthouse. What was he doing back in our woods?"

I said, "That *was* Gert speeding past the Grocery to Go. I thought that was her head I spotted through the window."

"I don't know," Christian answered. "He's on his way to Mercy." *The same place they'd taken Art.* "This is a bad business. I need to get back. Trudy and Darnell have a whole lot of cops with them, but I don't want them alone long. We need to go out and find that ape before he gets killed."

"All right," I said. "Can you take care of Lucy?"

He nodded. "We'll quarantine her and I'll get a proper crate to get her to the Ohio Zoo tonight. My staff can deal with the pregnancy there."

"No pressure," I said, causing him to bark a dry, sarcastic laugh. "But she's probably going to deliver soon."

Christian turned his head to look at me, but at first he didn't say a thing. Finally, he asked, "How do you get that?"

Lance briefly recapped our conversation with Ace, ending by saying, "That's all we know, and we all have to leave right now."

"Yes," I said. "We've got to get to Mercy. What if Stan is dying? He's every bit as old as Art is, and he's more frail . . . was. If the . . ."

"We aren't going to the hospital," Lance said.

"What do you mean? We have to go to the hospital. The man's the president of our board. If he's still alive, we need to be there to support him, and if he's not . . . if he's not . . ." I couldn't finish. Too many thoughts of Art batted around inside my skull threatening to descend and silence me.

"People are going to have to understand," Lance said. "It's ten till five. We're half an hour away from your parents' house, and that's if the detective flies back to the station to get us back to our car as fast as he drove to get here. Noel, we're about to miss our wedding."

"But . . . but . . ." There was Stan; there was Lucy; and right here was Christian. And all of them needed us. "Where did the *day* go?"

Lance looked at me, asking with his eyes if I really needed him to enumerate our hours. Really, he didn't. I had been keeping track until we left home. That was close to three o'clock. We caught an orangutan in under two hours. That was something like a miracle schedule. Now, it was down to the last moment, really the last moment, and Marguerite was going to kill me if I got to Mama's house much past five. But there were so many other needs. Art couldn't take care of Stan. Art couldn't take care of Lucy. And he couldn't go looking for Chuck. If Lance and I weren't getting married . . . If Art weren't dead . . . If it were anything like a normal Saturday, we would have divvied up the duties between the three of us. I probably would have seen to Lucy, Lance would have gone looking for Chuck, and Art would have gone to Stan.

But if it were a normal Saturday, there would be no Lucy, no Chuck. Stan Oeschle wouldn't have been hospitalized. Art would not be dead. And our wedding wouldn't be on the agenda. It wasn't a normal Saturday, and I had a decision to make. I could go out and try to save Chuck and establish Lucy in our quarantine for the few hours she would be in our care, or I could go to the hospital where I wouldn't be able to make a bit of difference for Stan Oeschle. Or I could go get married.

I didn't care what my guests thought. Now that it came down to what mattered, I didn't even care what Marguerite and my parents thought. I already had input from the one other person who mattered. Lance wanted to get married. And so did I. "Let's go," I said.

We exchanged a few more words with

Christian about Lucy, the radio, and our quarantine facilities. Lance gave him Ace's number, and I went over to promise Olivia that I would get her son's radio back intact. It was a lie. I was already planning a replacement purchase. In her house, I could feel the pairs upon pairs of little-boy eyes watching me, even though the owners of those eyes were strangely quiet.

As I was about to leave, I realized why things had fallen silent. "It's going to take us a few weeks," I said to the faces in the bedroom. "But we'll have you out to see the primates. We'll have a primate party."

"Promise?" a single five-year-old voice asked.

I said, "Absolutely," and left the house to a roar of children's cheers.

Out front, Lance had explained our predicament to Detective Carmichael, who had delegated Deputy Greene to our service. He was waiting for me at the curb. "If it's all the same," the young deputy said, "I think I'd better take you straight to your destination."

"Thank you," I said. "That would be wonderful."

Shuffled into the squad car's backseat, once more like a couple of prisoners, Lance and I wrapped our arms around each other.

As Deputy Greene took off for Mama's house, I laid my head on my fiancé's shoulder.

As suddenly, I sat up and pulled away, "Oh, Lance!" I said. "What's going on with your mother?"

He groaned. "She and Dad got on a plane around the time I left to meet you at the house this morning."

"Are you sure she got on? Is she even allowed to leave the state?"

"We aren't pressing charges," he said.

I thought, *We aren't?* But I didn't interrupt.

"The insurance company hasn't made a determination yet. And she was doing nutso stuff in the clink, stripping and putting on nude dances for the jailers. She was a problem child for them. The police released her into psychiatric care. Dad accompanied her as far as the plane, a caretaker from a Columbus inpatient facility actually got on with her, and she's agreed to go straight into care. I tried to talk to her for a few minutes, but nothing she says makes any sense. I can't believe how fast she deteriorated."

The police car accelerated as Deputy Greene wove deftly around parked cars and out onto the larger county route. "She was fine when she got here," I agreed.

"No," Lance said. "I've barely talked to Dad, but he says not. He says the novelty of our house may have snapped her back for a little while, but she's been heading in a bad direction for the last six months." He pulled me close to him again and continued. "She spent time in a psychiatric facility when we were kids. She's got medications she's supposed to be taking. This has happened a couple of times since Alex and I went to college."

"Wait a minute," I said. "Your mom has been in and out of the hospital and you never told me?"

He shrugged. "I didn't like to talk about it. Mom and I weren't all that close," he said. "You know that. I didn't want to know, myself. I'm so sorry it's come anywhere near you. I've tried to keep all of my family's crazy away, and I let her guilt me into inviting her to stay at our house before the wedding." Now he pulled away from me. "I should have *known* better," he said. "I can't believe I let her destroy your car."

I said, "I'm the one who let her drive it!"

"But I should have been the one . . ."

"No," I said. "This isn't your fault, Lance. You aren't responsible for your mom any more than you're responsible for your

320

brother. I don't blame you."

"Thanks," he said. "But I feel pretty responsible right now."

"No," I told him again. And then, because he seemed to have the case against himself all written up and certified in his own head, I pulled him into me and kissed him hard on the mouth. It was one of those dizzy kisses like the one we had exchanged in front of the spider monkey enclosure yesterday, and it served to silence him.

We kissed like that until Deputy Greene sped up again and cut on the siren. Then we cuddled together in the backseat, loving each other as we rode to get married.

CHAPTER 22

And so it was that I arrived at my wedding in a police car. Deputy Greene seemed to enjoy it very much that I should be as uncomfortable today as he had been yesterday. He turned on the lights and sirens once we got out of Olivia's neighborhood. "I only waited because they hear too much of us around there as it is."

"You don't need that at all, do you?"

He grinned and pretended not to hear me.

I looked up at Lance, who shrugged and then pulled me in tighter. "I'm glad you're not mad at me," he said.

"Of course not," I said. "Why would I be mad at you?"

"Over Mom."

"Lance," I said, "I've been worried that *you* would be angry with *me* about your mom. Up until last night, I thought I was responsible for keeping you apart from your family. Now, I'm beginning to understand that you and Alex *both* came to the Midwest to get away from them."

He nuzzled his nose in my hair. "About Bub," he said.

I found that I was a lot more open to hearing about Alex now that I had seen him looking shamefaced on my parents' lawn. I almost wished I had been at yesterday's dinner to see him struggling with their mixed emotions. But then, if I had been there, I don't think I would have felt compassion toward him. Plus, I'd still have a car. Like Lance, Alex very clearly blamed himself for his mother's behavior. "Yeah?" I said. "What about him?"

"He offered to go with Mom," Lance said. "To make sure she got there. But I told him to stay. I asked him to come to the wedding. Having him go would be like . . ."

"Letting her win," I finished.

"Yeah. I should have asked you before I told him anything, but you didn't pick up your cell in the middle of that surprise shower, and I had to tell him *something* before he got on the flight, and we've been going nonstop since . . ."

"Lance, it's OK," I said. "I'm not angry."

"Really?" He stretched his neck around and look at me half upside down, one eyebrow raised, the other scrunched over toward his nose.

I laughed at his peculiar face and kissed the lips he had put so conveniently near to mine. "Really," I said, and settled back against him.

Of course, the siren brought everybody out onto the front lawn when we pulled down my parents' street. And "everybody" was a *lot* of people. The road was lined with cars, and someone had started parking people in the yard away from the flower garden. Mama might have been an only child, but Daddy was one of eleven. My aunts, uncles, and cousins, our friends, and the small delegation from Lance's family all crowded around to see Deputy Greene open the door and usher us out like some kind of chauffeur. He shut the door behind us and made a sweeping gesture. "Let that be a lesson to you," he said. "In this county, it's *illegal* to try and run out on your wedding."

Then he got back in his cruiser and drove away. "My God, what were you thinking? You're a *mess*," Marguerite scolded.

"You don't really believe that, do you?" I said. "If we'd wanted to duck out, there's no law about it."

"But your hair's a wreck, you smell like a pigsty, and I doubt anybody will be able to get that stain out of your white shirt!"

Lucy hadn't smelled good, no better than Chuck did yesterday, but she didn't come close enough to leave her scent on us. Technically, I supposed Lance was the one who smelled like a sty. Working in the enclosures tended to leave one with a distinct odor. Lance was also responsible for mussing my hair on the ride over. And we had both somehow gotten the watermelon smeared all down our fronts. I doubted Marguerite would like to know the number of white shirts I had ruined working at the primate sanctuary.

"We're here," I said. "It's only a little after five, and we have most of an hour to get ready."

"You nearly gave Nana a *heart attack,*" Margie snapped.

"Oh, no, Nana!" My grandfather really had left her at the altar. She knew what it was to wait and hope for nothing. I bolted through the crowd toward the house, as if by hurrying now, I could alleviate an entire day's anxiety for her.

"There you are!" she said as I pelted through the front door. But her tone wasn't scolding. She sounded wryly amused, and she was smiling. Not at all the picture of a woman on the verge of a heart attack. To my look of surprise, she laughed. "Oh,

Marguerite's been fussing over me all afternoon. I knew you'd get here sooner or later. But do tell me, how did you arrange to come by police car? Most couples choose a limousine these days."

"Much more economical," Lance dead-panned. "You know us. Wouldn't want to waste any money on a wedding."

Everyone who had gathered in the foyer with us laughed, then Marguerite resumed her role as wedding coordinator, shooing us upstairs and guests back outside to wait near the rose garden. "I don't remember hiring her for this," I muttered to Lance.

"Let her have her fun," he said. "Saves us from having to deal with it."

We separated then to shower. I had barely rinsed out the shampoo before Marguerite was at the door hurrying me along. "Come on, come on!" she said. "I've had the girls dressed for twenty minutes now. Poppy is *going* to spill something. You're the only one left. I brought down my hair dryer. Or do you want me to try and pin you up while it's wet?"

"Senior prom," I said.

"What?"

"You reminded me of senior prom."

"*Your* senior prom," she corrected. "*I* was a sophomore."

"Yeah, OK. But you came."

"Of course!" Marguerite had attended both my junior-senior proms as well as her own. I was no social misfit, but she flitted and flirted and had connections in nearly every class. In ninth grade, she coaxed her way in as a volunteer by nominating Mama to the parent committee. Mama refused to repeat her role the next year. So in tenth grade, Marguerite challenged the captain of the chess team (a junior at the time) to a match. If she won, he had to take her as his prom date. I never found out what she was supposed to do if she lost.

That chess captain was outside decorating Mama's lawn right now, helping Bryce seat (and now reseat) the various guests. He was still the same hotheaded, overconfident fellow he had been two decades ago. And he still adored my sister shamelessly.

That first date, for prom, she wanted finger curls, so she slept with her hair in tiny rollers and wore them around the house all the next day. She got in the shower with the curlers still in her hair, and when teen-aged vanity caused her to try and wash the hair without taking it down, her nails caught and she had both hands tangled screaming, "Mama, Noel, get me loose or I won't be able to dance!" We freed her, she danced, and now she needed to leave the bathroom so I could finish my own hair.

"I meant that my hands aren't all caught up in my curlers, OK? They can't exactly start without me, and I'll be out soon."

Marguerite sighed heavily, but presently I heard the door bang shut behind her. I re-sudsed my scalp, letting the hot water run down my back. Outside the shower, I could hear my phone ringing in my pocket. I ignored it. Whatever it was, it would wait. I was getting married.

The door popped open again. "Margie, *go away* I said."

"It's me," Rachel said.

"Oh. What's up, honey?" With my eyes closed, I fumbled for the conditioner.

"Two things."

I added conditioner and scratched my hair. Rachel did not continue, so I said, "What's the first?"

"OK, first, Lance's brother Alex sent you a message. He said to tell you 'Mom is absolutely in Seattle.' I guess he's worried you'll think she's coming to blow up more cars or something."

I rinsed, then opened my eyes, looking for a razor and not finding it. With everything else that had happened, I had hardly processed my car's untimely demise. From the back of the deputy's cruiser, I had noticed the blackened patch by the curb in a distant way, almost like it didn't relate to me at all. "To be honest, honey, she's not even on my radar."

My legs were hairy like an ape's. I tried to remember if I had shaved them yet at all this year. Mostly, I left off shaving sometime in late September when the shorts went up into the attic and picked up the razor again in April. I was pretty sure I had forgotten to start up again this year. Oops.

I moved assorted soaps and shampoos around without finding any razors. I was tempted to skip it, given our current hurry. It was a hygiene ritual I engaged in largely for Lance's benefit anyway. In bed, he liked to reach down and run his hand around from my calf to my shin and up to my knee. He never said so, but I knew he liked it best when the path was smooth.

"Does Grandmama have a razor over there in the medicine cabinet?" I asked my niece. Her grandmama was my mama, and Mama didn't ever leave her legs unshaved.

Sounds of rummaging while I lathered up my legs. Then, "No. Do you want to borrow mine?"

"It will probably be the last thing the razor ever does if I do," I warned her. "I haven't shaved since last fall."

I couldn't tell if the sound she made was smothered laughter or not. "It's OK," she said. "It's disposable."

When Rachel opened the door to go get it, Marguerite said, "Is she hurrying up in there?"

"Yeah," my niece said. "But she still has to shave."

"That's going to take *forever*!" my sister wailed. "She never mows that down. You can't see the forest for the trees on her legs!"

I definitely forgot to shave this year. The only thing surprising about that was that Lance would normally have fixed the problem. If I didn't shave my legs for too long, he was apt to do it for me. I didn't hear Rachel's answer to her mother, because she closed the door, but whatever it was, it drew Marguerite down the hall, and their voices retreated. A few minutes later, in which time the soap had run all off my legs, the door opened again. "Thanks, honey," I said, poking one hand out of the curtain for the much-needed implement and reaching down again for the soap with the other.

"Oh, you're most welcome."

It wasn't Rachel.

I heard the lock snick shut, and I stuck my head out of the shower in time to see

Lance drop his borrowed robe. "Trust a man with a razor?" he asked.

If the shower hadn't been so hot, I think I would have broken out in gooseflesh. I know I felt his words with an electric jolt. "I trust you not to cut me," I said. "And that's about all."

He said, "Give me your leg."

At home, this ritual could last until the shower ran cold and had to be turned off. Lance was a leg man, and our thick bathroom rugs had been a purchase dedicated to that pursuit. "We don't have time to fool around right now," I said.

"Then I'll have to hurry up." He followed that statement with a positively wolfish smile.

Our eyes locked, and it was only a few seconds before I handed him the soap. The wedding was going to have to be delayed by a few more minutes. My sister shouting at us on the other side of the door only added to the thrill. She had absolutely no idea what was really going on in the bathroom. She didn't figure it out until Lance and I emerged, either.

"You said you did this all the time at home!" Marguerite accused him. "You said you could get it done for her faster than she could do it herself!" Somewhere around the middle of that second sentence, the double entendre finally stuck in her prudish mind, and she suddenly flushed scarlet.

"My legs *are* shaved now," I told her. "And it's not like we ever agreed to wait until the honeymoon."

The sound she made was a cross between an angry teakettle and a coach's whistle.

I pecked Lance chastely on the cheek and said, "Come on, Marguerite. Help me with my hair."

Up in the sewing room, my wedding dress faced me from its dressmaker's form. Beside it, in an inelegant pile, I found my stockings and petticoats. (I would need two, the second meant to give the skirt a little bit of flare at the bottom.) I got into the hose and the first petticoat before someone knocked.

Marguerite, who was already tugging on my bangs, pinning them back as she got ready to put my wet hair in its French braid, said, "I'm hurrying," around a mouthful of bobby pins. "I'll have her down there as soon as I can."

Because of the pins, it was doubtful the person on the other side understood her. "It's me," Rachel said. "You decent, Aunt Noel?"

"Yeah, reasonably. It's safe to come in."

She did. Her bridesmaid's dress was even

more stunning on her than it had been laid out this morning. Now she had a shiny matching jacket with three-quarter sleeves. The dress hung lower in the back than the front, so it framed her body and emphasized her curves. "That's breathtaking," I told her.

"Thanks," she said. "I wore it to prom, too, without the jacket. It works as more than a bridesmaid's gown."

"That's wonderful," I told her. Then, to my sister, "Hang on, Margie. Let me get the top petticoat on before you do anything drastic up there."

Marguerite let go of my head long enough for me to tuck it through the topmost layer of underwear. She said, "What do you need, Rachel? Can you tell everybody we're about fifteen minutes out?" Again, most of her message was lost to the pins in her mouth.

"I'll tell them," she promised. "I had two things to say earlier," she said to me.

"Yeah," I said. "Margie, do you want me to sit down?"

"No, I can reach the top if you're standing." Some handy things about having a tall little sister.

"What was the other one?" I asked my niece.

"You sounded so supportive earlier," she began. Marguerite groaned and Rachel trailed off.

"I meant it, honey," I said quickly, trying to drown out my sister's obvious dismay. "If you don't want to wear the jacket, your tattoo is welcome to be in our wedding." Margie groaned again and jerked my scalp pulling back the bangs. "Ouch!" I said.

She mumbled an apology.

"Not that," Rachel said.

"What is it, Rachel?"

She started again. "You sounded so supportive earlier. So I called up Lisa and invited her down. I hope it's OK."

Marguerite spat out the bobby pins. They speckled into my hair and down my back. "No, it is *not* OK!" she told her daughter.

I cut her off. "Margie, shut up!" I jerked my hair free from her braiding clutch and turned around to face her. "It's not your wedding, and it isn't yours to say." I glared at her for another moment, waiting to see whether or not she would advance her argument. She looked away first and began collecting her bobby pins.

"Rachel, it's fine," I told my niece. "I'm glad you did. If Lisa were your boyfriend, I doubt anybody would have thought twice about it. And if I'd known in the first place, I'd have sent the invitation myself."

For an instant, it looked like Rachel might

cry. Marguerite exclaimed, "For God's sake, don't ruin your makeup."

So I hugged my niece instead. "It's good," I said. "We'll talk later."

I gave myself over to my sister's none-too-gentle ministrations, and she dispatched Rachel to make sure everyone else was in readiness. I seriously considered telling her to leave my hair alone. She was still peeved and yanking on me like it was her wedding I was screwing up. The clock on Mama's wall said six forty-five. We would be an hour late. Not bad, considering.

With a grunt of frustration, Marguerite let go of me again, swearing under her breath because I was the only person she knew whose hair was harder to work with wet. While she went for the dryer, I pulled my dress off the model and over my head. I could have stepped into it, but if I was putting on the dress ahead of the hair, there wasn't any reason to do it the other way. Mama had replaced the button loops with a zipper hidden under the row of pearls. It simplified things tremendously to only have a few buttons for Marguerite to hook up above the zipper, which she did as soon as she returned and collected the last of the bobby pins.

While she braided, I thought hard about

the day. Our final discovery had completely collapsed my joy at having captured Lucy. What had happened to Stan Oeschle? Why would the police think he had hidden something in our barn, and what would that something have been? Did they think *he* had beaten Art to death? Did they still think it, if he had been carried out on a stretcher?

It would have been easy to get mired in the questions again, and I didn't want to. I wanted to enjoy my wedding. Margie, hired or volunteered, had put an enormous amount of her own energy into making this wedding come off. It must seem as if I didn't value her efforts at all. She deserved an explanation for my erratic behavior. Some of it, anyway. She wouldn't ever understand the shower delay.

"We found one of the orangutans, Marguerite."

"Do you think you'll be able to catch it?"

"We *did* catch it. We got it, and it's safe, and it ran us a little late, OK? I'm really sorry."

She turned on the dryer and blew it around my scalp. But she stopped pulling quite so hard on my hair, so I knew she heard me, that I was at least partially forgiven.

CHAPTER 23

Downstairs, Nana was waiting to approve me before I could go outside. "Yes," she said, and smiled. "That's how that dress was meant to be worn. It suits you." That had been almost exactly my own thought when I first put it on. Good. She embraced me carefully, then pecked both my cheeks. "Now," she said. "Let's have a wedding."

"No, hang on!" This time it was Brenda, trailing me down the stairs, waving my cell phone.

"What?" Margie demanded. "We don't have time for any more *hang ons.* The men are all in place, and all they're waiting for is us to come out the door before they start the bride's march."

"Sorry." By her tone, Brenda evidently wasn't sorry at all. She seemed to be quite a bit more versed than I was in ignoring my sister's moods. "Here." She handed me the phone.

"Hello?"

"Noel! I'm glad I caught you." It was Rick on the phone. Art's forgotten nephew. That was probably who tried to call in the shower, too. "Did you get my message?" he asked.

"No, I'm sorry."

Margie glared daggers and I turned away so I couldn't see her.

"It's fine," he said quickly. "I know you're trying to get a wedding on. But when I called the sanctuary, they told me you found *one* of the orangutans."

"Yes," I said. "The female."

"Congratulations. I had no idea there were two!"

"No," I said. "I suppose at the hospital yesterday we still only knew about the one."

"That makes sense. Anyway, I'll be brief." I was glad he would. Margie had come around the side to continue sending out malevolent vibes. Rick went on, "I told your friend Christian my little piece, and he said you would want to know too. I should have said yesterday, but nothing was right then." His voice rose a little, then fell toward the end. I agreed. Nothing was right yesterday.

"What is it?" Margie or no, he certainly had my attention.

"I wanted you to know you have somewhere to put her."

He *did* know what Art had been up to! "What do you mean?"

"You have an enclosure for the female orangutan, once her health is stable. Christian figures he'll care for her at the Ohio Zoo here at first. But you've got room for her. The male, too, if you can catch him."

"What are you talking about?" But I knew. We were right. Lance and I were right. "That isn't mall construction we've been hearing!" I said.

"It is," he told me. "But not *only* mall construction. And we've been entering the property through the back of the mall to avoid arousing suspicion. We've been back there building an orangutan enclosure and new administration building. The admin building's got to be finished, and we need to get an inspection. But we're done with the major work. I wanted you to know . . . I *know* Uncle Art would have wanted you to know . . . if you can catch that other animal, they both have a home."

My God, Art. Tears welled and threatened to fall. I held them back largely because Marguerite was still giving my phone and me the hairy eyeball. I had a thousand questions and Rick probably only knew the answer to a hundred. But the joy of finding Lucy, of capturing her alive and still probably pregnant, all rushed back in. "I want to see it," I said. "First thing in the morning."

"You got it," he said. "Call and I'll take you out for the tour. Go get married, Noel."

"Thank you, Rick. I will."

I flipped my phone shut and looked around at the assembled family. Margie rushed in with tissues to dab around my eyes and absorb the tears that still threatened to run down my face and spoil my makeup. "There's room at the inn!" I blurted out. I tried to explain more, but nothing I said made any sense, and Margie finally took away my phone and steered me to the kitchen door. Outside, she whistled sharply with two fingers, and Bryce materialized to take Nana's arm and lead her away toward the flower garden.

Across the way, standing outside the garden, I saw Lance and the minister arranged at the end of an aisle of roses. The space was made for ceremonies, though we all speculated that the ceremonies in question were funerals, rather than weddings. A separate part of my mind, one that refused to focus on marriage, wondered whether we could hold a memorial for Art here, then nixed the idea because we would need to hold it at the sanctuary.

The rest of me seemed to be operating

without that one part of my brain, which began compiling a list of people we still hadn't called to tell about Art. I was sure Rick would take care of the people from Art's personal life and the department secretary would cover the university. But that still left a huge number of professional contacts that Lance and I would be responsible for getting in touch with. And we needed to do it right away. Although Lance and I hadn't discussed it, I thought we would have to delay our trip to Ecuador until the center's future was more certain. Especially with a new enclosure.

A new enclosure. Art! No wonder he had been so secretive about the orangutans. That final piece fell into place for me, now that I was certain about his and Stan's "big reveal." No wonder he had delayed their delivery. If he thought they were safe, in good hands, and would soon have a place at his primate sanctuary, then Art would have taken the risk of leaving them where they were.

More than that, he would have gone down to the enclosure as soon as possible to get it ready for their arrival yesterday. He didn't go out front at all. He went around to the side and probably tramped up around the mall. I wondered where the new enclosure was located.

"Noel?"

We were at the top of the garden, and my father was offering me his arm. Forty years old and my father was walking me down the aisle and "giving me away" to the man I'd been living with for a decade. As Dad and I linked arms, another part of my brain splintered off to wonder about marriage customs and rose garden weddings.

I barely saw my nieces start in with their mismatched groomsman partners, only had a few moments to feel guilty because I hadn't said so much as hello to those groomsmen, who had come a long way especially for this ceremony. But Bryce and Poppy started off at a fast walk and the others followed quickly. Long before I had collected my scattered thoughts, the music changed and Dad tugged my arm gently.

Quickly, I leaned over to peck him on the cheek. "Thank you for the flowers," I whispered. "They're lovely."

I could see the tents a few feet away, next to the rose garden. Those roses that weren't lining my aisle filled yesterday's hastily purchased centerpiece vases under the tent's white canopy. Simple and old-fashioned, they suited the wedding the way Nana's dress suited me.

"Are you ready?" he asked.

I nodded. But really, my mind was still scattered over half the countryside, planning a memorial service, mentally apologizing to the groomsmen for being out of touch, and wondering how brides in India balanced the amount of gold their families often loaded upon them by way of bridal attire.

As Dad and I started forward, I took mental note of my own ceremonial clothing. The dress was both old and borrowed, so that covered two old superstitions. My shoes were painfully new and already rubbing a raw spot on my heel to chastise me for failing to break them in ahead of time. And after she had finished braiding my hair, Margie had presented me with a pair of delicate sapphire earrings. I had feared I wouldn't be able to get them through my holes, since I only wear earrings on occasion. It's not wise to give primates anything shiny and inviting to snag, especially not something attached to your body. But my piercings had ultimately yielded to poking and opened enough to allow me something blue.

My father kissed my cheek and looped my arm through Lance's as the minister said, "Dearly Beloved."

Lance whispered, "Your dress is extraordinary. I shall remember to trust your mother on all such decisions in the future."

"You mean you'll let her pick your next wife's dress?" I asked him *sotto voce.*

"I mean I won't complain when she decides to outfit you when we renew our vows every year from now until eternity."

I tried to refocus and concentrate on the wedding, but my distraction level only elevated. To my left, Bryce fidgeted in his tuxedo, then reached around to scratch his butt in front of everyone. Poppy saw it and started to snicker. I knew Marguerite must be squirming. *Sorry, Margie,* I thought at her. *I'm with Poppy. At least he's scratching the back and not the front.*

We had planned an extremely short wedding, with most of the evening to be devoted to the reception. Lance and I were much more invested in celebration than ceremony. Before I knew it, the minister indicated that we should face each other and exchange vows. He handed me Lance's ring and said, "Repeat after me."

I did so, but I didn't even really know what I was saying. My voice was on autopilot while my eyes studied my parents' street. Beyond the rows of parked vehicles, a sleek black car turned down the lane. It was hard to tell from a distance, but it *looked* like Stan Oeschle's car.

Then I slid the ring on Lance's finger and Lance repeated the same set of motions, unaware that bad news was driving our way behind his back. Because it *was* Stan's car. It crept between the lines of parked cars, its driver significantly less deft than Deputy Greene. Gert Oeschle should have been with her husband at the hospital. If she wasn't, he was dead. Simple. And if she was at the hospital, then who was driving her car? Natasha? She should be at the hospital, too. Bad news either way.

As the car finally pulled off the street and added itself to the lines in the opposite lawn, the minister said, "I now pronounce you husband and wife." Then Lance's face filled my vision, and he kissed me. It was a kiss like the one he had delivered yesterday morning at the sanctuary. His lips pulled at my schismed mind, uniting me in a way the whole ceremony had not done.

He swept me backwards, and I leaned into his arm, and we kissed and kissed again. I heard nervous titters from the audience, and Poppy's snicker progressed into a laugh. I suspected most of them believed a middle-aged couple like us should restrain ourselves to a less ostentatious display. If Margie had been squirming before, she must be writhing now. Her own wedding kiss had been a chaste peck, which was appropriate for a couple who had put a chess king and queen on their wedding cake. But my old-fashioned dress didn't indicate an old-fashioned attitude about romance. Finally, I righted myself, and Lance helped me regain my balance. If I had retained doubts about getting married, that kiss would have eradicated them.

I pulled him close to me, and we held each other a while longer. While I breathed in the warm smell of his cologne, the laughter faded in the audience. "Honey," I breathed into his neck, "Art built the enclosure."

"What?"

"I talked to Rick right before I came out. That's what he's been trying to call to tell us. That hasn't all been mall construction we've been hearing."

"We were right? Are you telling me we have a place to put these orangutans?"

"Rick's words exactly. He's already talked to Christian."

Lance pulled back and kissed me again, even less chastely than before, if that was possible. He laughed out loud and turned to face outward with one arm around me. "That's the best news I could have imagined," he said.

Gert or whoever had driven her car did not appear in the field. Someone who had heard Lance whispered to her neighbor, "Is she pregnant? At her age?"

I withheld my own laughter. Considering Lucy, I thought, *No, but pretty soon, with any luck, I'll be finding out whether it's a girl or a boy.*

I scanned the yard. I could see the car, but I couldn't tell if anyone had gotten out of it. So the person was either sitting there doing nothing or else already out and walking over, hidden by the house. On an impulse, I cleared my throat. The groomsmen and bridesmaids, who were supposed to fall in behind Lance and me for the recessional, all stepped back. I scanned the audience, then made eye contact with my sister. "Marguerite, could you come here a minute?"

She eyed me skeptically, but bound by the tradition of obeying the bride's wishes (as long as the bride wasn't delaying her own wedding), she joined us. I turned her around to face everyone and looped our arms together.

"First of all, I wanted to apologize for making you all wait so long," I began. "I'm sure you have heard what a stressful couple

347

of days we've had." I felt Marguerite's shoulders tense. This was beginning to sound like a speech, and speeches were supposed to be saved for the reception. I squeezed her gently. "I know it's getting late, and some of you will have to go before dark." Margie relaxed. If I was doing this for the benefit of the older generation, then she could understand it completely. Whatever it was.

"I won't go into the particulars," I said, "but I will say this. You may have heard that an orangutan was abandoned at the primate sanctuary where Lance and I work. It was actually a *pair* of orangutans. Before we got here today, Lance and I participated in the safe capture of one of those animals. And a few minutes ago, I learned that we have an enclosure suitable for housing them." The audience made appropriate sounds. These were our friends and family, after all. They knew how dear we held the sanctuary. Some of them were volunteers. Trudy and Darnell would have been in their number if they hadn't been taking care of the apes now.

I heard an old woman's voice say, "That explains what was happening at the Grocery to Go today."

"Because we have been so distracted," I continued, "not only yesterday and today, but ever since we got engaged really, other people have had to do most of the work for this wedding. A lot of professionals have put their effort into things like the food and the cake. Mama and Nana sewed my gown. You'll see Daddy's flowers in the middle of your tables under the tents." Marguerite had figured out where I was going, and she had started wiggling, trying to escape to one side. I clutched her elbow with my own and held her still.

"But the vast majority of the work to make this ceremony a success came from the woman standing with me. Margie, you were working from Cleveland with almost no idea what I really wanted, and you made everything perfect. Thank you."

I let go, and Marguerite turned to face me. "Thank *you*," she said. And when she didn't say anything else, I realized she was about to cry.

Beyond her, beyond the house, the door of the familiar black car finally opened, and Gert Oeschle got out. Bad news, then. Surely the worst.

I pulled Margie in between Lance and me. We all hooked arms, then walked down the aisle together.

At the end of the aisle, I stood aside and let the rest of the wedding party stream past us. Then I tugged Lance and Marguerite around the edges and back around to the front, where we needed to pose for a few pictures. Lance and I had stressed that we only wanted to take a few formal shots. Mostly, we wanted informal photographs to commemorate our marriage.

"Do you see her?" I asked Marguerite, pointing to Gert's lurching body. By the way she was walking, this was hitting her very hard, and I wasn't at all sure she should be driving. I briefly explained the situation to my sister. "Can you do me a favor?"

"Yeah," she said. She knew what I wanted.

"Come over for two family photos, then catch Gert up and get her settled somewhere. See who is taking care of her granddaughter." Surely even a teenager needed someone for the death of a grandparent. "Find out who can come get Gert. If she wants to come over to the reception and cry her eyes out, it's fine with me, but don't let her go driving off again in that state. I don't know how she got parked without hitting anybody, and I don't want her to get herself killed getting out again."

We all hurried up front to pose. A woman in a wine-red dress lingered in the audience, as did a dark-haired girl who looked around Rachel's age. The red dress likely belonged to Xian's wife (when had he gotten married? How did I know that? Was she a girlfriend? Friend? No, I was pretty sure they were married). And the young woman was almost certainly Lisa. It was unlikely they knew another living soul here. They were planning to sit through the photos so they could go in with their dates.

Marguerite might have the market on long-term planning cornered, but I can roll with almost any developing situation and adapt quickly. I scanned the exiting guests and spotted Chesley's wife, Annie. Ches was a grad school buddy, one who we stayed in closer touch with than Xian, who now lived in New York. Annie knew all of our school friends and had plenty of people to sit with. I waved a little and caught Annie's eye.

"Stay a minute for pictures?" I called out.

"Sure!" she called back to me. Then she said something to the three women she was with, who I belatedly realized were my own dear friends Hannah, Mina, and Jan, and they headed into the tent without her.

"Lance, get your brother."

Lance asked, "Are you sure?"

"I thought you weren't taking many pictures," Marguerite said.

"I'm not," I told her. I nodded to Lance. "I realized I want to do one with the wedding party, one with family, and one with spouses and partners."

Behind me, Rachel made a strangled sound, sort of a cross between a gasp and a laugh.

To my right, Margie said, "Oh Noel, why do you have to *encourage* this. High school kids are still in that uncertain stage. This could all go away next month for all we know."

Now Rachel sighed. An oft repeated argument, then. I stopped, forcing Marguerite to stop also. We looked at each other. "First of all," I said. "It's my wedding, and if I want to get Mama's dogs out of their run and add them to the picture, I'll do it." Margie looked somewhat chagrined, but I wasn't finished. "Second, I don't think someone who celebrated her twenty-first anniversary with her high school sweetheart has any place claiming that teens don't know their own sexuality." Now Margie wouldn't meet my eyes. "And third, I'm not 'encouraging,' I'm 'supporting.' Now come on, we've only got a couple of minutes for the family shots."

Nobody else argued, because by now everyone had seen poor Gert staggering across the lawn to us. Half the guests were staring out of the tent. Gert probably would have gotten to us long before we got so much as a single picture lined up, but with a glance toward me and a quickly interpreted wave, Hannah, Mina, and Jan all took off in her direction. Thank God for good friends.

The family pictures were awkward. I gritted my teeth and insisted on a sisters picture. And a brothers picture. And a spouses with their siblings picture. That one was worst, because Alex in his well-heeled suit seemed to be trying to catch my eye, and I was doing everything in my power to look away from him. He could, after all, still be the man who had killed Art and Stan Oeschle. I *thought* he was innocent. He *seemed* different. But I didn't trust myself where he was concerned. And I certainly didn't trust *him* where *I* was concerned.

As soon as the family photos were finished, I sent Marguerite up to the house to figure out what was happening with Gert, and we proceeded with the pictures of the wedding party. Mercifully, Alex faded into the tent.

We finished, then turned around and headed into the tent. Mama's voice cut through the crowd chatter before the DJ could introduce us. "You did *so* tell them a flavor!" she called out.

"Ah, you've seen the cake then?"

"Yes, I've seen the *cupcakes,*" she told me. "I think you got every flavor they sell!"

"Do you like them?"

"Of course I do. You got me lemon pastiche." A flavor the bakery had sold and Mama loved long before the trendy cupcake shop had moved in out at the bypass.

Then the DJ finally said, "Announcing Mr. Lance Lakeland and Mrs. Noel Rue," following the carefully worded instructions we had given him. We passed through an artificial arch, nothing so beautiful as the natural arch in the garden, but still effective for the purpose.

As soon as I stepped into the tent, the smell of dinner struck me. Curried chicken with mango. The name of the dish Lance made for our engagement flooded into my mind along with its smell. "We only ordered last week!" I protested.

"I ordered it eleven months ago," Lance said. "You confused everyone last week when you called up and asked them to send us whatever was on hand."

If Gert Oeschle hadn't been lingering in my mind, the moment would have been perfect. We swept into the room laughing together. I completed a fast round of the guests, maybe ten minutes to cover the most populous tables. I made my way toward the front, but Poppy tripped and crashed into me with glass of punch. The drink missed us both and splashed onto a white linen tablecloth. What happened to my plastic? Mama, no doubt.

I bent over to fix her shoe, a patent leather Mary Jane that had come unbuckled and caused the fall. "Put your foot up here."

Bending over to chair level in the dress was tight, but manageable. As I finished the buckle, I saw Margie's feet approaching. Perhaps if I had seen her face first, I would have been prepared.

Instead, when she said, "You have to go," in a strangely choked voice, I jerked back so hard that I nearly pulled Poppy off her feet.

"What are you talking about?"

Poppy took down her leg and dashed in another direction as I met Marguerite's eyes.

They were wide, and her face was flushed red. She held out the cell phone she had confiscated from me earlier. "Now," she said. "You have to go *now.*"

CHAPTER 24

"Go where?" I asked. There was nobody on the phone when I brought it to my ear. Apparently, she just wanted me to have it.

Instead of answering, Marguerite grabbed my elbow and tugged me off toward the house. As soon as we passed out of the garden, she broke into a rough run. The wedding dress, with its double petticoats and ankle flare, was not designed for running. I lost my balance and stumbled right out of my chafing high heels. I probably would have toppled if Lance hadn't been running right beside me. He grabbed my arm, steadying me before I could land in a face-first heap of lace and tulle.

"Marguerite, what did Gert say?" We were running again, even though the house was nearby.

"It's bad," was all she would tell me. I had guessed that much. Only a little while ago, Marguerite had been offended by my tardiness to the wedding. Now she wanted me to go somewhere. I had no trouble believing that Gert's news was bad. But, as heartbreaking as I considered it, Stan Oeschle's death held no urgency for me. Not in the way Art's did.

I knew Stan socially and professionally. But now that I wasn't sitting on the curb with Christian, I didn't feel any need to go rushing off to the hospital. I had never crashed on Stan's couch in a dissertation haze. He had never picked Lance and me up from the airport and talked African primates for six solid hours in his living room until we tumbled upstairs to sleep, too tired and jetlagged to even consider going home. I didn't think Marguerite would consider Stan's death urgent for me, either.

In fact, my sister was probably uniquely wired up to avert such a disaster. Where a lifetime of living with Mama and her charts left me averse to all forms of planning, it had given Marguerite planning superpowers. She anticipated things that could go wrong, developing outrageous worst-case scenarios that would have left others feeling terrified and helpless. Margie did this so she could figure out the solutions. She was a long-term planner in the strangest sense of the term. So if Margie's solution to

Gert's news was, "You have to go. Now," then she had predetermined a situation that would require me to leave. So I had to go. Now.

Inside, Gert hunched over the kitchen table, a collection of glossy pictures scattered in front of her. She had a walker shoved over into one corner of the room. I didn't realize she had a walker. I hadn't seen one yesterday at the courthouse. My three friends sat with her, and Nana stood over by the sink bobbing a teabag up and down in the cup in her hand. "Hurry," Nana said when we clattered through the door. "I hope your mother picked up more than one change of clothes in that overnight bag yesterday, because we don't have a thing to fit Lance in this house."

"But what . . . ?" I tried to ask.

"There isn't time. We'll talk while you're changing." Hannah scooped up all but one of the photographs and herded us along.

In the hall, she handed half the stack to me and half to Lance. I took a moment to glance at them, but only that long, because in the next instant I threw them all on the floor and stopped dead in my tracks. "Jesus Christ, what was that?" I demanded.

I looked at Lance, but he had thrown his pictures down too, and he was gagging into his arm. Without a word, Hannah picked up one of those Lance had dropped and held it out to me. I wouldn't touch it. But I looked. Reluctantly, I looked, and then looked away, bile rising in my throat as Hannah dropped it. My picture was bad enough. It showed Stan and Gert Oeschle's granddaughter Natasha posed provocatively in panties and garters, hands instead of a bra covering her breasts.

Lance's picture was worse in a terrible way. Natasha was outright nude, crouching with one hand on the ground between her splayed knees. Her head was cocked coquettishly, lips shaped in a pout. Everything about the print, from its glossy sheen to Natasha's bright pink lips, screamed professional. I processed that certainty to avoid the rest of the insult, which lay in Natasha's other hand. That other hand was stretched out ahead of her, hooked through the bars of a cage. Looking back out at Natasha was a monkey. *Our* monkey. The girl was stripped naked, gazing lustfully at the rhesus monkey Lance and I had spent the past two weeks rehabilitating. The one that had thrown its stinking feces at him yesterday morning only a few minutes before actually eating in our presence for the first time.

I reeled between nausea and absurd realizations: *No wonder it's taking so long to normalize him. Did it bite her? Is that why she had a bandaged hand?*

"Noel!"

I didn't realize I had fallen down until Lance's face loomed into mine.

"Art, what have you done?" I said.

"I don't think it was Art." Gert stumbled in from the kitchen. "He was the one who brought them to my attention. He delivered an envelope yesterday morning. I didn't have time to open them before that blasted adoption hearing, or . . ." She cut that thought short and said, "I think he found them in your new building."

"But why not turn them over to the police?" I had not gotten up, so I remained tangled in my wedding dress at the foot of the steps.

"I did," she said.

"But Art . . ."

Lance gripped my elbow and hoisted me up. Gert said, "Art gave them to me first, God knows why. These aren't even the ones he gave me. Those were alarming, but not damning. He wrote a letter. He said there was worse but asked me to come to him if I felt I really needed to see them. By the time I opened the envelope, he was . . ." Gert cut herself short. Then, she continued, "I

360

found these in the basement." Then she started to sob, though she continued talking.

I couldn't initially understand Gert's words. They were lost to her tears. I went back down the hall to her, and I started to understand what she was telling me. The first thing I got was ". . . had her with him."

"Wait, what?" I asked. "Natasha? Who had her with him?"

"Stan! We fought when I showed him the photographs. I shouldn't have done that. He had her swearing up and down she *wanted* to do that!" Gert waved at the pictures. "And then they drove off, and I went to the police." I noticed my friends retreating to the end of the hallway, returning to the kitchen even as Nana joined us, my family closing in around me to listen to Gert's horrible story. Gert's face was oddly puffy, I supposed from crying, and when she continued, her voice was hoarse. "When I found out Art had been . . . was dead . . . I thought Stan killed him." I pulled the old woman into a tight embrace, my own shock driving me to hold onto her as she continued. "But then, the police came and got me this afternoon. And someone has beaten *Stan* half to death." She dissolved back into tears.

"Surely he'll be all right," I told her.

She stopped crying, pushed me away and seized my shoulders. "That goddamned pornographer!" she burst out. "If he ever wakes up, I'll rip out his throat myself. He destroyed my Linda and now he's taken away Tasha." Linda was Natasha's mother, the one whose instability and eventual death had led to Natasha's becoming Gert and Stan's ward in the first place. I didn't see what she had to do with this, but before I could try to work it out, Gert wailed, "And I was so blind! So blind." This acknowledgment seemed to deflate her. She sank against me for a moment. "She's gone!" Gert whispered. "Tasha's gone. He had her with him. The police are combing the area around your facility, but they haven't found a thing. They don't know how to search. He has her stashed somewhere in that new building . . . somebody *has* told you about the new building?"

"Yes," I said. "How did *you* know?"

Gert revived momentarily. "Stan paid for it, for God's sake!" As Lance and I had suspected, Stan Oeschle and his personal fortune had once more stepped in to save us.

"But surely you told the police?"

"They couldn't find a thing."

"Then why do you think we can?" My baffled horror wasn't only fueled by the fact that we had no idea of the new building's layout. It was that we were no longer facing something inexplicable at the center. When Art had been killed by someone violent with an unknown motivation, I didn't fear going to the sanctuary with appropriate company. But pornography was nasty business, and I had to believe these people were behind Art's death. If he had taken the time to contact Gert, then who else might he have told? Who might he have angered? And how could he have exchanged such a banal e-mail with Stan?

Oh, Art. Why hadn't he gone at once to the police? It was the orangutans all over again. He tried to give people time to act appropriately on their own and instead exacerbated two bad situations. And this one had surely led to his death.

Marguerite was pulling on my arm. "You have to go," she said again.

"Go get killed?" Stan may not have been a very physical man, but Art was strong. Neither Lance nor I would stand up long against whoever was out there if that person could kill him. But it was Marguerite demanding that I go. The woman who barely an hour before had been adamant that I

363

stay. I knew where her urgency came from. It wasn't that hard to figure out now. Natasha was a year younger than Brenda, three years younger than Rachel. My sister had spent her children's lifetimes protecting them from exactly this sort of exploitation. The danger to a girl a little younger than the two oldest of her babies would be like an ice pick in her gut.

"You have to *find* her," Gertrude implored.

"The *police* have to find her!" I insisted. "This is horrible. But I don't see what Lance and I could do that they couldn't. I don't even know where the new building *is*."

"Rick knows," Lance said. "He'll take us."

"He can take the police!" I said. "We cannot do anything that they are incapable of."

"Since when did you trust them so much?" Marguerite demanded.

"Since when did you *stop* trusting them?"

"This argument is pointless." Nana's voice sliced through Marguerite's and mine both. I had nearly forgotten her, even though she was standing directly behind Gert. "Noel, the way I see it, you have a choice. You and Lance can either call Art's nephew and ask him to escort you, or you can tell the police that he will know where to look." I had forgotten she knew Rick, but Nana knew everyone, so I shouldn't have been surprised. She went on, "And if you want my opinion, I think you ought to do both."

Lance asked, "What?" while I stared.

"Clearly, you can only risk your own lives so far, no matter what the situation," she explained.

"They've combed the whole forest. They can't find her," Gert said. "Please, help me find Natasha. She's all I have left."

I breathed deeply and tried to set this emotional appeal aside. "Nana, what were you saying?"

My grandmother continued. "You and Lance know how the building is designed . . ."

"No, we don't!"

"Not specifically," she agreed. "But generally. You know what your sanctuary is like. Niches that would seem secret to a law officer . . ."

"Would, to us, be someplace where we could quietly observe the animals. Predictable, maybe, if Art had a hand in the design." Nana, at eighty, looked so much younger than the sixty-year-old Gert right now.

"Precisely," my grandmother said. "And I worry that if you don't go first, the police won't welcome you to come look. Better sometimes to beg forgiveness than ask permission."

I didn't trust the police at all. Not to let me look, not to find Natasha if she was in plain sight instead of hiding, not wanting to be found. "Dogs!" I said. "They need dogs."

"I'm sure they do," my grandmother said. "Maybe they have them. Maybe they have already found her. Maybe they are trying to find Gert to tell her that right now."

Lance said, "And maybe not. I'll go."

"Not without me!"

"Noel, wait . . ."

"Now don't you . . ."

"I'm taking Bub," he said. "Somebody with a club is going to snap either one of us in a blow. But there's not much Alex can't handle. And I don't want you in with him."

"I'll cope."

"Noel, if he has to protect me, he's going to do it with *rage*," Lance said.

"And maybe he'll direct it where it belongs for once. I'm going up to change my clothes, Lance, and if you aren't waiting for me when I come down the stairs, then I'm going . . . I'm going to be angry." I had almost said, *I'm going to get an annulment,* but the lie wouldn't leave my mouth. We were married now. For better or worse, till death do us part. "Don't you dare go get yourself

366

killed without me."

"Right," he said. "Because dying is so much more pleasant in company." His soft smile took the edge off his words. I hugged him quickly, then hitched the skirt up a little and headed up the stairs.

He followed me closely to get changed, calling down behind us, "Somebody find my phone so I can call Rick." I handed him mine.

Even getting undressed in record time and with Lance's help, I still scurried down the stairs too long after my new husband, whose suit came off much faster than my dress. He was flipping my phone shut after having called Rick, and someone had Marguerite's minivan idling in the street, Alex in the passenger seat. He hit a button that opened the power door on the side so I could get in back.

I pulled myself up. "OK, Margie," I said. "Tell Nana to call the police, now. She'll . . ."

Marguerite swung around into the driver's seat before I noticed she was wearing street clothes too. "Nana knows what she's doing," my sister said.

"What are *you* doing?"

"If we find that little girl, she's going to need a *mother*," my sister snarled. "And all

367

of you need to buckle your seat belts in my car."

Alex never wore his belt, but under Marguerite's glower, he stretched the belt across his midsection.

"Let's go."

My new husband said, "Rick's going to meet us by the mall site and drive us in. I guess I should tell you we own a brand-new already-defunct strip mall now."

"What? Don't you mean the sanctuary . . ." I corrected him.

"No, *we* do. This whole thing was Art's idea of a wedding gift to us."

"Oh, *Art*!" I clapped one hand over my mouth and sagged back in my seat. "How do you know?" I asked Lance through my fingers.

"There's more."

"What more?" What more could there possibly be? What possible more? I had been asking that question for the last two days.

"I'm sketchy on the details, but Rick said Art was going to sign it over to us at the surprise grand opening tomorrow. Rick has a copy of Art's will. He hasn't been to the attorney's office yet, but he knows the details. He's the sole heir and executor, and he plans to honor his uncle's wishes."

"So . . . what? This isn't even part of the

rest of the sanctuary?" I asked.

"I don't know," he said. "I think it is. I think he assumed we would turn around and donate the land to the society."

"But why give it to us in the first place?"

"Rick says to get around the board."

"What getting around do they need?"

"Art was retiring. He wanted to give us negotiation power so one or both of us could assume his position formally. Rick said he was getting some kind of pushback."

I shook my head, as if physical motion would clear this whole conversation from my mind. "I'm not thinking about this right now," I finally said. "Later."

"Later," Lance agreed.

We fell into an uncomfortable silence as Alex squirmed in the seat belt. He had always claimed they chafed him, something I had never questioned. But his discomfort seemed more intense than a strap across his chest might justify. Sure, he pulled at the belt, arranging it on the outside of his shoulder and tugging it away from his stomach like a pregnant woman. But he also kept twisting his head, like he was looking over at Lance, though he was really darting his eyes back to me.

CHAPTER 25

I hated the feel of Alex's eyes. He used to be able to cut me with a glance. Now, it seemed more like he was wounding himself. "What?" I finally snapped. "What the hell is eating you, Alexander?" I hadn't really meant to use his full name. But I didn't apologize for it.

"I'm sorry, Noel," he said.

"You're not seriously doing this right now?" I had half suspected it was coming. I had seen it in his stance last night while my car burned (a distant event that felt like it had happened to someone else). I had seen it in the way he stood away from the other guests while I walked down the aisle with Dad. In the way he kept trying to get my attention during the family photos.

"I wasn't going to," he said. "But you asked."

"Yes," I conceded. "I did."

He took this as license to continue. "Most

of these conversations were less complicated. They were nine years ago, and they
all started out 'I'm an alcoholic.' But I don't
need to tell you that."

No, he didn't. I ground my teeth and let
him keep going, hoping he would be quick.

"And I thought probably the best kind of
apology I could give you was to stay away.
But when Mom called, and I had to come
. . ."

As soon as I had made it, he snapped my
resolve to be civil. "You did *not* have to
come!"

"I *did* have to come." His voice had an
edge I didn't like at all. A familiar edge that
made me want to tell Marguerite to stop
the car so Alex could get out. But I think he
heard it, too, or else felt it, because he
stopped talking to draw in a long breath
through his nose and exhale through his
mouth. He breathed in and out one more
time, then repeated in a level tone, "I *did*
have to come. You don't know my mother,
Noel. Lance never should have let her invite
herself to your house like that."

"He didn't," I interrupted. "He didn't
want her at all. That was my mistake. I
thought it was a fence that could be
mended. Clearly not."

"No," he said. "But it's a fence that's got

nothing to do with you. Bub, have you ever
. . . ?" Alex let the question hang, and Lance
mutely shook his head. It drove me nuts the
way they called each other "Bub." Always
had. "Then I'll try not to," Alex said.

"No," Lance said. "But I should have. And
now isn't the time for it, but if you want her
to understand why you had to come, I'll try
now."

"What's with the brotherspeak?"

"Short version, OK?" Lance said, and I
realized he was talking to me.

"Yes, fine, short version." Short version,
long version, this wasn't what we needed to
be talking about right now. I could see them
going further off course, and Marguerite
doing nothing to help redirect them.

Lance said, "Mom's destructive. Bub and
I spent about a year in foster care one time
while she tried to get it together."

"Foster care?" That was Marguerite.
"What about your father? Wasn't he a
competent caretaker?"

"Wouldn't leave her," Lance said. "It hurt
him to let us go, and he fought like mad to
get her in shape and get us back, but that's
not really the worst part."

Not the worst part? "And you've never said
word one about this to me?"

"I've never said word one about this to

anybody. I try not to think about it."

"Not the worst part?" Marguerite echoed my thoughts. "What could be worse than that?"

"The worst part," Lance said, "is that a week after we got to come home, she tried to kill herself, and then she spent a year inpatient."

"I'm sorry," Marguerite said. "And I'm sure it sounds cold, but she blew up my sister's car yesterday, so I'm not feeling a lot of sympathy for *her* right now. At least you were home with your father, not off with a bunch of strangers."

Alex shook his head, much in the way I had shaken mine earlier, like he hoped to clear it. "OK, but you get the point," he said. "She hasn't ever been stable. And neither have I. Not until . . . Noel, you saved my life when you prosecuted me. I know you think rehab wasn't good enough, but I'm telling you, I was suicidal. What I did to you, that was my rock bottom. I would be dead. I would have killed you and then myself. It was a lot like Mom. And I'm more like her than I . . . she and I have the same triggers, or a lot of the same ones. I thought I could predict her and stop things from getting out of hand."

The more he talked, the less I cared. The

less I wanted to hear his voice. Trying to kill me saved *his* life? "Narcissistic, oblivious asshole! Could you get to the point?"

"I just did!" This time, he turned around fully in his seat to look at me. And there was that edge again. I had an idea that I was one of those triggers he was talking about, that by opening my mouth, I pushed my brother-in-law to anger. He might be trying to apologize, but he was really telling me that he still blamed me for his nearly murdering me.

"If you think for one minute," I said, "that I'm going to fall over and be grateful you showed up, you can forget about it right now. It is *not* my fault your childhood sucked, or that your mother is a nut job, or that you drink . . ."

"Drank!"

". . . or that you spent eight months in rehab when you came after me with that telephone. Do you want to know something, Alex? I had two facial surgeries to reconstruct my nose and cheekbones. I *still* have bursitis in my left shoulder. You mumbled apologies to a couple of athletic directors and had another job within a month. I spent an extra half *year* working on my dissertation and missed three unique research opportunities because of my delayed graduation date. So don't you dare come down here and act like I ought to want you here, because I don't, and I'm not ever going to."

He closed his eyes while I was speaking and did some more of that nose breathing. When I stopped he said, "I deserved that. And I don't think you want me here, and I absolutely know it. Bub asked me to stay. And right now, I can help you find that kid. I hope. Or if I can't, I can at least look imposing so you and Bub can look."

Lance said, "Listen, Noel. Mom tried to take Alex with her when she tried to kill herself. Dad and I were out back, and he wouldn't eat the pills she was shoving in his face. She forced several down, though, and he had to have his stomach pumped. By the time he got loose to run outside to us, she was chasing him with a knife."

None of us said anything for a while. I stared back and forth between Lance and his brother, slack jawed.

Finally, Alex said, "I've always been the only one who could pull her back. When she called me, she wanted to burn your parents' house. She was acting stupid but not . . . crazy. I thought if I stepped in and talked sense, she'd back down long enough that Dad and I could get her out of town before she screwed over your wedding. She's screwed Lance and me over from day one, and I didn't want her to sour this. I owe him that. I owe *you* that."

I could not imagine a sense of responsibility for a family member as strong as the one Alex seemed to carry with him. No wonder his drinking. No wonder his violence.

Abusers, especially abusive parents, often focus on one child. It sounded like Sophia had focused on Alex. Lance had, perhaps, been a little more sheltered. No wonder Lance hadn't said anything.

And the simple fact was that today, we needed Alex. Two men had been beaten, one to death, in our woods. It was even odds whether we would find Natasha or something far more brutal at our new enclosure. Lance was strong, but he was no fighter. I had self-defense training, still spent Monday evenings in Tae Kwon Do classes. But I was strictly studio. I had never participated in anything resembling a street fight. And I really didn't know how I would fare against someone big enough to smash Art's face in like that. We needed Alex for brawn.

Our argument had carried us to the mall site, and Rick's faded work truck waited for us now. He got out. "You folks want to follow me? Or do you want to ride along? It's not far, but it's a pretty bumpy ride."

We piled out of Marguerite's minivan. As I walked the short distance to climb up in the truck bed, I studied the ground.

Rick and Lance clasped hands briefly and Lance got in front while everyone else got in back. Rick and Lance talked through the open cab back window with the others about Natasha, the enclosure's layout, and the most efficient way to go about searching the property as we thumped down a dirt track through a grassy field. "We've been moving the equipment around out front here every day so you folks would think we're working on the mall. We've got done with the enclosure proper. All that's left is the barn structure. Not much to look at there right now . . ." Rick went on. He had a great deal more to add, and Lance had several questions, but I tuned him out. For all the attention I paid, they could have changed over to talking politics and the national debt.

Something had caught my attention as I was getting in the truck, and now I hung over the side, watching the ground. Finally, Alex said, "Are you all right Noel? You're not getting sick, are you?"

Without looking up, I said, "What? No."

"There was scat all over the ground back there," Lance said. "She's trying to see if there's any other sign of the orangutan."

"Oh, God," Margie groaned. "I forgot about King Kong."

Lance said, "Kong was a gorilla."

Then the truck lurched to a stop, and Rick said, "Do you see that?"

I pulled my head back into the truck and stood up so I could look out over the cab. I rose until, at the bottom of the hill, I saw our new enclosure, domed with black mesh and blended into the forest exactly like Art had surely planned it. "It's beautiful," I said. But I was distracted, and I pulled my eyes away quickly to look nearer to the truck for any sign of Chuck.

Instead, my eyes lighted on a corrugated metal shack. "Rick," I said. "Do you have security cameras here?"

"Yup," he said. "Mr. Oeschle was kind of paranoid the whole time this place was being built. I guess from what you say, he had some cause."

Lance asked, "Can we get at the video?"

And I explained, "Art said . . . the last thing he said to us was to watch the security video. We didn't see anything really helpful on the center's video. But maybe this . . ."

"It would explain why he went out back," Lance said.

"After we find that *girl,*" Marguerite said.

"We've got maybe fifteen minutes to look before the police get here."

"Right."

Rick pulled down the hill and we all clambered out. I was unsure whether we should make a lot of noise calling or not, but Marguerite solved that problem. "Natasha!" she shouted. "Natasha honey, come out if you're here. We're here to help!"

In the distance, police tape fluttered around a tree. Was this where Art had initially been beaten? What about Stan? The grass was trampled down as if many people had passed through the area. Had the police already come and gone?

And then we all started yelling, even Alex, whose bellow had always had a bull-like quality. We circled the enclosure twice on the outside. "I don't see her. We can't help someone we can't find," I said.

We walked back toward the truck, an absurd little posse dejected because we had failed without even trying.

"No, we need to go inside," Marguerite insisted.

"Rick, are there keys?" I called.

He threw down his entire ring by way of answer. "It's the only padlock key on there," he said.

Lance, who had caught them, fumbled a

little, then walked over to unlock the door. He handed them to Marguerite and she went without being asked back up the hill to give them to Rick. "Go back and check out that security shack," I said to her on an impulse. "I'll call if we find her." I waved my cell phone. As we walked into the enclosure, I heard Rick's diesel rumble back to life to carry Marguerite back up the hill with him. I felt better with her gone, though I couldn't say why.

Art had already prepared spaces for the animals, which surely proved he had been expecting them. He had ropes strung throughout and huge branches. The space's defining feature, though, was a domed center built around an existing tree trunk. The tree spiraled up beyond the top of the mesh, and the wire ended in some kind of metal circlet that kept it from either wounding the tree or being an easily removed obstruction to escape.

"If she's anyplace, she's up there," Lance said. He started up the tree, leaving Alex and I standing below. And then, when he was halfway up the trunk, I heard faint rustling in the imported browse off to my left.

"Shh," I told Alex.

A quiet voice said, "Don't go up there.

Please, don't go up there."

"Natasha?" I said.

Lance stopped climbing.

I strained to see into the foliage, which had, I now realized, been dragged into something of a nest. "Please don't go up," she repeated. "You'll be able to see straight down on me, and I haven't got . . . I don't have . . ." She took a loud, shuddering breath. "He took my *clothes*," she wailed.

"Oh God, Lance, get *down*," I said. But it wasn't necessary. He was already descending, dropping branch by branch more rapidly than he had climbed them.

"Where are you?" Alex demanded. I realized he hadn't found the nest yet, and I pointed.

Natasha didn't say anything. I had an idea she was crying. "You can have my shirt. Give me a minute," Alex said. Rapidly, he unbuttoned his shirt, fumbling with the cuffs and jerking loose the central panel so fast he popped a center button. "Is she very tall?" he asked.

Lance said, "No," and indicated my height. In fact, she was slightly taller than me, but that was something I was more apt to notice than he was, I supposed.

"That ought to cover her up, then," Alex said. He was probably right. He was as tall as Lance, but a whole lot broader, and I had a sudden memory of sleeping in his shirts, which he wore long. They never quite lost the smell of his cologne and came down to the middle of my thighs.

He stripped his sleeves off, exposing his forearms. He still had my name tattooed across his shoulder. "Oh dear God," I said. "I would have thought you would have done something about that by now."

His eyes met mine in silent apology. I had to give him credit. A thing like that would have driven the man I knew a decade ago to glowers and pursed lips, if not outright violence. "The other one says 'Joyous,' " he said. "Most people think it's a Christmas thing."

"You can afford to have it taken off," I said.

"Yeah." He handed me the shirt. I didn't think he was really agreeing.

"Go get Marguerite," I told him. As he left, I said, "Natasha? I've got something you can put on." She didn't answer. "Can I bring it to you?" Still, she didn't say anything. I started over to her hiding place holding the shirt out in front of me.

When I got there, I had to negotiate my way across any number of branches. She was a clever builder, and I was reluctant to destroy her sanctuary. Natasha sat in the middle of her circle, in a place she had padded with leaves. She was facing away from me, her knees drawn into her chest, and her face buried between them. A raw rash across her back suggested an allergy to some of the bedding that made up her protection.

Why had I sent Marguerite back up the hill? She had been right about one thing. Natasha needed a mother. I had no idea what to say to a child so badly damaged and obviously suffering. When it came to the deep hurts, my motto had always been to give my nieces and nephew back to my sister. Same thing with my friends' children. I was good at friendship. I could listen to sadness and offer general comfort. But the closest I could come to a deep connection with this kind of pain was Rachel's ongoing experience. Maybe that. And as bad as that was, I felt like it paled next to what Natasha was enduring right now.

Her whole body shook with silent tears. I had an idea she never would have revealed herself if Lance hadn't started up the tree. I opened up Alex's shirt and wrapped it around her bony shoulders, trying to figure out how I could access her kind of pain.

And then I knew.

CHAPTER 26

I couldn't connect to Natasha as a child. She probably hadn't been a child for a long time anyway. I tried to imagine myself at that point in my life when Alex had been my overlord. I tried to consider the words someone could have said to get my attention. But I didn't think anyone could have said anything. I wouldn't have believed. So instead of trying to talk to the girl in front of me, which clearly wasn't working, I sat beside her.

I drew my knees up like Natasha's and laid my head across them, looking at her. After a long time, she turned to me. Her face was tear-streaked and puffy. I couldn't tell if the purple on her cheek was smeared mascara or a bruise. I hoped the former. I feared the latter. She was still silently crying, swallowing and breathing in jagged but silent gasps. I wondered how long she had been crying like that. How many years.

"He's coming back," she whispered. "He put me here to wait for you."

"No," I said. "Stan is . . ."

"Not Stan. I don't know what's taking him so long."

I could see that she wasn't going to leave. That it didn't matter if she was in danger. She seemed to be in shock. Then I registered the first part of her statement. My stomach suddenly knotted. "Who?"

She shook her head, and I thought at first that she didn't intend to answer. Then she said, "My cousin — Gary," in that same whisper and turned her face back to her knees.

"Who?" But even as I spoke, my mind was running through images and names, coming to the conclusion that I only knew one Gary and that, yes, he would have been Linda's cousin if his mother was Gert's sister. My mind hadn't bothered with this before, even though I should have realized it.

"The one that finished his degree," Natasha said. "I think he maybe went to kill Gran, even though he promised to leave her alone if I came with him. But he never got done killing Stan, and . . ." She drifted into silence.

I thought a little information was in order.

"I guess he beat Stan up pretty badly," I said. "But your gran is OK . . ."

"You're lying." She said it in a matter-of-fact tone, as if she was making an observation about the weather. *It's sunny. You're lying.* All the same. And she went on crying. She looked back at me. "And I bet you think it's all Stan's fault anyhow . . ."

"Well, he *did* . . ."

"He's my *grandfather*! Or the closest thing to one I'll get. He wouldn't do that. Gary and Aunt Gretchen are spreading around that he had something to do with this, but it's because they're caught."

"What are you talking about?"

"It's too bad you don't know. Then he'd at least have a *reason* to lure you out here."

"Know *what*?"

"Those two volunteers of yours."

"Which two . . ."

"Trudy and Darnell."

"What?" Had we left Art's killers in *charge* of the sanctuary?

"They're some kind of federal agents."

I stared at Natasha, opening my mouth and closing it again.

"When Uncle Gary's passport was blocked, it didn't take him long to figure out they were behind it, but he figured you, and Granddad, and Mr. Art had to be involved. He's been hiding with Aunt Gretchen ever since she fell."

I had visions of the dozens of interns Art had brought through the center over the years. "Natasha, how long . . . ?" I wanted to ask her how long this had been going on, how deep it went, but I wasn't sure she knew, or that I wanted to know even if she could tell me.

"Mom brought me into the films when I was ten. She was aging out. And then she went and OD'd, so it was only me. I guess Gary's been using your monkeys ever since Granddad bought into his sob story and got him into the graduate program at the school. It made a good cover, and Art's such a putz. He never thought his best buddy's nephew would be anything but perfect." My heart flared in defense of my friend. But Art's focus *was* almost entirely on the monkeys. It wouldn't have crossed his mind to ask why Stan's nephew wanted to study primates. It certainly hadn't crossed *my* mind. I hadn't even thought to find out how closely the two of them were related.

Now that she was talking, Natasha didn't seem able to stop. She showed no urgency to leave, and I didn't know how to break into her trance to get her out. She said, "But Gary thought Stan would give him his own

387

monkey house. And when Stan found all those pictures . . ." Natasha strangled a sob.

"Wait . . . Stan found the pictures? Not Art?"

"Yes! Weeks ago. He's been after Gary to turn himself in, and he wanted to call the police, and I should have let him, but I don't want the kids in school to find out I'm *that* kind of girl. And now he's killed Gran because I couldn't get her out of the hospital. He'll get in there and finish poisoning her."

"Your grandmother's not in the hospital," I said.

"No I guess not, now. She's dead," Natasha responded.

"She's fine . . ."

"She's not. He's killed her."

I tried, "How else would we have known to come looking for you?"

"Because Gary sent Aunt Gretchen in to get you."

It clicked. The walker. The stumbling gait on uneven ground. The way she had leaned into me and looked so old in comparison to my grandmother. The woman in my parents' house was *not* Gert Oeschle. It was her sister.

"She was supposed to go in pretending to be Gran, hysterical since your friend dropped off those pictures for her. Her job was to get the two of you out here so he could get you out of the way. And when Gary gets back here, he'll kill you. Then I'm going to get to star in my own personal snuff film."

Finally, some of her message reached me. I knew the term "snuff film." It referred to fetish pornography in which women were killed and their bodies sexually assaulted. I had been listening for ways to help Natasha. I should have been more concerned with ways to get her moving. The police had never been called until Nana called them. *If* she called them. I had left an impostor at my house. With *my* grandmother. Sooner or later, Gary *would* come back, and Lance and I had sent our defense arm up the hill to get my sister. We needed to go.

And then I finally knew what to say to her. "Natasha, this isn't your fault." She didn't believe that. I knew by the way she blew out a breath and shook her head. But it was still the right thing, because she unclenched one of her elbows from around her knees and started sliding her arms into Alex's dress shirt.

She shifted onto those knees to button it up.

"Come on," I said. "Let's get you to your

grandmother. Wherever she is."

Natasha froze, and for a moment, I thought I had spoken wrongly, but she said, "Shhh." And pointed. She was smiling. I expected to see Gary standing behind me, but all the fear had relaxed away from her face. "Look," she whispered. "That's why Gary never finished Stan. I'm sure of it. But . . . he took my clothes, and I've been here since yesterday afternoon, and I can't really think . . . and . . . but, *look,* will you *look*!"

It was the first passion I had heard in her voice. Slowly, I turned my head. "Ohh."

Natasha's protective circle of greenery extended to the mesh, but she had made a half-moon shape that left one edge completely open to the outside where the greens met the enclosure's sides. From the outside, it looked like nothing was there, even though she would have been clearly visible from above. She could easily move to hide from anyone outside of the enclosure, leaving her nest empty and looking no more manmade than the other plant life Art had dragged in from the forest.

And now, on the other side of the wire, stood the orangutan we had been hunting for two days. I could smell him. I had been smelling him for some time, but I had been so wrapped up in Natasha's words that I had not paid attention to my other senses. Chuck poked his fingers through the mesh, palm up. Without prompting, Natasha reached out and tapped them with her own fingers. One, two, three, four, five. Tap, tap, tap, tap, tap. Natasha sucked in her lower lip, and I knew she had forgotten me. Then, she made a pincer out of her hand and used it to tickle Chuck's fingers. One two three four five.

The orangutan peeled back his lips from his teeth and gurgled breathy laughter. At close range, his grin didn't look at all funny, and his burble would have been easy to mistake for a threat. I had a sudden insight about why Gary hadn't come back. Art had told me, "It tried to save me." Chuck tried to save Art. Natasha said something about Gary not finishing Stan. Chuck did that. The orangutan bought the injured man time. Chuck went after Gary when Gary beat Art, and he intervened again to help Stan. And now he was protecting Natasha, and by extension, us. It was impossible to know what he understood, but he wasn't incapable of emotion, and he had lived with humans for probably his whole life.

"Look at that," I heard Lance whisper. He was right behind me, though I hadn't heard him approach.

"You do this much?" I asked Natasha.

"All night," she said. The ape pulled out a hunk of cantaloupe from behind his back with the other arm and mashed it against the mesh. "He's been feeding me," Natasha said. "He's so sweet."

In my hip pocket, my phone trilled. I had barely picked it up when Marguerite shrieked in my ear: "You've got to get out of there! That wasn't Gert Oeschle at the house! I don't have time to explain . . ."

"Nana!" I shouted.

At the noise, Chuck reared back.

"She's OK. Your friends did something to that other woman and they called to warn me. But listen, we're all three locked into the shack up here, and he's coming after you and Lance." A loud crash echoed across the line.

"What? Who?"

"That was Alex. He's going to bust down the door, but it's taking a while."

"Who slammed it in the first place?"

"How should I know? He slammed the door and yelled at us after Alexander came in. Go! He's going to come find you next!"

Standing as close as he was, Lance heard. "We have to go," he said.

Natasha's joy vanished as fast as it had come. "It's Gary, isn't it?" she said.

I nodded. I was afraid she would retreat back into herself. But she said, "We can't let him hurt the orangutan." She spoke in a tone I wouldn't have believed possible a few minutes earlier. "Go, go!" She made shooing motions at Chuck, then darted away, exiting her nest in the same way I had come. "He'll leave if I go," she shouted to Lance and me.

Barefoot as she was, she still ran ahead of us to exit the enclosure. What happened next felt like it came in slow motion. She bolted out into the woods, the door crashed shut behind her, and for a moment Gary materialized, slamming home the padlock in a fluid motion, then turning toward Natasha. She heard the noise, looked over her shoulder once, then kept running. "You can't catch me!" she shrieked. But Gary could catch her, and he meant to. She had barely a two-step lead on him, and youth wasn't giving her much in the way of speed. Gary moved to close the distance between them.

And then Chuck exploded from beside the enclosure, loping easily alongside the human he perceived as a threat to his girl. He backhanded Gary in almost the same way he had smacked Art out of the way yesterday, only harder. And where Art had flown out of the way and then bounced back to his feet, Gary spun all the way around. His body made an impossible arc and flipped over. He landed on his head with a crunch audible to Lance and me, trapped behind the enclosure's mesh. I think he was dead before he struck the ground. I think he was dead as soon as that giant hand connected with his face in that backhanded slap.

Natasha stopped running and looked back at Chuck, who threw back his head and started a longcall. He emitted the initial screech, then his body suddenly stiffened and he crumpled inches from the human he had inadvertently killed.

"Everybody OK?" Christian asked. "I can't believe how long he fought the dart. I think it may have caught in his hair. And when he got that burst of energy at the end, I thought he wouldn't give in." Then he indicated Gary. "Sorry about *him.*"

As he spoke, Christian clambered down the hill from the other side, skidding around tree stumps. Natasha stared from him to the fallen Chuck. Then she screamed, a sound of rage entirely worthy of her orangutan friend, and threw herself up the hill at Christian.

"He's fine, Natasha," I yelled. "Christian tranquilized him."

"You're lying," Natasha screamed. "You're lying, you're lying, you're lying!" She changed course and threw herself on top of the prone animal instead of attacking Christian. "You're lying!" she screamed again, then in the same hysterical tone, "He's breathing! You didn't kill him!"

"He's fine," Christian said. "Look." He turned the dart gun so Natasha could see it. But she wasn't looking. She buried her face in the ape's fetid fur, like he was possibly her only friend left in the world. Maybe he was.

In the distance, I heard the wail of approaching police cars. "Art's nephew has the key," I said. "If you can get him out of the security shack, he'll help you let us out, and we can maybe move Chuck in here until you can get a truck down to get him."

CHAPTER 27

Sunday dawned clear, and my mother and grandmother's voices drifted up through the floor. "Pancakes," Mama said.

"Waffles," Nana argued.

I groaned, "Neither," and buried my head under my pillow.

Margie said, "Sausage."

Last night had been another long one, and the sky was barely light now. Marguerite, Alex, Lance, and I had been tied up with the police for hours after sunset. We would be dealing with the chaos resulting from Gary's pornography ring for a long time, but remembering the way his body had twisted as it broke still made me shudder. Nobody deserved to die that way.

Tranquilized, Chuck had been moved into the temporary enclosure, and Christian planned to move him to the Ohio Zoo until our barn was finished and the whole complex passed inspection. Christian, ever the optimist, assumed our facility wasn't about to be shut down for its inadvertent role in the scandal.

We did find out that Stan Oeschle was alive. He was airlifted to Columbus, and the full extent of his injuries was still unknown, but his condition was listed as serious but stable. Gert Oeschle was located, alive, in a Columbus hospital, recovering from the effects of poisoning Natasha said was administered by Gretchen. We were only able to obtain limited information on the phone, but the consensus seemed to favor Gert's ultimate survival.

And then there was Natasha.

She retreated into herself as soon as the police arrived. She sat outside a cruiser on the ground and refused to speak. Marguerite tried to mother her, but Natasha shook off my sister's hands and turned away from her words. I was busy with the orangutan when Marguerite stalked over to me. "You see if you can get anything out of her."

"What? Who? The detective is a man."

"Natasha." She projected disgust with my misplaced priorities.

Natasha had curled back up with her head against her knees, and she was rocking slightly. Someone had provided her with a sweat suit, and Alex had regained his shirt.

We had Chuck on a makeshift litter, and Lance and I were helping push him while Christian tugged him forward. He was heavy, and even with Christian's strength, the progress was slow.

"Tell her to come down here." I turned back to the animal.

"Noel! What are you doing? Isn't a child more important than a monkey?"

"He's an ape, and Natasha doesn't want our *pity.*"

"What are you talking about? She's in *shock*!"

"She's in misery. There's a difference."

"You have no *idea* . . ."

"Oh, yes I do." I finally gave up pushing the orangutan and stood up. "When he," I pointed to Alex, "pounded me into my apartment floor, do you know what hurt the worst?"

Marguerite shook her head.

"Watching my family watch me afterwards. You couldn't hide the *pity,* and that made the humiliation so damned bad. So go up there and tell Natasha to come down here, and don't get all maudlin about it. Tell her we need help getting the orangutan to safety, and she won't hesitate." I bent back down and flopped one of Chuck's arms onto the stretcher.

Within a minute, Natasha was standing beside me. "She said you needed help."

"This is going really slowly. The cops are busy doing police stuff, and we don't have enough people pushing."

"Why not get him?" She pointed to Alex.

"Because he tried to kill me one time, and I prefer to keep my distance." I looked up at her as I spoke, but in the darkness, it was hard to gauge her reaction.

Finally, she said, "So what do you need me to do?"

"He's so big, it's hard not to drag the stretcher right out from under him. He keeps sliding off. If you get back here with me and help push and flop, Lance can go up with Christian and pull."

She took Lance's place, and we worked together until Chuck was a few feet from the enclosure door. My shoulder and back begged for our golf cart. "He tried to kill you?" Natasha asked.

"Damned near succeeded."

"Well, how come he was with you earlier?"

"He's a lot nicer now . . ."

"They all say that."

She was protecting me. She was protecting the ape. She was protecting everybody but herself. "I know. That's why I prefer to keep my distance. But we needed his help

399

to find *you.* We knew there might be trouble here, and he wouldn't be too easy to beat up."

"I don't guess so."

Chuck was in. We pulled the stretcher free and exited, locking the door behind us. Christian would have a truck here before the orangutan woke, since a padlock would be a small obstacle to our new ape.

"What about you?" I asked her. "Your grandparents are both in the hospital. Will they let you go home alone?"

"No, and I don't want to."

"Are you going to stay with a friend?" I pressed.

She huffed through her nose and looked away. "I haven't *got* any friends. They can probably find one of Gran's friends, or I can go back into foster care for a few weeks. I've been there before. It's not so bad, really."

I didn't realize Lance was listening until he spoke. "Stay with us."

"Yes!" I echoed him immediately. "We've got a spare bedroom, and one way or the other, we're going to need extra hands out at the sanctuary in the next few days."

"I guess . . . I already know some of the smaller monkeys." Her discomfort seemed to come from our offer, rather than from

400

the way she had developed her familiarity with our residents.

"Good," Lance said. "I'll go figure out how to make it happen."

Now, downstairs, Natasha said, "I can *cook,*" in a tone that suggested someone was trying to baby her out of the kitchen. We owed that kid something, and I struggled out from under the covers before Marguerite or my mother could drive her to anger with their pity. She needed our help. Everything she'd been through, and it was her hysteria that would probably save us from a media outcry about our homicidal ape when word of what happened last night reached the public. If Natasha was vocal enough, maybe more people than Lance and I might recognize Chuck's heroism. And if I didn't get downstairs soon, she was likely to get very vocal indeed with my mother and sister. Or else very quiet. I didn't like the thought of either.

Our connection, slight though it was, felt real. And I had an obligation to protect her from their pity. I thought I might be able to help her better than anybody, even my sister. The girl might have a shot at recovery if she could maintain that relationship with the big ape. I doubted she could continue to maintain the illusion she had held up ever

401

since she had come to her grandparents. School was liable to be hell when she went back in the fall. I didn't see any way for her to pretend away the last four years of her life. I knew how much the sanctuary had helped me when I was broken and recovering, how much it mattered that I could throw myself into the needs of creatures who needed me. I hoped she could take similar comfort, if only for a little while.

The center. I groaned. We were surely going to be shut down. Even if we didn't have to close because of our role in the pornography gang, I doubted the college would be interested in continuing to fund an institution with such an uncomfortable reputation. And Stan and his money couldn't save us from everything.

It wasn't all bad. Natasha was safe, and Art's murderer lay dead. If Lance and I were allowed to keep it, we had a little home for two orangutans. It wasn't a big space, but it was a beginning. I hoped it was one Natasha would help us foster into something larger.

The argument downstairs had expanded to include Brenda's voice and a proposal of bacon. Then the doorbell rang. "Enough, I'm up!" I said to the room.

It was probably Hannah, Jan, or Mina.

After we left to find Natasha, the false Gert — Gretchen — pulled a pistol on Nana to stop her from calling the police. She thought they were alone in the kitchen when she did it, but Jan had not gone with Hannah and Mina to break up the reception. She was actually in the bathroom. Jan was my Tae Kwon Do partner. And unlike me, Jan *had* been in her fair share of street fights, albeit many years before.

Coming from the hall, she got up behind Gretchen and kicked the gun out of her hand. Gretchen staggered for the back door, but she burst out upon Hannah and Mina returning to the house. My three friends tackled the would-be murderess, who went down in a heap screaming about her broken hip and multiple sclerosis. *Broken hip indeed. People with broken hips don't go shambling around pulling guns.* Nana called the authorities. After we left the police at the orangutan enclosure, we came home to the remnants of our reception and another police investigation. Mama had saved us some of our dinner and a cupcake each, but I had only limited appetite for either.

Now, I pulled on yesterday's shirt and shorts as Lance rolled over behind me in bed.

I opened the door to the sound of Darnell's voice downstairs. "We really do need to ask them some questions," he said.

Yes, I supposed we did owe our volunteers and interns, the honest ones, answers. And maybe they owed us some as well. I hoped Darnell was honest. "You let them sleep, young man," Nana said.

"It's all right," I called. "We're up. We'll be down in a minute." I waited while Lance dressed, and then we started down together.

"Is everything OK at the center?" Lance asked. Darnell and Trudy stood side by side in the doorway.

"It was fine when we left it with Christian last night," Darnell said. "Is there someplace private we can talk?"

I led them into the back parlor, the one where Lance had first seen my wedding dress. We sat down opposite each other, Lance and I on the sofa and they in matching yellow armchairs that only my mother could have made work in a room. That was when they flashed their federal badges. Natasha had been right, then.

Darnell said, "We'd like to formally extend our thanks to you and the staff of Midwest Primates for helping us conclude a federal investigation. We can only release limited information because prosecution will be ongoing for some time."

Trudy said, "It's a lot to process, isn't it? Federal agents are making a dozen arrests this morning in conjunction with a case we've been pursuing for several years."

Lance leapt to his feet. "So what you're telling me is that you *knew* what you were sending Art out to find Friday afternoon?"

Darnell was up as fast as Lance. "No," he said. "Absolutely not."

"But you had reason to believe . . ."

"No. None. We believed until yesterday afternoon that Friday's events were unconnected with our ongoing investigation. You have to realize, Lance, Art was assisting us. He knew. After your center helped break up that exotics ring last year, he got suspicious about the zoo up in Michigan. The one where it seems Chuck and Lucy came from."

"The one where all the animals got out?"

Finally, something I did know. Until last Friday, the primate smugglers had been the biggest thing to cross into our territory. And Art *had* expressed concerns about any number of unregulated private zoos in our relative area. The Michigan zoo had folded after the animals' release revealed unsanitary living conditions.

Darnell continued, "He passed along his suspicions to an agent. At the same time, our agency had been following Gary Buchanan for several months before he came to work at your facility. He was suspected of involvement in the illegal animal trade, but nobody knew about the pornography.

"Our agency had been tracking the exotics ring for some time after Art helped break up that one arm, but the case wasn't a large priority for the government. Illegal exotic animal trade doesn't typically crop up in Midwestern America. So a lot of our initial work, Trudy's and mine, involved data collection until we met your director. When Art told us he suspected one of the animals from the zoo in Indiana wound up at the facility in Michigan, and we then connected Gary Buchanan with your facility, there was finally enough evidence to assign Trudy and myself to surveillance.

"But we got here and . . . nothing. Gary knew he was under suspicion, and he got more crafty about his activities. He graduated and left, and we were getting ready to move on. He falsified documentation for his passport, which allowed us to prevent him from leaving the country temporarily. But if something hadn't come to light soon, we would have been forced to go home and abandon our investigation."

Neither man sat back down, and Trudy

stood up behind Darnell, so I got up too.

"I brought you all coffee!" Mama materialized in the doorway complete with a tea tray, four cups, sugar, cream, and tiny stirrer spoons. "I wasn't sure how your friends took theirs" — she made this sound like a deliberate insult on our part to her hospitality — "so I brought all the fixings. Now what are you all having for breakfast?"

"Oh, we won't be staying long," Trudy began.

"Oh, no, I insist," Mama said. "You all have done so much for Lance and Noel these last couple of days. We wouldn't have extracted them from that sanctuary of theirs for the wedding yesterday if they hadn't been able to trust you to run the place."

"No, well . . ." Darnell was obviously flustered.

"Place the order," I said, sitting back down. "They've got waffles, pancakes, scrambled eggs, bacon, and I think sausage."

From the doorway, Poppy added, "And now Nana's got Natasha making hash browns and Rachel and Lisa cutting up cantaloupe."

I said, "Lisa's here?"

"Yes!" Mama said. "What a sweet little girl. I don't know what your sister is so up

407

in arms about. Have you seen Rachel's tattoo?"

Before I could answer, Trudy said, "Bacon and scrambled eggs would be wonderful."

Darnell shook his head but said, "Sausage."

"Waffle or pancake?"

He looked ready to resist an answer, but Trudy shot him a look and he said, "Waffle. Fine."

After Mama left, the others sat down again. I perched sitting forward, as I tried to make sense of what they were telling us.

Darnell went on, "Things went bad up in Michigan, and we lost track of a large number of animals and suspected individuals when the saboteurs released all the animals. Art had only recently seen the net result of allowing police to interact with wild animals, and his primary concern in his interactions with federal investigators was to save those animals. So after the police killed the animals in Michigan and northern Ohio, he was feeling frustrated with us, as well."

I said, "God, Art." It would be just like him to invite investigators on-site in hopes of saving an animal, but to shut them out if they were even remotely connected to the people who had harmed another animal.

Beside me Lance said, "We always thought he couldn't keep a secret to save himself. Now it looks like he kept them left, right, and center."

Darnell said, "I really think he could do anything where Midwest Primates was concerned. He kept working with us because he feared Gary was trying to smuggle animals through his facility without his knowledge. None of us realized Gary was simply using the animals already on-site for a much darker purpose."

Lance glowered across at someone we had recently considered a friend. "And thanks to your lack of knowledge, there's a good chance our center will be closed for creating inhumane conditions where animals could be involved with child pornography."

Neither Trudy nor Darnell said anything for several minutes. Finally, Trudy said, "Approximately the only thing we can tell you for certain is that we will do what we can to ensure the animals' safe placement if your facility is closed down."

That hung between us. Ensuring the animals' safety. Lance said, "You can't think that closing Midwest Primates will benefit the animals. Not after . . ."

Darnell said, "What do you know about Sally Williams?"

And then Mama came in with Poppy and breakfast. She had Bryce and Daddy drag in a card table and went to elaborate lengths to set out our food, refill the coffee, deliver juice, and lift up the room with running commentary about the disaster of our reception. I remembered that yesterday when Lance and I tried to have a private conversation, the whole family had eavesdropped on every word. It was what my family did. We didn't keep things from each other. And if we did, Mama or Nana shamelessly ferreted them out.

Mama hadn't come into the room right when she did by accident. She popped in the first time when she thought things might get dangerous. She came in now to buy Lance and me time to think. It wasn't much, but I would make it enough. I had been on the verge of telling the agents everything I had ever known about Sally Williams.

Instead, when Mama left, I said, "What do you want to know about Sally?"

Trudy looked at me. Darnell looked at me. "Where she is, for one thing," they both said.

I answered with absolute honesty. "No idea. Before yesterday, I would have told you that Gary was somewhere in Africa and

Sally was at the National Zoo in Washington DC. Yesterday, I would have said Gary was with his elderly mother in Pennsylvania. But Gary, very clearly, was not in Pennsylvania. So who knows where Sally is. Is that everything you needed?"

"You said you spoke with her," Trudy began.

Lance started to say something, and I mashed his foot under the card table. "Did I say that?"

"What the hell game are you playing?" Darnell snapped.

I stood up, nearly flipping the table, but ultimately only pushing it forward so that Darnell couldn't stand up. It wasn't planned, but I took advantage of it. Standing was a position of power. I leaned forward on the table. "I'm not playing a game, Darnell. You walk in here and say you've been watching the situation that got our best friend killed. That nearly got *us* killed. You walk in here and tell me you've been watching everybody who came through our facility for the last who-knows-how-long. And you expect us to fill in the gaps in your knowledge because you flash a badge."

Darnell said, "We didn't *have* to *tell* you anything. We could have gone right on anonymously. We could have asked you casually if you'd talked to Sally since Art's death, and you would have told us out of friendship. We are trying to give you a sense of the depth of the problems you and Lance are going to be facing as the facility's acting directors in the coming months. If you *don't* get shut down, and there's a good chance you won't, you're going to be answering questions like this for some time."

I leaned harder on the table. "And you can come in with a subpoena and get what you need for all I care. Sally can't be very hard for you to find. The best you want to offer us is safe placement of the animals, but if you want our willing cooperation, we need a little more help." I sat down. "And to start off with, I want to know what Sally Williams has to do with anything."

Trudy started to say something, but Darnell waved her off. "Come out to the car a minute," he said.

CHAPTER 28

I was tempted to refuse. The federal badges had looked official enough, but in the long run, there was nothing to say they weren't forgeries. I didn't think they were, though. I thought Darnell and Trudy were on the up and up. I also thought they could do a little more than offer to shuttle our animals somewhere safe.

So we all four went out to Trudy's beat-up sedan, where they had a picture to persuade us to help them. Clearly, they had expected my pushback. It was a graphic image of Natasha and Sally in a clinch. At least there wasn't a monkey in the shot. I pretended indifference. "And you can't find her."

"She's the only one," Trudy said.

Darnell added, "And you have her phone number."

I said, "It's in the staff files at the center. I'm sure you'll find her quickly."

Darnell said, "If you talked to her Friday,

you have a number that isn't in the staff records. That number was disconnected at the end of May."

I said, "Let's say I do. By now, she knows who you are. Gary certainly did. Natasha told me yesterday." I didn't let my pleasure at their visible surprise show. "She's not going to answer a call from Trudy and Darnell at the center."

"As long as the phone is on, we can use the number to track it using its internal GPS."

"Wouldn't it be better to know she's *with* the phone first?"

"That's not your concern. Maybe we'll call it."

"And maybe she'll hang up and run. What do we know," I went on, "about what Art said to try to save his own life? We know Chuck the orangutan came in and attacked Gary, and that gave Art a chance to flee. We know it probably happened near the new enclosure because Art thought it would be on security video. Gary clearly thought Lance and I knew more than we did. He risked a great deal to send his mother in to lure us out to 'save' Natasha. What if that was because of something Art said? And what if Gary called Sally up to warn her off?"

Trudy didn't say anything. Darnell was also quiet. It was a plausible theory. Finally, Darnell asked, "What's your point?"

"It's this. I don't like those pictures, but I have every confidence you can find Sally without me. However, as you note, I talked to her Friday night. She is still answering the phone for me. She may think I can give her information. If you want my help, then I need something better than safe placement for my animals."

"We're not authorized . . ."

"Oh, can it." Marguerite's phrase. "You can help us if you want to. We need two things if we're going to stay open. We need the authorities not to shut us down, and we need the college to perceive the sanctuary in a positive rather than a negative light. We need you to spin-doctor this for us. Art sacrificed his *life* for your operation. If you want my help to tie up your loose end, then you need to make that sacrifice worthwhile."

"Wait a minute," Trudy said. She gestured, and then she and Darnell got back into her rust bucket. I saw her place a phone call from the front seat, and when they got back out, she said, "What can you offer us in return?"

"Sally's number, obviously. But why don't I call her once you trace it, so you know whether or not she's with it?"

Darnell and Trudy quickly located Sally's phone. It was *not* in DC. I was not supposed to know where it was, but I clearly heard "Columbus." While we waited for permission for me to call her, Alex phoned Lance to let him know he was on a plane back to his own home in Texas. We spoke to Christian briefly, but he had imported some of his own staff from the Ohio Zoo to help the afternoon volunteers, as he himself returned to the facility. Lucy was in labor.

Darnell and Trudy waited with us, ate the breakfast smorgasbord, and finally received authorization for my phone call. Part of me wondered if they stayed to make sure we didn't do anything to warn Sally, but they seemed to genuinely accept my logic. They spent the time coaching me to act natural and to tell the truth without giving anything useful away.

Sally answered on the first ring. I forced myself to stay casual. "Hey," I said.

"Noel, hi!" Her voice was unnaturally high and fast. "Did you get my texts?"

Oops. "No. You know I don't text, and it's been crazy here. I guess I'll get to them. What did you want to tell me?"

"Oh, just that I couldn't get in touch with Gary on Friday, and I wondered if you had made contact?"

That was it. That was my entire job. Sally was with the phone, and I could hang up as soon as I could get her off plausibly.

"No," I said. "Never found his mom's number." I doubted if I sounded any more remotely normal than she did. But I was pretty sure I knew why she was so uncomfortable. I didn't think she knew the same about me. I finally said, "Listen, I'm calling because we're having Art's memorial service next Saturday, and I thought it might be nice if you and Gary could come and say something, assuming Gary's still in the country then." He was in the country all right. His body was, anyway. The rest of him would never be in *this* country again. "You were his last graduates."

She didn't say anything at first, then, "I can't, Noel. I . . . can't."

"It's OK," I said quickly. "I'm sure you haven't got a lot of spare change right now. We'd cover your ticket."

"No, really, I couldn't." Her discomfort was evident. And I *liked* it. I wanted to hear her squirming for a thousand years. My mind blossomed with a hundred strategies to keep making her refuse to help us out.

But then she said, "Um. I've got to go. Somebody's at the door."

That quick, then. As I hung up, my mind suddenly flooded with images of Art. I thought of him on Friday, leaping up after Chuck batted him aside. I saw him throwing the watermelon and bolting back around the building, as alive as ever I'd known him to be. I saw him giving Lance the white wedding suit that he probably had gone out and purchased for that express purpose. And from thoughts of revenge, I fell instead into despair.

Darnell pulled me out of it. "You kept your end," he said. "Now it's our turn. Here's what we're going to do. You need to call your board members and set up an emergency meeting. As far as we know, none of them were involved in this, but Gary *had* been cultivating all of them for some time."

I was pretty sure I understood then what Rick had meant about Art getting pushback about handing his job down to Lance and me. I thought Gary had been trying to engage in a little politicking behind Stan's back and bring the rest of the board around to making him Art's successor. I wondered if he had known or surmised anything about Art's planned retirement. In any case, the board would hopefully be easy to win back now, because we were going to need their full backing to keep the college on board with its funding.

"And you need this." Trudy removed a computer printout from a binder she had been carrying under her arm.

It was a letter from Art. Or part of one. It said:

Dear Lance and Noel,

I want to congratulate you warmly as you celebrate your marriage. Soon, you'll be in Ecuador, and I know you will learn tremendously there. But I'm afraid that will be one of the last trips you'll be taking for some time. I have an opportunity to live in Africa for several years, my dears, and I would be a fool to pass it up . . .

The letter said more about working with primates in the wild and using the things he learned to come back here and launch the next phase of his interconnected research facilities. It was clearly the beginning of a speech, probably the one he had intended to make when he unveiled the unfinished new orangutan center. I finished reading in tears.

Trudy and Darnell waited as Lance and I spun through this final gift of Art's words, recovered from his hard drive. Then Darnell continued, "Tomorrow, we'll get a couple of news crews out to posthumously award Art for his assistance in bringing a federal investigation to a successful close. That's about the best we can do."

"And federal authorities won't be swooping in to shut us down?"

"No," Darnell said. "There will be formalities, but the end result is that Trudy and I can both attest to the quality of care your animals receive and that will go a long way toward quieting the ruckus. This won't go away quickly, but I think you will be able to continue your operations."

He had other things to say, but I barely heard him. We weren't being shut down. The center would survive for Lance and me to win over our board and the college. The worst of my fears would not be realized. They could not, or possibly would not, explain much else about the pornography ring, but Trudy did tell me we would need to hire a different security firm, and she drew my attention to an article on the Internet that said the head of Baywater Security had been arrested in a federal sting. By the time Darnell and Trudy left, I had a much better feeling about them than I had when they had identified themselves as federal authorities. I thought we might someday in the future consider them friends again.

Before Lance and I could gather our things and our new foster daughter and leave my parents' home, we had one more call to make. Like Sally, Christian answered on the first ring, though I was much happier to hear his voice than hers.

"You finally got my messages!" he said.

"Did you text? No, look . . . It's been another long day here. We wanted to know how Lucy's doing."

"Well enough," he said. "Well enough. She's delivered a healthy male baby."

"Can she mother him?"

"No, not yet." That was no more than we might have expected of any captive-raised animal. When primates had no mothers to model with, they had no idea how to care for their young. "We've got a good surrogate, though," he continued. "We had a mama come to us last year, and we're trying her out to make sure she remembers how to act before we give her this little guy for a while."

"Do you think Lucy can learn?"

"We'll see," he said. "No reason to think not. She responds to the clicker, and she's got good rapport with the trainers. Right now, we're going to stabilize her health. We'll put her where she can see everything and see if we can't get her back together with this baby soon."

And finally, everything was done. I hung up and turned to Lance. "Let's go home."

"Absolutely."

"Oh, no, you don't." It was Mama. "You two and those blasted monkeys. You've conspired to ruin your own rehearsal dinner, your wedding reception, *and* our little brunch. You are going to stay for supper, and you are going to tell us *everything* starting," and here she turned to Lance, "with when your mother lost her mind and your brother somehow looked sane by comparison."

She turned and walked away, leaving us to process her admonishment. Lance looked at me and shrugged. "It looks like we're staying for dinner," he said.

We were in the back parlor again, sitting together on the couch. I leaned into my new husband, and he pulled me in close with one arm. I said, "What do you say we postpone our honeymoon?"

He buried his nose in my hair and wrapped the other arm around my back. "You know," he told me, "I was thinking the exact same thing."

ABOUT ORANGUTANS

Orangutans are an endangered species whose existence is threatened by deforestation of the rainforests on their native islands, Borneo and Sumatra. To find out more about them, and to learn how you can help slow or prevent their extinction in the wild, search the Internet for great ape sanctuaries in the US and abroad. Your local or regional zoo might also be a good resource to learn more about an extraordinary creature that is losing ground against human intrusion.

ABOUT THE AUTHOR

Jessie Bishop Powell grew up in rural Ohio. She now lives in Montgomery, Alabama, with her husband and their two children. She has master's degrees in English and library science from the University of Kentucky.

Jessie's first book, *Divorce: A Love Story,* was published as an e-book in 2011. You can find out more about her and her family on her blog *Jester Queen* at http://jesterqueen.com.

The employees of Thorndike Press hope you have enjoyed this Large Print book. All our Thorndike, Wheeler, and Kennebec Large Print titles are designed for easy reading, and all our books are made to last. Other Thorndike Press Large Print books are available at your library, through selected bookstores, or directly from us.

For information about titles, please call:
 (800) 223-1244

or visit our Web site at:
 http://gale.cengage.com/thorndike

To share your comments, please write:
 Publisher
 Thorndike Press
 10 Water St., Suite 310
 Waterville, ME 04901